MW01277810

MURDER IN THE MEADOWS

MURDER IN THE MEADOWS

John E Sjoberg

Edited by Brenda Garton

Copyright © 2012, John E Sjoberg

All rights reserved. No part of this book may be reproduced, stored, or transmitted by any means—whether auditory, graphic, mechanical, or electronic—without written permission of both publisher and author, except in the case of brief excerpts used in critical articles and reviews. Unauthorized reproduction of any part of this work is illegal and is punishable by law.

ISBN 978-1-105-43971-1

To my wife, who encourages
and inspires me
forever and a day.

With special thanks to Barbara Garton for her guidance and talent. Original oil painting for cover, by Barbara Garton.

CHAPTER 1

I have always envied people who break the ordinary, everyday mold. You know, the unpredictable, eccentric types, who keep you captivated by their every word and move. Oh, Kirk was by no means "ordinary." He was so intriguing, so complex that he could fill a case study curriculum for a college psychology course. I never knew what random and spontaneous adventure would enter my life when he was around, but it was always something.

Kirk Preston was one of those "thirty something" playboys who never left his hometown after high school, never had a long term relationship and jumped from job to job, more out of boredom than of necessity. He had a kind heart and a gentle, delicate way about him.

He was just as popular today as he was when he broke the Meadows High School football record for touchdown passes and led his team to a triumphant New England Championship. Kirk had always exhibited and exuded that intangible star like aura; it surrounded him and charmed everyone's attention, especially from the ladies.

Maybe it was that magnetic popularity that kept him in Meadows, still living in the glory of the improbable dream of '92. That and a healthy trust fund handed down from his grandfather, one of the barons of the paper industry, I am told.

Meadows, Massachusetts loved winners. It was a tradition to be the best at whatever you did, whether it was playing the fiddle or playing football. If you were the best, you were loved. Kirk was the beloved son to the proud townsfolk. He could do no wrong.

The quaint town of 15,000 is an idyllic "bedroom community" of upper middle class New Englanders, with a keen and resonant sense of history. In many ways, it is a town that time forgot. Even the new fire station, police station, library and school buildings had to conform to a resemblance of Colonial American architecture. The picturesque old tree lined streets and majestic lawns once harboring horses and carriages, remain the same, now hosting modern modes of horse power amidst the historically preserved fifth generation homes.

There are two country clubs, two golf courses and absolutely no fast food restaurants. While surrounding communities deal with murder, arson, dropouts and gangs, Meadows' residents engage themselves in heated debates over the town's fall leaf pick-up schedule. It is a great place to soak your socks and butter your bread. And it suited Kirk's laid back lifestyle just fine. In less than two hours, he could hop into his convertible and be in Boston, New York, Cape Cod or the Berkshires.

I guess I always felt sorry for Kirk in some way, even though I vicariously lived through his thrilling "edge of seat" escapades. I don't really know why I felt that way. Maybe I was just trying to smolder my engulfing and burning jealousy of him.

If you took away his entourage of "bombshell" girlfriends, his endearing fans, his 67 Corvette and his turboprop Piper Plane, he really was very alone. Just another perfectly chiseled, 6 foot 4 inch, blonde haired, blue-eyed, GQ cover, multimillionaire . . . borrrrrrring, at least that's what I kept telling myself.

It's been a few years now, but it might as well been yesterday. Perhaps it's because I have endlessly replayed every detail of those days in hopes of understanding how my rope unraveled and snapped so quickly, spiraling my life out of control.

When Kirk didn't come by my apartment to pick me up one Saturday for a day of rock climbing on Mount Tom, I didn't think too much of it. After all, it had been a week since I had spoken to him and you never know what kind of Friday night Kirk might have had. My cheap answering machine had been on the fritz, too.

It was just as well. I really didn't have the time to risk my life on the side of a mountain cliff two days before a huge business presentation I was to make in front of my new boss in Indianapolis.

When he was two hours late, I called Kirk and recorded a sarcastically berate message on his voice mail. *"Hey Kirk, it's Jesse. You know I'm gonna kill you one of these days. You stood me up for the last time you bum. You could've called."*

I hung up the phone and headed to my office to prepare for my business trip, a trip that would lead to a fall, that is.

I didn't travel much, but when I did, I loved every minute of it. Travel gave me a chance to anonymously be anyone I chose. Sometimes I would bring a medical book along from the library and stage an urgent hospital phone call on my cell phone in the crowded airport waiting area, always talking just loudly enough to be intriguing, but not annoying. Other times I might broker a million dollar business venture with a foreign sports star, much to the delight and entertainment of my nosey, ease dropping audiences. I didn't have delusions of grandeur; I just thought of it more as a "drug free escape" from reality.

My otherwise mundane existence was often lifted by my fantasy portrayals. The façade, however, would ultimately fade and lead to an even greater sense of depravity when forced to face my real-world-view through dulled and cracked glasses. But this trip would be different; I could feel the positive energy burning within me.

I had planned it for weeks. I even attended a class at a technical community college in Springdale to brush up on my PowerPoint skills. Springdale is the 3rd largest city in Massachusetts and the urban neighbor to the upscale Meadows.

I had a new suit, new haircut, new shoes and a borrowed gold and diamonded Rolex from Kirk, just to impress. I had a resourceful repartee of witty lines and clever small talk all memorized, including the requisite elevator speech, if necessary. I knew that a failure to plan was a plan for failure.

This was going to be my premier solo spotlight for thirty minutes on the sales stage of my career. I would perform in front of an important client and in the doting watchful presence of the new national sales manager, whom I had not yet met. I was only days away from being known as the amazing Jesse Thorpe, "the wonder kid of the sneaker world."

I was ready for everything and anything. In fact, I was so certain of my imminent success that I only booked a one way coach airline ticket heading out to Indiana because if all went well, as I knew it would, I would buy a first-class ticket returning to celebrate in style. I was also looking forward to boasting my success to my friends back home.

I went to the Meadows' schools growing up, although I never lived in Meadows. I was part of a school choice program that allowed students to choose other school districts if their school was determined to be "underperforming." My old school buddies were great and many of them are still my closest friends, but my insecurities always left me with a feeling that I didn't really belong, perhaps because I didn't live in town or play sports on any of the in-town teams.

That feeling only polarized further as my friends went on to graduate schools and meaningful professional careers, while I had little success as a manufacturer's sales representative. My future had always been uncertain, in fact, so uncertain I wouldn't even buy green bananas. But that was about to change.

I'll admit I had trouble fitting in with the Meadows' crowd. It's what made my friendship with Kirk so important to me. Kirk didn't care that I didn't play sports or that I wasn't particularly popular with the girls. We just had fun hanging out together and Kirk was the king. The others at school called me Hanky. Partly because they said I looked like Tom Hanks and was just as funny. The nickname also came from my nose's propensity to unexpectedly bleed. I always kept a hanky nearby.

I might've looked like Tom Hanks, but that's where the similarities ended. Encouraged to do so, I once tried out for the drama club. The theater coach, however, made his opinion of my talents crystal clear. He told me if I ever wanted to see my name up in lights, I should change my name to EXIT. Ha ha, not very funny. It didn't matter. I was content with my real-life high school role as best supporting actor, cast as the "Invisible Man" in the shadow of a star named Kirk Preston. I loved him and hated him.

This year's 20th high school reunion would definitely be my turn to be noticed. I may never be the town's beloved son, like Kirk, but my catharsis from the tolerated step child was about to unfold. I envisioned arriving at the reunion in my new Lexus LS460, dressed in Armani, walking in Ferragamo and best of all . . . followed by Kirk.

I was on my way, a new dawn was breaking and my forecast was exceptionally bright. Life was good. Soon, I would no longer need shoe lifters, blond highlights, fake tans, blue tinted contacts or my cubic zirconium pinky ring. I would be unveiling to the world the real deal …just call me J.T.

CHAPTER 2

When I arrived in Indianapolis, I asked the taxi-driver at the airport to drive by the convention center, where my meeting and huge presentation was being held, before heading to the Holiday Inn. I wanted to get a sense of where I would be going and exactly how long it would take me to get there from the hotel. As it turned out, the convention center was just two blocks away and I wouldn't even need a taxi to get there from the hotel for my presentation in the morning. I always kept in mind the advice of a former teacher who said, "If you can visualize yourself succeeding, then you likely will."

After checking into the hotel, I timed myself walking to the convention center and walked up to the conference room area. I knew it would calm my butterflies if I could picture the room where I would be presenting. I had everything covered; this was it, my turn to impress my friends. Everything was right, but little did I know that everything was actually terribly wrong.

I headed back to the hotel and called room service for an evening snack and then I made my perfunctory call home to check my messages. I rarely had any, but when I was away I always checked a few times. The sound of the phone gave my dog exercise. Whenever she heard my voice on the machine, she would run around the one bedroom apartment and jump up onto the couch and over the back of the couch to the floor and then circle around the side and jump over again and again.

When I called this time, I was surprised to hear that I had received nine phone calls. Nine phone calls? I figured they must be tele-marketers or wrong numbers or something. They couldn't have been for me. Kirk and my friend Suzie both knew I was away and they were the only ones whoever called.

Unfortunately, I could not decipher a single one of the messages. The gurgled recordings sounded like an underwater talking game I used to play with my friends at the community swimming pool when I was a kid.

I made a note to myself on the hotel stationery that priority number one, when I get home, was to buy a new answering machine. I also thought it would be a good idea to get a new phone and have new telephone wires installed too, my phone always sounded scratchy. I made a note to *"get rid of the phone wire"* on the hotel stationary note pad, so I would remember. I'm a list kind of guy and need to be reminded of things. I definitely needed all new equipment, especially since I would likely be the new regional sales manager for Olympiad Shoes and I would probably be conferencing all over the country, maybe even the world.

When I arrived at the conference room the next morning, I began to set up my equipment for my presentation. I was the only one there, besides a uniformed maid who was vacuuming the carpet and dusting the chairs. A churning feeling of malaise was settling in my now sour stomach. Something didn't seem right. The meeting was scheduled to begin in less than an hour and the room didn't look nearly ready for a new product seminar.

Usually the corporate office was meticulous and thorough to every detail. They would customarily send an entire team in the night before to set-up banners behind the podium and hang advertising literature and posters. Even the traditional gift baskets as center pieces on every table were missing. None of it was there.

My heart began to pound like a marching band drum. Where was everyone? Is there more than one convention center in Indianapolis? I asked the cleaning lady if she knew about the seminar and if I was in the right room? She wasn't sure. She did know that there were basketball people coming in a couple of hours as she pointed to the clock on the wall.

That's when I realized that I had not set Kirk's watch back an hour on the flight out to the Midwest's central time zone. Thank

God, I thought. I took a deep breath and sat down for a moment at one of the tables to review my notes for the one hundredth time. It's good to be this early.

Loosening my tie, I took off my jacket and hung it over the back of the chair. My nervous sweat had made my self-tanning spray run onto my white collared shirt and my nose began to drip blood all over the front of it. I don't know why my nose would always bleed when I experienced sudden stress. Doctors told me it had something to do with the rapid opening of blood vessels in the temple of my head, caused by a sudden rise in body temperature and blood pressure. I never told the doctor, but I always believed it was due to picking my nose too many times as a kid and somehow making my nostrils too big to hold the blood in. Either way, it would never happen at a convenient time. It may be the reason I was never comfortable with close intimate relationships. Nothing puts a damper on a romantic interlude faster than a blood dripping nose, trust me.

I was always prepared for my fickle nose with a nearby handkerchief. When most kids got socks and underwear as un-welcomed gifts, I would gratefully receive bulk-packaged handkerchiefs. I was prepared for the unexpected wardrobe malfunction too.

I took my newly discovered extra hour and went back to the Holiday Inn to change my shirt. I threw the stain ruined shirt and used bloodied handkerchief in the trash and headed back to the convention center. This time when I entered the conference room, my projector had been unplugged and moved to the side. The room was beginning to fill with a cavalcade of officials from the NCAA Basketball League, all wearing navy blue golf shirts with gold embroidered NCAA insignias on the left breast pocket.

Yikes! I thought. This really is an important client. It wasn't the client I was expecting, but it didn't matter to me, my presentation would be perfect for any group. Remain calm, be cool, I told myself.

I instinctively and overtly began to work the room, without my colleagues. I couldn't worry about where they were. There was no time to waste. I was by far the shortest person in the room, but I confidently felt as though I stood the tallest. I was the center of attention and welcomed everyone to the meeting from the podium. I was thinking fast and knew I needed to captivate the crowd from the start.

I grabbed a nearby metal waste basket, turned it upside down and removed the microphone from the podium stand and stood on top of the basket. I heard a chuckle from the audience and then I heard the murmuring whispers asking "who is that guy and what in the world is he doing?"

After several minutes of promoting a new running shoe design, I was not so politely escorted out of the building by security guards. I was informed I could be charged with trespassing and unlawful soliciting of goods if I didn't cooperate. To make a long story short, it was the worst day of my life and I just as soon forget the entire ordeal, if only I could.

Stumbling outside, I immediately called Olympiad Shoes corporate office to find out where everyone was and why I wasn't notified of any changes. I was connected to the Vice President of Human Resources, never a good thing, who told me point blank . . . I was terminated. What? When I asked him for an explanation, he replied in a draconian voice,

> *"Explanation? How about this for starters; your presentation was in Minneapolis not Indianapolis. We just lost one of biggest sales opportunities because you failed to show up."*

And then he abruptly hung up the phone. I thought maybe I had been disconnected or maybe I misunderstood what he had just said. In complete disbelief, my comprehension shifted into neutral and I stood stone-like still, replaying the sequence of events which had just unfolded. After a few minutes, I re-dialed the number and heard a recording from the cell provider stating that my cell phone service had been cancelled. No further information was available. Wow, that was fast. What the hell just happened?

How could I have screwed up so badly? Am I a complete idiot? Is this a bad joke or prank? Someone at corporate must have set me up for failure to get my job. That's got to be it or was it my stupid answering machine? My new found circumstance was too much for my six pounds of chicken-colored goo to process. It didn't matter now anyway. It was too late. Nothing mattered now.

So, just like that, my promising career was over. Done, clean up your locker, check please, done. There was nothing left. It was over. Period. Maybe it was all for the best? Yeah right. I lost it. My composure boiled over and my pressure cooker blew its top, not just as reaction to my present experiences but from everything that had been festering in my hollowed soul for years. I slammed my worthless cell phone down on the sidewalk, where it came apart and shattered into the street only to be symbolically crushed by a new Lexus sedan. Unbelievable.

I sat down on the curb to swallow my pride and digest my helpless thoughts. With further insult to my injury, I received the blessing of an overhead passing Pigeon, ah yes, the urban black sheep of the Doves. In classic McEnroe style, I stood up and I looked up to the sky and yelled at the top of my lungs…**"You can not be serious!!!"** Somehow this was not what I had visualized. Little did I know it was a harbinger of far worse things to come. It only served to reaffirm, the only thing I ever succeeded in was failure, I was the best.

I didn't have a booked flight home and didn't feel much like traveling anyway. With nowhere to go and nothing else to do, other than drowning my memory and coming up with some lame excuse to tell my friends when I got home, I decided to aimlessly walk around the circle city.

I didn't bother going back to the hotel to get my stuff. I didn't need any of it. Instead, I dragged my pitiful self around the downtown business district and against a flow of people down Market Street. I felt like a lonely spent salmon struggling against an unfriendly and formidable downstream current, except my sacrifice had no purpose in life.

When I saw all the businessmen and women walking and talking on wireless headset phones, as mindless robots, I felt a little better, freed from all the crap they were forced to contend with from the corporate establishment. It was never really for me. There had to be more. There had to be. I always found a way to sugar coat the sour events in my life. It's what kept me vertical.

In Massachusetts, we have a saying, "if life gives you lemons - squirt 'em on Lobstah." So my pitiful failure in joining the ranks of successful yes-men, now would, instead, give me a chance to reinvent Jesse Thorpe.

I ended up at the famed, iconic Monument Circle, in the heart of the city. I remember peering up at the huge limestone and bronze testament to the veterans of every war since the American Revolution and thinking how small and insignificant my own little world really was, in the grand scale of life.

After buying a bag of chocolate at the South Bend Chocolate Factory and riding the elevator to the monument's observation deck, I was ready for some stronger and more mitigating medicine. I definitely needed some mind and pain numbing comfort, especially after a chocolate covered caramel pulled off my front dental cap leaving me looking like a veteran hockey player in a visitor's penalty box.

I entered a bar that reminded me of an elite New York City Club on Park Avenue complete with a burgundy canapé, velvet roped partitions, red carpet runners and a doorman in a long coat with a Lincoln style top hat. I knew I would find my old friends Jack Daniels and Johnny Walker waiting for me inside.

I sat down at the bar, rolled up my sleeve so the bartender could see my Rolex and I bought a round for everyone in the room on my Olympiad credit card before it too was cancelled by corporate finance. I figured they owed it to me. A few of the cosmopolites came over to me and thanked me for their drink, some just nodded from a distance while raising their glasses, but most didn't even look my way.

I could have been in any high class downtown bar in America and seen the same lonely souls simply trying to get through life, each with their own stories of unfulfilled dreams. I sat at a beautiful old mahogany bar until closing. The wall of top shelf bottles was neatly aligned in front of an antique etched mirror which extended all the way to the patina tiled copper ceiling.

For hours I tried to avoid looking at myself in the mirror and facing my every flaw. I was depressed enough. It was the same torment I faced every month when I went for a haircut, being plopped in a chair in a well lit room four feet away from an unavoidable mirror. Instead of seeing who I am, I would become haunted by who I was not.

Day quickly turned into night and I didn't care much about getting home. I had nowhere to go, and no one waiting for me back home at my apartment except for Casey, my lovable Beagle.

I don't even remember leaving the bar or how I ended up spending the night on a cement park bench outside the Indiana State House. But I do remember when the sun broke. The sunlight rays streamed between the cold skyscrapers and reflected off the towering windows into my half opened and encrusted eye lids. I was awakened by the prod of a night stick by one of Indiana's finest and told to get up and get out before the "real" businessmen and elected officials came into the city.

I must have looked like a derelict bum. The dew from the foggy morning air had properly wrinkled my clothes and curled my hair. My head was pounding, my money and credit cards were gone, and I had a nasty cut under my eye. I didn't have a memory of the night in my mind. That was probably just as well.

After clambering to my feet, begging for a spare quarter and searching for a pay phone, I found myself in a coffee shop, calling my dearest friend Suzie. Suzie lived in the same complex as me and had a key to my apartment. Suzie wasn't home, but I left her a message, I asked her to pick up Casey and take care of her for a few extra days.

Kirk had given the dog to me last Christmas as a companion when I broke up with a girlfriend named Casey. He thought the dog had her eyes, and would be a lot more loyal. She was. Kirk could be a real wag when he wanted to be. This time, he also happened to be right.

I loved that dog. It was the only living thing that actually completely depended upon me for its life, and I wasn't going to let her down. It doesn't seem like a huge responsibility, but for now my dog was the closest thing I had to a family.

I have known Suzie Dillon for half of my life, we grew up together and in my salad days, I dreamed of making her my girlfriend.

That desire ended though in my entrée years, when we were separately invited to a wedding and assigned to the same family table. We were 2nd cousins and didn't even know it. It was hard to swallow, because I always had a crush on her. Suzie would become more of a sister to me, unfortunately literally.

I knew I could count on her for anything. We saw each other nearly every day. She was my loyal running partner and would knock on my door every morning at 6:00 AM to get me up to run with her.

Her dream was to run in the Boston Marathon. I was just happy running along the Connecticut River in the serenity of the early morning hours and it didn't hurt that I was with Suzie. She was drop dead gorgeous, easy on the eyes. Occasionally, when we ran, there would be an early morning commuter driving by and I imagined that they would think that the silky blonde was my wife.

When I called, I asked her to wire me some money from my checking account. I told her to go into my apartment and where to find my checkbook and that she should forge my signature, cash a check and send it Western Union. It wasn't the first time she forged my signature. We were very close; sometimes, when I was away, she'd even paid some of my bills. I told her I might be a few days and perhaps I would take a train home, since I had lost my credit cards and couldn't board a plane without any money.

Maybe I would even take a detour on my way. I always wanted to see New Orleans, but never had the time. I figured that if I went right home and found another job, I probably wouldn't have any vacation time for at least another year, so why not?

Good ol' Suzie came through and I picked up $2,000 cash at the Western Union on State Street, later that morning. I was so anxious to get on my way, I didn't even read Suzie's note which was printed on the telegraph in the memo section of the wired money voucher.

Before heading to the train station, I bought a football jersey, a pair of Levi jeans and a bottle of aspirin. I was beginning to feel a little better and was actually trying to make light of losing my job. I kept telling myself that selling a running shoe was a pretty worthless contribution to make with one's life and who knew what great opportunities my future might now hold? This was not what I was about. There had to be more.

As a kid, I believed that anything was possible. As a young adult, I still believe in dreams, but the path had become obscure and no longer illumed. My greatest fear is an acceptance of mediocrity, a surrendering of my desire to be significant in life, or my will to leave a lasting footprint in the sand, a legacy resolute to the washing tides.

Abraham Lincoln had a great quote, "the best part about the future is that it comes one day at a time" and that was the way I would approach my destiny, one day at a time.

With my head held high I entered the Indianapolis train station and looked for a restroom so I could change into my new fresh clothes. I emptied the pockets of my suit pants and while changing, I finally noticed Suzie's note on the Western Union receipt. It simply read:

"Kirk is dead/ police are looking for you/ don't call/ hide"

What? I froze. What the hell is that supposed to mean? I starred at the note for what seemed like an eternity, unable to take a step and barely able to breathe. I kept reading each word in frantic doubt, like a lottery player would look at a winning million-dollar ticket in disbelief.

I kept starring, everything else in the room had blurred out of focus and the note seemed to grow like the image in a zooming lens of a camera. I could feel my heart beating in the temple of my head. My eyes dried from the absent blinking and began to burn in disbelief. I crumpled the note up and threw it in a paper towel receptacle. I splashed water in my face and stood stone-like, looking at the mirror, searching for meaning, trying to think-images of my best friend, Kirk, flashing in my mind, questions, questions.

It was a numbing "out of body" experience where time stood still, but viscerally imploding in my gut. Could it be a sick joke? That's not like Suzie. What do I do? Police looking for me? For what? Why? Why can't I call? I heard the muffled voices of people coming into the bathroom and the sound of the door opening on a squeaky hinge. My instinct was to retrieve the note from the trash and go into one of the vacant stalls, so I did.

I shut the door, read the note one more time and then flushed it away. I grabbed some extra toilet paper for my soon to be bleeding nose and headed out of the bathroom, out of the train station and back on the street.

Please God let me wake up from this ghoulish nightmare, I pleaded. Please tell me it's not true. I wasn't so concerned about myself, but the thought of Kirk dead, felt like I had been kicked in the stomach and a lump in my throat was growing like an enveloping atomic mushroom cloud.

My mind was flashing back to reckless near death precipices I had with Kirk when he was fooling around in his plane or topping a hundred miles per hour in his Corvette. WE had skirted death and loved every minute of it. I had worn out the edge of that suicide machine's passenger seat and warned him that the odds would catch up with him sooner or later, but truth be told, I never really thought they would. Kirk was larger than life. He always lived as though he was dying, while never living to die. It just didn't seem possible. Wow, Kirk dead. It just can't be. I needed to speak with Suzie and she needed to explain her bizarre message to me.

I never thought of death too much. Everyone feels immortal when they're young; it takes the loss of a close friend or family member to remind us how precious life is. Mark Twain said, *"Each person is born to one possession which out values all his others – his last breath."* There were times I loved Kirk and there were times I hated him, but never did I ever imagine, I would mourn him.

I had to know what had happened to my best friend and why it suddenly involved me. I stumbled and maundered around in a daze for the better part of the late afternoon, confused, searching for answers in my mind, still hoping I would just wake up from this bad dream. I asked a stranger who passed by, where I could find the nearest library or Internet café. I could no longer wait to conjure my own answers. I needed to find a computer so I could find out what the hell was going on. I knew I could straighten everything out. I just needed to know.

There was a dark inner voice that was torturing me. A subconscious conscience that somehow controlled every thought I invoked. It would vanquish my good thoughts and replace them with evil. The demon would question my real deep feelings for Kirk, the feelings that would infuriate me about him. Yeah, I was jealous. He had it all. Sometimes I wanted him to fail. Whether it was football, academics, girls, it didn't matter. I wanted him to feel failure. Just once, I wanted him to see and feel life through my eyes and in my shoes. What kind of friend wants you to fail? No friend at all.

The voice told me I was a despicably selfish being and I only cherished our friendship for what it brought me. It was right. Kirk was infinitely better than me on every level. Kirk was a true friend. He asked for nothing and nothing was what I gave him. And now, he's gone. He didn't deserve death, I did, and I had earned it. I should be the one that people are crying for. Instead, my inner voice would accompany and nourish my guilt forever. It was fitting that I lose, again.

How could two opposing worlds co-exist within my tortured soul? I knew right from wrong, but the reality was always a living lie, a day to day canard to fit my external circumstance and a Jekyll and Hyde spinning wheel of misfortune turning within my heart. If we really are the sum of our experiences and the source of my most memorable experiences is now gone, then a part of me has died too. So, this is it, whatever I am - I am and all that I have is the past.

I couldn't think straight and decided to start running instead of taking a taxi the eleven long blocks to the library. I think the running gave me comfort, it always had. When my legs moved, serenity flowed. I used to think it was the endorphin high or running through nature's stadium that dulled my stress, but now I realized it wasn't the dangling carrot before me, but the demons behind that propelled me. It seemed I was always running away from something in my life, but this time was different, a run up Kilimanjaro wouldn't be enough to escape my formidably blanketing shadow.

By the time I made it to the library, it was closing. Out of breath and panting, I gaspingly pleaded through the door window with the librarian to let me in. I told her I had left my iPod somewhere in the stacks earlier in the day and it would only take me a minute to retrieve it. She agreed it would be all right to let me in and flicked back on the humming fluorescent overhead lights.

I sprinted around the corner and out of the librarian's sight, logged onto a computer and went directly to the Springdale affiliate TV news web-site. The lead breaking news story was "Murder on the Mountain." Kirk had died near the rock climbing mountain where we were planning on going last Saturday. His lifeless body had been found by hikers. Foul play was immediately suspected. His neck had ligature markings that indicated he had been strangled with a wire or a cord and the article noted that he was not wearing his Rolex Watch or his famed diamond football ring, both of which he rarely removed. He was discovered at the bottom of a rock crevice on Mt. Tom.

Good Lord. I couldn't believe what I was reading. My heart began racing again.

When I clicked on the "read more" icon, I was greeted by my own picture, freshly taken only hours ago by a security camera at the Circle City Western Union store on State Street, complete with the nasty cut under my eye, missing front tooth, ruffled hair & unshaven face. Holy-cow, even I thought I looked guilty. There it was… the home page window to the world, with Kirk's prophetic face on one side and my pathetic one on the other. There was even a zoomed image of Kirk's Rolex on my wrist. I was the prime suspect for my best friend's murder.

It was impossible for me to fathom the gravity of what was happening. How in the world could my photo get posted within hours after it was taken? My name must have been entered into some sort of national data bank, and because I was receiving a large sum of money something must have automatically flagged my name during the transaction to alert authorities.

I wanted to read further in depth, but I heard the sound of the librarian's high heel shoes clacking coming my way. The sound resonated through the empty marbled room and echoed louder as she neared. She tapped me on the shoulder just as I exited the screen displaying my wanted picture. I kept my eyes and face low to avoid eye contact with her, and thanked her for letting me find my iPod. I headed directly to the doors without another word, stepped outside and began the marathon run of my life on the lam. But where would I go? What should I do? The answers to these gut-wrenching questions would slowly unfold into a dismal and uncertain future.

CHAPTER 3

Even though I had nothing to do with Kirk's death, I somehow felt responsible for what Suzie was about to go through. I should have been there for her, to answer questions for her. Police Chief Tommy O'Donnell was two years from retirement and volunteered to the Mayor & district attorney's office to take the lead role in investigating the death. The case would be handled by the county law enforcement offices and ultimately tried in Springdale.

O'Donnell was a somewhat bitter, but affable man, who longed for the years when he first came on the force, the years when the first generation Irish and Italians ruled the streets of the city and crime was limited to a respectable Mafia, enforcing gambling debts while intolerant to drugs. Today, the once great "city of homes" languished with an insurrection of ruthless murders between periling ethnic gangs, or as O'Donnell referred to them, "cockroaches." They were nothing more than slaves and soldiers besetting to Satin's silver spoon.

The pragmatic Chief came to work every day, kept out of certain neighborhoods, ate too many doughnuts and visited the Mayor's office every morning for coffee and his innocuous daily dose of city dirt. Mayor Sullivan, "Sully" to his friends, grew up with O'Donnell in "the good ol' days." Their wives were sisters.

Now they both tried to stay out of trouble and with a little Irish luck collect their municipal pensions in a few years somewhere on the Gulf of Mexico. The case looked like an easy one, and more importantly to O'Donnell, it would keep him off the menacing streets for a while.

The streets at night were too dangerous for a senescent veteran like him, especially after a weekend when the top reputed drug kingpin in the region had been found stabbed to death and another leader had been arrested with 1 kilo of pure cocaine in a stolen car. The cockroaches were buzzing. Gang violence had reached a feverish pitch and O'Donnell wanted no part of it. His exterminating days ended a long time ago.

O'Donnell's disheveled desk was mired in dozens of cases left to freeze, mostly inter-gang violence, sadly, with forgotten victims. Some aspects of modern day urban policing had become so meaningless and loathsome that the stewards of law had lost all sense of purpose or any conceived notion of scripting a moral biography of their professional lives.

Occasionally, a case would come along that would awaken their call to justice and stoke an otherwise smoldered fire to burn with a flaming vigorous purpose. The Kirk Preston murder case had the feeling of a defining moment in time in the lives and careers of the local force and no one involved in the investigation would be pressing the snooze alarm until the final judgment hour.

As the lead investigator, O'Donnell had the authority to delegate the entire homicide detective's division on the case, and he did. He was content sitting back in his torn and weathered black leather chair, waiting for the young energetic cops to bring him evidence. Some information he would keep, some he would throw away. That's just the way it was.

His door was always closed. Most at police headquarters assumed he was coercing informants or protecting witnesses, but most times he was whiling away the tedium and boredom looking at brochures of the Gulf Coast and listening to a Red Sox game on the radio. And if he had his druthers - that's the way it would stay until his retirement day.

It wasn't to be the clear cut case he was anticipating, after all, a hometown hero was dead and the sensational news story had spread throughout the region and even made Boston's evening news. Overnight it went from a local tragedy to a tabloid foddering national water cooler story. In the heart of the Midwest – the manhunt had begun for Jesse Thorpe.

In the first 24 hours, following the discovery of Kirk's body, detectives had searched Kirk's Blackberry, which was attached to his climbing belt and discovered on his calendar, *"rock climbing/Jesse/Mt. Tom"* for the same Saturday that his body was found and at the foot of the same mountain.

They had also listened to an un-played message I had left for Kirk, telling him I was going to kill him for standing me up. I wasn't a suspect at the time. They just wanted "to talk" to me, but, when they sequestered my bank records and found that Suzie had forged a check and wired $2,000 in cash to me in Indiana, they became very curious and my status was elevated to a "person of interest." Suzie told detectives I had an alibi that I worked for Olympiad Shoes and was away on a business trip.

When detectives called to confirm the story that Suzie provided, they were told that Jesse Thorpe never made his business meeting in Minneapolis and had been recently terminated. Credit cards traced to Indianapolis located the room where I had stayed at the Holiday Inn.

Local Indiana authorities were asked to check the room. They reported back to Springdale detectives that the room was riddled with incriminating evidence strewn and scattered about like the remnants of a once filled piñata at a child's birthday party.

They found my abandoned bags in the room and a one way airline ticket receipt inside a briefcase. The hotel staff indicated that I never officially checked out and had just disappeared without a trace. They all thought that was odd.

They also discovered the bloodied and stained shirt rolled up and discarded in the trash, along with a bloody handkerchief. One of the detectives dusted some charcoal on the hotel note pad on the night stand. The imprint left from the previous sheet read *"get rid of the phone wire."* On the night stand, next to the bed, sat an empty Rolex watch box with the gold embossed initials K.P. for Kirk Preston.

Further credit card transactions led police to interview the bartenders in the classy bar near Monument Circle. The doorman and the entire staff described the depressed stranger with the Olympiad Credit Card and Rolex watch, who left the bar at closing time, with seemingly nowhere to go. The paradigm of coincidental evidence against me was overwhelming and tantamount to a lifetime lunch pass in prison. In a word? I was "screwed."

The police had no choice, but to issue a nationwide manhunt for me, prime murder suspect and now fugitive, Jesse Thorpe.

CHAPTER 4

Don't ask how I ended up going to New Orleans. Something just beckoned me there. I remember sitting in the Amtrak train heading toward Louisiana. My face shielded from the other passengers as I leaned my head toward the window. The staccato sound of the tracks and stropping lights as we passed them by, were hypnotizing.

I couldn't help but feel sorry for myself and my situation, even if I could talk my way out of it and explain all of the circumstances, at best, I faced the grim reality of being an unemployed man who just lost his best friend in the world. Never mind being his accused killer.

As the hours passed, my visual focus alternated between the passing sceneries outside to a closer reflection of my face in the window. The contrasting images of an outward world set in a cinematic fast forward mode and the inward stillness of a ghostly transparent face. The long trip gave me therapeutic pause to allow an introspective look at life, but it didn't help.

It didn't seem fair. I suppose it's only natural to feel a sense of guilt that the world should keep turning day after day as if nothing ever happened, as if nothing really mattered. I could faintly hear a young couple laughing in the seats behind me; their world was happy and carefree. We were in the same place at the same time, but in different worlds. Kirk was an incredible guy and in my own esoteric being everything was now diminished.

How can I ever laugh or party again in the same way? I will never be the same, so, how can I act the same? If I did, it would be living a lie. I don't deserve to be the same. It only further degrades who I really am now and what Kirk was. Nothing can ever be the same.

So, do I just become someone else? Do I leave the old Jesse behind to pity, deservedly? I don't know. I was always good at pretending to be someone else; maybe it was time to put my skills to work. I needed time to sort through my deepest feelings and my own fundamental existence. Time, it's always about time, too much, not enough, too slow, too quick. Past has passed, tomorrow is never, and time is only now. Now is not good.

Maybe I should just keep running. Ah yes, old faithful running. Running always gave me comfort, but running for my life? Now that's a motivating purpose. Maybe I could hop on a ship in the port of New Orleans and stow away to some exotic island and start a new vagabond life, my old life had nothing worth saving anyway. But then again, if I ran, everyone would surely believe I did it, and even worse, the person who really was guilty of killing Kirk could be golfing with O.J.

I decided once I found a safe place to stop running I would try to figure out who killed Kirk Preston and exonerate myself from afar, or return home in a disguise like some exciting Hollywood drama and find the killer or killers. Before any of that, however, I would have to call Suzie to make sure she knows that I'm all right and that I had nothing to do with any of this. She was now my only trusted friend in the world.

The District Attorney's office wanted to tap Suzie's phone. They were certain I would try to contact her, but O'Donnell refused. Suzie was not a suspect and wire tapping her phones would not happen unless she volunteered. O'Donnell liked Suzie and wanted to shield her from as much police harassment as possible. O'Donnell knew Suzie's father when he was still alive. He was the only remaining mechanic in Springdale who could work on the Chief's vintage Indian motorcycle.

The Indian motorcycle was one of the finest bikes in the world and was made in the city. O'Donnell's Indian was one of the rare originals. That bike was O'Donnell's baby. When his wife had died, he got through life by taking long weekend rides in the countryside surrounding Springdale. He was his happiest when he was riding. I'm sure there had been a bug or two flatly mounted on his smiling teeth over the years.

He was once profiled by an evening magazine television show as one of Americana's unsung heroes. His pot belly physique and handlebar moustache combined for the perfect portrait of a gregarious old cop. He had a Wilford Brimley look that left an indelible image etched in your mind. His nostalgic ways and colorful personality had the media enamored. He was also a damn good cop, revered, as he was respected.

Suzie had an infectiously scintillating personality, and an effervescent "Breck Girl" smile that would light up any room, people liked being around her. She was a cheerleader for the same championship team that Kirk had played on and proud to be known as the only cheerleader who had not slept with Kirk. She was pure and striking. Together they were the King and Queen of the prom and prom night was the only time Suzie could ever remember a passionate kiss with her now lost prince.

Suzie always had dreams of meeting someone special and leaving Springdale behind. She hoped it would be Kirk, but worried that he would never "grow up" to notice her in time. She wasn't planning on waiting forever. No one felt safe anymore. Springdale was quickly becoming known as an insidious gang-haven frontier. It was no place to live.

She told the Chief that I couldn't have been involved with Kirk's murder, but had no answers to offer him. She pleaded with him to look at the Latin Kings. She remembered Kirk having a run-in with one of their leaders over a stolen gold chain. O'Donnell remembered it too. He told her not to worry, but that if she did speak to me . . . she must call him on his private line.

CHAPTER 5

When I arrived in New Orleans, I headed straight to the French Quarter. This would prove to be the best place for me to blend in with the crowd of tourists. I needed to take a shower, get a meal and get some sleep. In the morning, I would make a plan and figure out a way of calling Suzie. I stopped at a couple of hotels and was turned away, told I could not have a room without a credit card.

I knew I couldn't stay on the streets, so when I was approached by one of the "ladies of the eve" . . . I immediately inquired whether I could hire her for the night and if her rate included a room with a shower or a tub? She looked at my Rolex, which I had forgotten to take off and said, ***"The whole night? For you sugar? I will do it for $ 1,000."*** I had never spent a thousand dollars for anything in my life, but at that moment in time, it seemed like a bargain.

I followed her around a corner and down an obscure side alley, where she knocked three times, paused and knocked again twice on an old wooden door with a small black painted window and a one way peep hole below.. It must have been some sort of Morse code signal.

A buzzer rang and we quickly entered into an open and smoke-filled, perfumed foyer where a middle-aged woman sat on a battered red velour antique parlor chair, playing solitaire. She had about an inch of make-up, false camel eye lashes, torn fishnet stockings and a masticating cheek of gum with a repeating bubble smack. Her caked-on bright red lipstick looked as if it had been applied with a child's crayon.

My escort walked over to the lady and asked for the room with a bath. The madam looked up at me, as if I was some sort of kinky customer and smiled. She handed the girl a key and she handed me a towel and a clean folded bed sheet. When we entered the room, I gave the happy hooker her money and told her she could take the night off, I just needed some sleep.

For the first time in days, I felt safe. In spite of incessant headboard banging and moaning from every wall around me, when my head hit the pillow- I was out like a light. The sounds penetrating into my subconscious state must have stirred an untapped memory bank. It had evoked a memory of a convention I had attended in Las Vegas years earlier, with Kirk.

It was my first year with Olympiad Shoes and I was attending the International Sports Apparel Show, IS-AS for short. Kirk decided to come along, just for the ride. In classic style, Kirk rented a fire engine red Ferrari Spider from an exotic car agency and we cruised "the Strip" looking for ladies of the neon night.

There was no way I was going to partake in Kirk's revelry with a stranger. My nose would never be able to handle it. So, I talked him into getting tattoos instead. He agreed that a tattoo would be a more enduring memory of our trip. I didn't actually want a tattoo. I was just happy to get his mind off sex. Kirk got a football on his forearm and I settled for the almighty "$" symbol on my shoulder.

Whenever I would see the tattoo in the mirror, it would motivate me to work harder and with a little luck - someday I could retire and buy a bar by the ocean and serve Margaritas all day while listening to Jimmy Buffett songs on a juke box. But now, when I see the tattoo… all I can think of is Kirk…and happier times.

When I woke up in the tawdry house of the rising sun off Bourbon Street, I took a quick bath and headed down the back stairwell leading to the entrance foyer. The same old lady was sitting in the same chair and was still playing a game of cards. The smell of her aromatic coffee barely pierced through the perfumed air, but it was enough to trigger a Pavlovian craving response. I had not had a cup since my hangover in Indianapolis and satisfying my caffeine fix would be my first order of business.

Walking out of the old house of pleasure, I was greeted by an intense wall of sweltering and humid heat. It was only 8:00 a.m. and the late summer southern temperature was a surprise to my northern thick skin. I had no plans except to find a new change of clothes and buy a disposable prepaid cell phone to call Suzie. I wasn't sure if one of those phones could be traced. I figured it was my best bet.

On one of the corners in the city, stood a coffee shop with a bright flashing sign promoting its new iced coffee. The beacon drew me directly to the store, a comforting lighthouse in my java fogged harbor. I entered and stood in line behind the counter to wait for my fresh brew. In the corner of the café was a small sitting area with laptop connections and a stack of daily newspapers. On the wall was a mounted flat screen plasma television, broadcasting the morning news.

From where I was standing, I could not hear the audio, but the national cable video was unmistakable. It was Chief O'Donnell on the steps of Springdale Police station headquarters in front of an unleashed barrage of intrepid reporters. A streaming headline was scrolling across the bottom of the screen alerting viewers of the "breaking news" **according to Amtrak officials, murder suspect Jesse Thorpe is believed to be somewhere in the Gulf area.**

I stood paralyzed; starring at the television, with multiple beads of sweat instantly sprouting on my forehead like a time lapsed video of mushrooms growing on a hill. I looked down at the carpet, and went blank. It was the same sensation I sometimes felt when I stood up too quickly and the blood rushed from my head. I lowered myself to one knee and steadied myself for a moment, until my vision returned. I was completely oblivious to my surroundings until the café attendant loudly repeated his request to help the next customer in line. I heard the rambling voices, but could not react. Instead, I stood up, turned away and darted out of the café without my coffee.

My desire for caffeine was replaced with a dire need for flight, a change of clothes and an urgent call to Suzie. I found a small touristy clothing boutique and a sidewalk news kiosk across the busy street and on the next block. Again, I began to run. It may have been my imagination, but suddenly I felt the whole world was watching me and everyone knew who I was and why I was running.

When I came out of the store, I lowered the bill of my new Saints cap to cover my eyes and shield as much of my face as possible. With my vision partially hindered, I walked directly into the path of a mounted police officer, on his horse, making his morning rounds. I looked up, muttered an apology for my clumsiness and inadvertently made burning eye contact with the cop.

The officer looked down at me and gestured for me to approach him. Fortunately for me, he was distracted by his horse's nervousness brought on by the banter of excited school children asking if they could pet the popular equine.

The momentary commotion allowed me time to turn and blend back into the throng of tourists. I quickly joined a nearby line of workers boarding an old green painted school bus. Sensing my exposure, I spontaneously got on the bus and headed toward the back row and sat down. I slouched down behind a husky man in the seat in front of me and bent down pretending to tie my shoe.

Before the bus could pull away, the officer rode his horse in front of the bus and flagged the driver to stay put. He slowly paraded his horse around the bus peering briefly in each window he passed. As he cleared the left side, I jumped over from the right side and took a seat on the left. Somehow, remarkably, I went unnoticed.

The officer waved the bus on and after a loud backfire from the exhaust and a grinding missed gear; we bounced and back lashed out of the congested city area. Just like my life, I didn't know where I was heading, but anywhere was better than where I was. The other men on the bus looked like migrant workers and most were speaking Spanish. Fortunately, they paid no attention to the uninvited passenger among them. I felt like a timid school child on his first day of school, surrounded by bullies peering at me from all directions through the corner slits of their conniving eyes.

This seemed to be as bad a time as any to call Suzie, so I did. When she answered, she sounded very nervous. Her anxious, quivering voice asked me if I was O.K. I told her I was fine and I was in . . . she interrupted me and said she did not want to know where I was in case someone was listening. She thought I should "lay low" for a while. She told me it didn't look good for me.

Apparently when the news had hit Boston, everyone in the media found out about it. It was just the kind of story that people loved and rating hungry news networks knew it. Even a national crime catcher's show had contacted the Springdale market and informed them of their interest in running a half hour segment on the murder mystery. Soon, everyone and anyone with a TV would know my face.

Suzie said she couldn't talk to me any longer, people were watching her. Before I said goodbye, I advised her to call a man named Wayne Alden, he worked for the FBI. I told Suzie that he could clear me. He knows what happened to Kirk. I quickly told her that I didn't do it. Before she hung up, I heard her reassuring and dulcet voice say,

"I know you didn't, hang in there babe."

Her voice was a soothing sound in my tortured sea of pain.

CHAPTER 6

October 19th was a quintessential New England fall day. The autumn foliage colors were exceptionally brilliant this year. Bright red sugar maple leaves cast upon the backdrop of a deep indigo blue sky, with rays of glorious sun illuminating the classic white steeple church in the center of Meadows. By all accounts this could be the model setting for a Norman Rockwell Saturday Evening Post cover.

But the dolorous visitors to the historic village town did not notice any of its colorful beauty. With weighted hearts, heads hung low and dressed in black, they filed into the picturesque church for the solemn funeral service of their lost friend, Kirk Preston.

The somber day had brought together hundreds of old friends, from all over the country, every one of them with their own stories of Kirk. He was instantly a best friend to all; he had never met a stranger. Kirk had no known immediate relatives. He was adopted at the age of ten when his biological parents died in a tragic New Years Eve car crash. His parents both suffered and battled with alcoholism for most of their adult lives

It was on a snowy night they drove their Bentley down the wrong side of the Long Island Expressway directly into the path of an unforgiving snow plow truck. They were returning, from a high-society party, to their palatial seaside mansion in the posh town of South Hampton on New York's Long Island. That's when their lives ended and the lives of their family changed forever.

Kirk's childhood was a very sad one. He would seldom talk about it. I never asked. Kirk never drank hard alcohol and vowed to never marry. I am sure that the memories of his childhood were the reasons for his silent and disconnected pain.

His Grandfather had arranged for him to be adopted by an elderly couple he had known during his travels. They were professors at an Ivy League college about 30 miles north of Springdale, but they lived in Meadows. The adopting couple did not have children themselves and in fact, didn't even like children. They accepted the adoption proposal along with a generous stipend from the wealthy grandfather, to care for the tragically abandoned child.

On the day Kirk turned eighteen his adopted parents endorsed the trust fund to a new executor and moved to France to complete a book they were writing on European history. Kirk remained in the modest brick ranch house, which he had completely gutted and converted into a swank bachelor pad.

No one was really surprised to see that his adopted parents did not attend the funeral. They had sent a simple wreath, with a note that read, *we will miss you.* Their absence at the funeral was akin to their absence in his life. It didn't much matter anyway. The church was abundantly filled from the towering oak doors to the stain glass altar, with unforgotten love mixed with anguished pain and sorrow.

The closed white casket, covered with yellow roses, was carried out of the church by members of Kirk's famed football team of 92' and placed in a white hearse. The tranquil sound of singing birds and the ringing of the 200-year-old church bell signaled the congregation as they made their way to the endless line of cars, stretching around the one mile verdant town green. The placid sounds were quelled by the roaring sound of Chief O'Donnell's Indian Motorcycle taking the lead escort position for the short procession to the town's historic cemetery.

Before arriving at the graveyard, the motorcade would detour to make a stop and circle around the town's football field-once Kirk's hallowed ground. At the center of the field was a ceremonial civil war company of five uniformed soldiers. They fired a five-musket salute and played an emotional round of taps on the bugle to a hauntingly silent crowd of mourners. On the final echoing note the quaint town of Meadows was painfully empty.

CHAPTER 7

The investigation was moving along, but too slow for the media. O'Donnell put the word out to his detectives to keep an eye and ear open among the city's gang leaders. He didn't want to be accused of rushing to judgment on me, without the due diligence of first exploring and following up on all leads.

One of the team members thought it would be a good idea to have the lab people scour Kirk's house. O'Donnell thought the house search was a waste of time; the crime scene was not the house. It was on Mt. Tom, and the mountain had already been searched with a fine tooth comb. Instead, he told the young detectives to hit the streets and hear what people are talking about.

The Chief was beginning to show signs of stress and the pressure was on from the DA, the Mayor and even more importantly, the media. He was already losing control of the case. On top of everything, producers from nearly every national cable news show were beginning their own independent investigations. The Chief's once adoring media now questioned and scurrilously attacked the older O'Donnell's experience in murder cases and his level of professional competency in directing a case as sensational as the Preston killing.

In front of a live camera, an overzealous reporter asked him to comment on his theory of why Kirk's plane flew from nearby Municipal Airport in Westford to Richmond, Virginia and immediately back again just one day before his murder. And why did Kirk Preston have a three million-dollar life insurance policy payable to his trust fund if he was the only beneficiary and a second new policy for a million dollars naming me as the beneficiary?

O'Donnell was stunned by the revelations, but, without chagrin, he was able to get out of it, like the seasoned and unflappable pro he was. He gave the standard answer: he was investigating all leads and could not comment during an ongoing case. The pressure had a sobering effect on O'Donnell though, and he was no longer completely confident of his task. When the cameras were turned off, O'Donnell closed his office door, leaned over his desk, put his face in his hands and asked himself,

"Why me? With just two more years, why me? Good grief."

Within hours, the police station switchboard was deluged with calls from nearly every television cable news program. All the evening anchor personalities were there trying to "scoop" the story from their competition. The onslaught of media mayhem to the city of homes took on a carnival atmosphere. The street in front of the police headquarters had been partitioned off to traffic to allow for the mini media compounds to erect camera locations and remote anchor studios.

There were mounds of cables and wires tossed about and piled like an electronic spaghetti buffet in the street. Springdale became "satellite city" overnight. News anchors were blinded in spotlights, shoulder to shoulder, while interns heavily powdered their weathered Botox faces and performed sound checks from live trucks. Soon, thirsty television audiences would be drinking from a fire hose of information and the news itself would become the news.

O'Donnell refused to take any calls, except for one that curiously came from a pawn shop in Miami, Florida. The voice on the phone was Nicky Cardoni, the owner of "Pawn n`Go Check Cashing." He had just accepted and paid for an 18-karat gold high school ring with a custom diamond inlay. According to Cardoni, the inscription on the inside of the ring read K. Preston. 92' HS Champs.

The store owner also told O'Donnell he had a picture of the customer on his security camera. He had seen the story on the news and wondered if the ring had a connection. This was the break O'Donnell was hoping for and it was a lead that he alone had received.

Something didn't smell right with the cheesy call though. The caller had somehow bypassed his secretary's phone and accessed an unpublished dedicated number in order to directly reach the Chief's desk. O'Donnell didn't want to share this information with the other detectives until he had seen the picture of the person who allegedly pawned Kirk's ring.

To the caller, O'Donnell tried to seem unimpressed with the information, but inside he knew the man was lying about accepting the ring. O'Donnell knew where the ring was and it wasn't in Miami. So why would a complete stranger want to lie to the police, he wondered. What's the motivation? O'Donnell was holding an ace in his socks. He would reveal it later, in an "all in" raise, when all the players were most vulnerable.

O'Donnell wanted to take the heat off of me, and this was the clue that would help move the case in a different direction. The Chief never believed that I was the killer, but the evidence was too overwhelming to ignore. The manager of the pawn shop offered to e-mail the picture when his daughter came back from shopping.

Cardoni said his daughter knew how to work the computer better than he did. Chief O'Donnell thanked Cardoni and asked him to send the picture to his personal e-mail, instead of the stations, as soon as possible. Cardoni was certain that the picture he had was that of Kirk's killer or at the very least, someone who knew the killer.

When he hung up the phone, he sent a unit over to the airport to check out and secure Kirk's airplane for possible evidence. If the detectives found anything unusual, he would call the boys from the state lab to give the plane their routine forensics dust.

CHAPTER 8

The bus on which I stowed away continued out of the business district and made a second stop outside the crescent city to pick up about another 10 workers from some sort of temporary compound. I watched as the able-bodied workmen left their tents, trailers and smoldering trash can fires to line up for the approaching bus. The bus was filling to capacity and I knew I would soon have to share my undeserved seat with one of them.

I slid over as the men walked up the aisle and offered up some of my space. I figured sitting alone would only attract more attention, and that was the last thing I needed. A young Hispanic fellow gestured at my seat as he approached and sat down. He nodded his head to me. I thought I would try my luck at Espanol and said,

"Hola! Como esta?"

I knew that my year of Spanish class would come in handy someday. The man replied,

"Sorry man I don't speak Spanish."

"Great! Neither do I. Can you tell me where we're going?" I whispered

"Same place as yesterday, the 7th ward area, by the lower levy. Where are your gloves?"

"I, ummmm, forgot them," I answered.

"I'm Cole, are you a new guy?" the stranger asked

"Yeah, I'm new. My name is . . . uh. Pete," I stuttered.

"Hi . . . uhpete nice to meet you."

"Sorry" I said, *"I'm a little nervous"*

"Don't worry about it, stick with me, I'll show you the ropes, it's easy work and better yet it's easy money, just the way it should be in the big easy, right?"

I smiled at his good nature and looked around continuing to assess my situation. I gathered that we were some sort of salvage crew on our way to clean up the rubble of destroyed homes from the aftermath of Hurricane Katrina. With everything on my mind, I had completely forgotten about the unprecedented devastation this area had encountered just a few months ago. I was shocked to see all the scars that still remained.

As I watched out the window, street after street, house after house was gone, with only a hand full in the rebuild mode. The only signs of life were the stray dogs, rats, birds and garbage, everywhere garbage.

I realized my selfish problems were actually quite petty when it came to the issues some people were hopelessly facing every day. I just needed to wait out my problems and everything would be fine. These people, on the other-hand, were fighting for their mere existence, a bright to blight turn of a page in a very real tragic story.

It all seemed so incomprehensibly cruel. Homes that stood as monuments to good people living the dream, now lay shattered from nature's war, a simple white X painted upon their once symbolic doors. It was enough for the most reverent to question this ungodly act of worthless suffering. Where did God's love go, when the Devil's tropical girl began to blow? Why, why? But there would be no answers, only a growing descent between a government and the people it purports to serve and protect.

When the bus stopped, everyone filed out. I just followed along with Cole and the crowd. The foreman at the site looked like a chain gang guard out of a Cool Hand Luke set with mirrored glasses and an unlit stubby cigar in his mouth. His shirt's lapel read FEMA. Super, I thought. I am now hiding from and working for the government at the same time. But I figured at least half of the other workers were probably illegal too. It didn't seem to matter to anyone.

I grabbed a shovel and got to work. Each work area of rubble would need to be sorted and separated into piles of wood, metal & plastic. When an area was cleared, we would spray-paint the dirt in front of the pile and a bucket loader, followed by a long row of dump trucks would remove the refuse. It was backbreaking dirty work, but a temporary clean escape. I felt safe. It also gave me time to think about my situation and to plan my next move.

CHAPTER 9

It was Wednesday morning, which meant that Suzie had to go back to work after taking a couple of days off for Kirk's funeral. I wish I could have been there for a formal farewell. I still can't believe he's gone and that I'm the one being blamed for my best friend's death. It was all too surreal.

The spa, where Suzie worked, is a renovated antique colonial located on the town green. It is directly opposite and in full view of the picturesque white church, the church that would never be the same to any of the town's residents, especially Suzie. Her co-workers greeted her with comforting hugs and supportive smiles as she entered the doors of the spa. They could not imagine what she was going through. One of her best friends was murdered. Her other best friend was the accused. What a hopeless world in which she found herself.

She wiped a tear from her cheek and thanked everyone for being there for her. Suzie took great solace in finding her desk full of sympathy cards and a large bouquet of fall-colored flowers. She opened one of the accompanying cards and read the note that had been sent from Chief O'Donnell. It simply read *"I am thinking of you, brighter days are ahead, I promise."*

She paused for a moment and looked out the window, starring at the church, remembering Kirk. The town green in front of the church was busy with a bevy of scampering squirrels chasing each other up and around the trunks of the 100-year-old oak trees and gathering acorns in preparation for the long looming winter months ahead. An occasional blustering wind would unhinge dying leaves from their summer loft and gently float them down to be joined amidst a parade of cart-wheeling color crossing the historic lawn.

This season, one most New Englanders longed for, would never be the same for Suzie. Reminders of the ever drifting change from life to death, light to dark, and warmth to cold would now dominate all other thoughts of beauty.

Suzie focused beyond the green and became affixed on the church's large brown stone steps and the eight foot hunter green double doors framed by oversized planters filled with bright yellow mums. A flashback she once had, of a dream, drifted her mind away. It was a dream where she would marry Kirk and they would walk down those very steps of the church with all of their friends tossing yellow rose pedals at them before they drove off to their new life. Instead, the storybook image had turned to a picture of six pall bearers, a white casket, and the very real death of her dreams, her pleasure, now replaced with her pain.

Suzie had always thought that some day she and Kirk might be together. Kirk and Suzie had strong feelings for each other, but it was sort of an unspoken love. Occasionally, when their eyes would meet, there would be a long drawn and deep stare, a silent gaze beneath the surface. It was a storied secret love for each other they never openly shared. For Suzie, the look was a window into a fragile and dark soul - a yearning call for love and understanding. For Kirk, the vision was a world of love he longingly dreamed for, but tragically feared - a rose bud never to bloom. His past was the bane of his existence and the emotional compass for his life's misdirection.

Her melancholy voyage ended with her co-worker informing her of her customer. It would prove to be a very busy morning for Suzie at the Spa, due primarily to all of the recent cancellations and rescheduling and also for the fact she was the most popular attendant.

She was happy to be busy on her first day back, it kept her mind off Kirk and me and it was also good for her to see her old friends from town. One of her nail clients was Lori Ferguson. She was also a cheerleader on Suzie's squad and worked as a bank teller in town. Lori knew Kirk well and had sat with Suzie during the funeral.

They talked briefly about the beautiful ceremony and about how all of the girls that had come from out of town, looked so old and overweight. That made Suzie smile. Lori then asked Suzie if she knew about Kirk's money troubles. Lori went on to tell her that Kirk came into the bank about a month ago, to draw money from his trust fund account, but that there were no funds available. Suzie said she knew all about that, even though she didn't. Suzie was puzzled, but suggested to Lori that it was just a technical issue with Kirk's executor's office.

Soon after Lori's appointment Suzie felt nauseous and decided she could not continue working. It had already been a difficult morning. She just wasn't ready to go back to the reality of work. Her life had changed and falling back into a routine as if nothing was different, was going to be difficult, if not impossible.

Suzie regrettably notified the staff she needed to cancel her remaining afternoon appointments. Before she went home to her apartment, she decided to stop by the police station and personally thank O'Donnell for his generous gift of flowers and for the thoughtful card.

CHAPTER 10

The police station had what seemed like a permanent TV satellite camp outside its front doors, waiting for a "breaking news" press conference, unless another big story broke somewhere else; Springdale is where the top journalists would remain. It had everything the media wanted in a juicy prime time story. The town hero…the star athlete…the young handsome and wealthy resident of a small New England town found murdered on the mountain. But O'Donnell had no intention of talking to the tenacious media, after the last ambush he had to endure from a reporter and in front of a live camera.

His office was beginning to look like a college dorm room during finals. There were empty Chinese food containers on the shelves, candy wrappers on the floor, and an empty bitterly burnt coffee pot still sitting on its hot burner. He had been working late hours behind closed doors, sifting through evidence and following-up on leads generated by my photo appearing on every cable news show for the past five days.

When Suzie came by, he jumped from his chair, buckled up his belt and cleaned a spot for her to sit. She was a welcomed visitor and a bright sight for his crusty sore eyes. He apologized for his office and for the odor. He explained that he had been working hard to find Kirk's killer. Of course, Suzie understood.

She did worry about him though. She noticed an open bottle of Nitroglycerin pills on his desk. Suzie's father had died of a heart attack which was blamed on stress and working long hours. Suzie knew the Chief's stress from this case was a metabolic time bomb. She didn't want to see anything happen to him, especially because he also espoused my innocence. He was the only one, in a position of authority, that hadn't already convicted me of Kirk's death. He told her not to worry, he was tired, but he was otherwise doing just fine.

She thanked him for the lovely flowers. His response to her was a straight, eye-to-eye non hesitating question,

"Suzie, I need to ask you, how is Jesse doing?"

They looked at each-other for a moment. His instincts told him that Suzie had been in contact with him. Although the whites of his eyes served as a palette for bloodshot lightening bolts, she saw a trusting twinkle that prevented her from lying. She thought about her dad again and his long friendship with O'Donnell over the years and she replied in her soft voice,

"He is doing all right, he's scared, but he's safe."

He smiled at her, leaned forward and whispered softly back,

"Tell him I need a few more days and for now, maybe it would be best if he stayed out of sight and didn't call."

Before Suzie could say another word, the Chief's intercom on his desk began beeping and flashing. O'Donnell asked Suzie to bear with him for just a second and he would walk her out. He pushed the "receive call" button on the system and announced his name,

"This is O'Donnell and it better be important."

The voice on the other end was detective Brian Murphy at the Westford Municipal Airport where he had been instructed to secure and possibly impound Kirk Preston's airplane for investigation. He responded to his bosses' comment,

"Oh it's important all right. I'm in Preston's airplane. You better get out here fast. We've got a problem, a big problem."

O'Donnell grabbed his jacket and hat and asked Suzie if she wanted to take a ride to the airport. He wanted to talk to her some more about Kirk and the 20 minute ride would be a perfect opportunity away from his office. She agreed and within minutes they were in a Springdale patrol car, heading to Westford.

CHAPTER 11

I hadn't worked this hard for years. It was nearly a 12-hour day, with only a 30 minute break for water and a couple of stale beignets. I felt like I was paying a debt to society with some sort of community service sentence. Occasionally, I would stand up and stretch my crooked back and wipe my brow and get a brief glimpse of the Gulf of Mexico.

It was hard to believe that this was once a thriving tourist destination. I could envision what the harbor area looked like before the hurricane. I imagined the bright lights of the seaside casinos, restaurants and shops, people everywhere. I heard the rising and falling sounds of classic jamming jazz escaping from doors as they opened and closed. I could almost smell the homemade jambalaya steam from the air vents of restaurant kitchens.

It was a spirit that filled you in every way imaginable. But the reality was it was all gone, just a faint light struggling to penetrate through a distant but deep soul. I couldn't help but think that my work was in some way helping to bring that all back again. It actually felt very rewarding to be making a difference, albeit a small difference, but a lot more purposeful than pushing expensive Chinese-made sneakers.

I was reminded of a line from a movie I had once heard, *if you're not living for something, then you're dying for nothing.* I promised myself that some day I would return here and proudly tell my kids that I helped to resuscitate the heartbeat of this place. Better yet, maybe I would just stay here and work in that Jimmy Buffet bar I always dreamed of.

I didn't see Cole for most of the day. He was asked to work on a secret copper detail when we arrived at the site. The foreman had figured out a way of making some extra money at the expense of FEMA by separating all of the copper tubing from the metal piles and placing it in his personal pick-up truck and using the paid workers to do all the work. When everybody left on their buses, he would drive to a metal scrap yard and cash in on the side for the valuable metal. Ah yes, our government hard at work.

The sun was gently setting over the Gulf and everything in its midst took on a warm orange hue. A line of flying Pelicans coasted by, silhouetted against the backdrop of the fiery sky. The sound of breaking waves blended like the percussion section of an orchestra and trumpeted by the horn of a shrimp boat announcing its return to the resting harbor. It was starting to get dark and when a bell sounded from atop a nearby tower, everyone dropped their tools and slowly started walking back to the waiting bus.

I waited behind for Cole, so I could board the bus with him at the same time. I was planning to sit with him again to learn what would be happening next. As I walked up the stairs of the modified school bus, I was handed a voucher by the driver and I immediately followed Cole to the back of the bus and quickly lowered my head and took my seat.

When I settled into my seat, the bus released its air-brakes and started off. I peeked down at the paper I was given. It was a government-issued coupon for $300 redeemable at any bank, post office or participating federal agency. I was stunned by the seemingly bottomless pockets of money our government had when it came to dealing with a problem.

Three hundred dollars, tax free, for one day's worth of work. It may have been commensurate with my physical and mental travail, but even so, this was a gig I could definitely work for a while, and go completely unnoticed. I asked Cole where he was heading and what he was doing after work. I was partly curious and I was also hoping for an invitation.

I didn't have anywhere to go or should I say "hide" and so far, he was the only person I knew. He told me he was staying at the work center and if I was planning on saving my earned money, I should consider it too.

The work center was a FEMA subsidized temporary housing unit for the workers and it was free. I could take a shower and pick up a free box dinner there. There weren't any more rooms available, but he told me to grab a tent from the storage trailer behind the building and recommended that I get my name on the list for the next open room. I wasn't planning on giving my name out to anyone, so the tent option sounded like a good one.

I ate my dinner outside, where I was more comfortable in the obscure early darkness of the night. It was difficult for me to know just how far the news of my manhunt had spread, but I wasn't taking any chances. The longer I could stay free, the better chances I had of Suzie and the others finding Kirk's real killer.

I followed Cole's suggestion and procured a tent for the night and proceeded to set it up. I decided to pitch it among another group of tents, where I would hopefully blend in, and not be noticed. My incompetence, however, and total lack of any mechanical ability to figure out the tent, made me stand out like a broken thumb. Fortunately, Cole was passing by at the time and came to my rescue, again.

I don't know why we became friends so quickly, maybe it was because we were the only two on our work crew who spoke English or maybe someone was just watching over me. I don't know. It didn't matter. Cole was a good guy and he had already served as a safe haven in my storm. He had just run into some bad luck and decided to work the salvage effort for a few weeks for quick cash. He didn't seem like the others.

Within a matter of minutes, Cole had anchored all four sides of the tent and raised the center with the provided metal support stakes. I thanked him for his help and told him I was going to lie down for a while and that I would catch up with him a little later.

Cole reminded me,

"Hey, don't forget about the bonfire tonight. It's a good time."
"Great, that sounds . . . good," I answered with slight hesitation.

I hadn't actually planned on going to the nightly party. It didn't seem smart for me to be outwardly sociable considering my situation.

"I'll come and get you around nine and show you where it is," Cole said.

"Uh..Great, I . . . uh..will be right here, thanks," I said.

I crawled into my tent and rolled up my sweatshirt into a ball to use as a pillow and I laid down for a short contemplative nap. I was completely exhausted from my day of manual labor and my body was feeling the effects of the heavy lifting. Even under these dire conditions and circumstances, I fell into an immediate deep sleep.

I was never a very good judge of time, particularly when I was sleeping. Sometimes an eight-hour sleep could feel more like a thirty minute snooze, and a two-hour nap could feel like a ten second blink. When Cole called my name, I didn't respond right away. For one thing, I kept forgetting that I used the name Pete as an alias.

Looking back, I feel kind of guilty for lying to my new friend. He had been genuinely kind to me. I was just confused and didn't trust anyone at the time. Cole pulled aside the canvas curtain door and raised his voice a little more.

"Hey Pete, wake up dude."

He startled me for an instant.

"Whoa, sorry Cole. I must have been really zonked. Is it nine o'clock already?" I asked.

"Oh yeah, come on get up. It's party time," Cole announced.

Before leaving the tent, I grabbed a bottle of water and poured a little into the palm of my hand and splashed it on my face and then I ran my wet fingers through my makeshift pillow-flattened hair. Cole led the way and I followed behind the main pavilion and down a narrow half mile sandy path through the woods leading to a dune clearing.

The soothing sounds of cicadas and tree frogs silenced momentarily as we hiked down the wooded path and then resumed their repertoire as we safely passed. From a distance, I could see a roaring fire and red-hot embers floating up in the air like dancing fire flies in a black summer sky, rising randomly and spiraling toward the still silver stars above.

As I approached, I could make out about thirty to forty people standing around the fire, each drinking a bottle of beer. Their faces glowed with a warm orange hue, each of them smiling, laughing and gazing into the hearth and its mesmerizing flames. The rhythmic soft sounds of mixing southern jazz came into a clear fine tune as we made our way closer.

"Hey this is really cool. I feel like I'm back in high school or something," I told Cole.

Cole turned to me and said,

"Oh you're gonna love this. Hey, have ya got ten bucks on ya?"
"Sure."

I reached into my shirt pocket and peeled off a ten-dollar bill and handed it to Cole.

"Thanks Pete, everybody chips in ten bucks for the band. They've all been out of work since the hurricane. We like to help em out, plus they bring the beer and the crawfish."
"Oh man, this is soooo cool," I repeated.

Among those gathered, were the workers from the salvage crew, some locals and four musicians. The band consisted of one bass player, one sax, one trumpet and a drummer with a make shift ensemble of upside down plastic barrels. Cole tossed our crumpled bills into the open bass case and greeted the members of the band, who in turn, tipped their hats and nodded their heads.

Cole looked over to me,

"How about a cold one?"
"Are you kidding? I can't think of anything better," I replied.

Cole opened a bottle of beer and handed it to me and then opened one for himself and raised it and clinked them together. I was feeling very relaxed and even started to mingle around with the other people. To the side of the large fire, was a smaller smoldering one, with another group of people surrounding it.

The fire had been covered by a layer of wet seaweed and then layered with a couple of bushels of spiced crawfish and covered by a wet mesh blanket. When the blanket was periodically removed, the rising plume of steam would billow and fill the air with a mouth-watering aroma from the delicacy below. It was the signal for everyone to get in line, scoop up a batch and pile them in their bowl.

This party was just what the doctor ordered for me to unwind from all of my recent stress. I have been a lover of jazz music all my life. I even played a little clarinet in a group, back in high school. My dad introduced me to the great legends like Charlie "Birdman" Parker and John Coltrane. I still listen to Miles Davis, whenever I "Getz" a chance.

Something about that music soothes my soul and brings me great comfort. Somehow it always unraveled those tangled lovin' blues that followed me and had become the tattered patch quilt of my miserable being. Music has a way of taking you away, a private endless journey that hypnotically lifts the shredded fibers of your spirit to anywhere you will allow yourself to go no matter where you are, or who you're with. For me, music was her name. Needless to say, I was grateful for Cole insisting I come along. What a night. What a trip - a welcomed, but temporary, escape from my troubles back home.

The band played for several hours and the partygoers became more and more festive as the brews continued to flow freely. Cole was impressed that I knew every selection the band played. It wasn't long before some of the party gals were slapping tambourines and playfully dancing around the fire. One by one, the ensemble would pick people out of the group to join them in a little percussion or a sing-along.

Maybe it was the beer that made me feel so bold or maybe just the good vibes I was absorbing into my desperate shattered world, but I moved to the front of the crowd and stood tall, in hopes of being chosen to join the band. When the bass player pointed to me, I jumped up and pointed back to a clarinet which stood on a stand next to the sax player. I can still hear Cole's voice like it was yesterday.

"All right Pete..take it away. Go baby go."

The bass player looked around at the other members of the band and then counted off four counts to start. I could have named that tune in three notes. It was one of my favorites, **Sweet Georgia Brown**.

We all played a stanza of harmony and then in traditional jazz keeping, each musician performed a solo rendition, with the others playing a supporting background accompaniment. Then we all joined in for the final harmonic finish. When the solo time came for me to display my clarinet ability, I went crazy with a progressive flurry of notes. My fingers moved like excited spider legs. I drew everyone's attention. It was one of the best times I had ever had.

When I finished, the crowd screamed, hooted, hollered and whistled. Cole came to the front of the cheering gang and raised his hands in the air for me to slap. It was great. I wished the night would never end.

CHAPTER 12

The ride to the airport in O'Donnell's police cruiser took Suzie and O'Donnell out of Springdale heading west about 10 miles into the scenic New England country side. It wasn't often that the Chief would leave the city on business and he welcomed the opportunity to get away from the station for a while, especially with the mounting pressure he was feeling from media surrounding the Preston case. O'Donnell savored the ride with Suzie. He was in no hurry. He didn't run his siren or flash his lights and didn't even take the most direct route to the small municipal airport.

About three miles away from the airport, O'Donnell pulled the cruiser over to the side of the road near a rest stop, overlooking the scenic Pioneer Valley and the Westford River. As he was pulling in, he said to Suzie,

"I used to stop at this rest stop with my wife every Sunday after church and have fresh apple cider doughnuts and coffee. I just love coming here. It brings me back to a happy time in my life."

Suzie looked at him and knew that something was wrong. She always knew that O'Donnell was a sentimental guy, but stopping on the way to an urgent police call, didn't seem characteristic, even for the laid back O'Donnell.

"Is everything all right? Shouldn't we be getting to Kirk's plane?" asked Suzie.

O'Donnell paused, took a big breath and exhaled. He reached down and shut off his radio and his mounted computer. He unhooked his seatbelt and shifted his body to allow himself to turn toward her. He took off his glasses and rubbed his eyes.

"Suzie, what I am about to tell you, only two other people know in this world."

"What is it?"

"I know what happened to Kirk and I am probably to blame for his death," said O'Donnell, with his head contritely slumped down and his eyes shut.

Suzie felt a shiver run through her body and wasn't sure what she had just heard. She abruptly placed her hand upon his and said,

"What are you talking about?"

O'Donnell told Suzie about a meeting he had in the Mayor's office about two months earlier. It was a Monday morning and O'Donnell stopped by City Hall to have a coffee with Mayor, as he had done every morning for years. But this morning when he walked into the Mayor's office there was another man sitting in front of the Mayor's old desk.

He stood up quickly when the police Chief entered the room and introduced himself as FBI Agent Wayne Alden.

Suzie interrupted him,

"Did you say his name was Alden?" she asked.

"Yeah, Agent Alden, he's from Boston, but had been working in Springdale," he replied.

Suzie told the Chief,

"Jesse told me to call him. He told me that Alden could clear him of the murder charges."

O'Donnell just shook his head and warned Suzie,

"This guy is bad news. You don't want to call him. I don't know how Jesse knows him or why he told you that, but stay away from Agent Alden. He's very dangerous and powerfully corrupt."

O'Donnell continued to describe the initial introduction in Mayor Sullivan's office. When the Chief shook his hand, he joked with him for a minute about the FBI still stuck in Springdale after two years of investigating corruption in city government and only finding a fraud case in the housing dept. Agent Alden snickered a bit, but was all business.

It was true what O'Donnell had said and Alden knew it. He was assigned to look into the city's dealings and find something to hang an indictment on, no matter what it was. After two years of running around, impounding records and computers from every department in the county, he kept coming up empty, and the Boston office was not happy about the wasted time and resources they had spent.

The Mayor spoke first,

> *"Take it easy Tommy. Remember when you were venting in my office a couple of weeks ago about the feds wasting time, and money, investigating us, while our own citizens were afraid to even go outside? Well, it looks like someone heard your cry."*

Agent Alden knew that if he didn't bring home something to the Boston office, his chance to make inspector someday would be "zip." Alden decided that his best chance to shake up Springdale was to take down the drug trade by the local gangs and that's where his focus would shift.

The Feds had always labeled Springdale as being a corridor for drug distribution in the Northeast. The FBI theorized that Springdale was the link between New York, Boston & Providence, and if any progress was going to be made in the battle, Springdale would be the logical place to start.

When the three men sat down, Agent Alden asked for their cooperation in creating a sting operation that would attract the drug kingpins to the area where he could bring them to justice. It would take collaboration from all jurisdictions while involving only the top level personnel, if it was to be successful. His proposal resonated loud and clear. The Mayor and police Chief were all in favor of getting a little help from the Feds on this one, and offered to do whatever he requested.

Alden's plan was to use someone from outside the police dept. and the FBI, someone popular who people knew had money, a high roller type who had nothing to do with law enforcement.

O'Donnell looked at the agent and asked,

"Isn't it against policy to use a civilian in a law enforcement operation, a dangerous one at that?"

The agent simply responded,

"Of course it is and the drug network knows it. We aren't forcing anyone to do it. It is strictly volunteer and top secret. He will be handsomely rewarded and will have complete protection from any danger."

Suzie sat in the police car in complete disbelief as she anticipated his next words about the conversation in the Mayor's office.

"Please don't tell me you recommended Kirk," Suzie pleaded.

O'Donnell admitted that he had, but with the assurance that Kirk would be protected at all times and nothing would happen. Suzie just starred out the side window away from O'Donnell and felt a tear fill in her eye and overflow down her cheek. O'Donnell offered her a tissue. Suzie looked at him and shook her head.

He started up the cruiser and pulled out of the rest stop. His mood had suddenly changed and as he sped toward the airport with siren and emergency lights fully activated. He looked over at Suzie and said,

"I'm going to get the cockroaches who did this, I promise. Kirk will not have died in vane. They're all going down. All of em, including that son-of-a-bitch agent."

Chapter 13

I woke up when I felt dripping rain on the back of my neck, seeping through my government-issued tent. Before I got up, I laid still and remembered an overnight boy scouting trip I had taken with my dad to the Mohawk Trail in the Berkshires, when I was just eleven. The smell of the wet canvas and the sound of the pelting rain triggered this cherished tangible memory of my childhood.

I remembered looking out of my tent and seeing my dad leaning over a pile of tinder and protecting it with his jacket and blowing as hard as he could to start a fire in the pouring rain and how proud of him I was when he got the only fire started at the entire campsite.

I don't have many memories of my dad, but those that I have I hold close and wouldn't trade for anyone's. Whenever I think of him, it warms my heart and I wonder if I will ever have a son who will look at me in the same way that I idolized him. He was the finest man I ever knew.

A voice from outside the tent immediately brought me back to the present time and unfortunately for me, my present situation. It was Cole, standing outside in the rain with an umbrella notifying me that because of the weather there wouldn't be any work today and he was planning on going fishing with a buddy of his and I was welcome to tag along.

I knew I couldn't stay in the tent all day, so I told him to give me 20 minutes and I would shower-up, grab some rain gear and be ready to go. Cole told me I wouldn't need the rain gear. The weather out in the gulf was just fine. He couldn't wait 20 minutes. He needed to meet his buddy right away and get the boat ready.

He suggested I grab a taxi and tell the driver to go to pier # 14 and for me to look for "T-dock 7." By the time the taxi arrived for me the rain was beginning to let up and the air was uncomfortably heavy with humidity.

I got in the back of the festering garlic infused yellow cab and gave the instructions to the driver. I felt very uneasy in the cab and insecure when I noticed that the driver was starring at me in the rearview mirror more than he was watching the road in front of him. Something didn't seem right.

The driver picked up his microphone on his CB radio and began speaking in slang French dialog in such a fast and excited pace that it would even have impressed Evelyn Wood. I gathered he might be alerting someone of his fugitive passenger. Could he have recognized me from the TV reports? Should I ditch the cab at the next slow turn or traffic light and make a run for it? I could taste the distinct flavor of blood on the back of my tongue, when I sniffled and knew that I would soon be bleeding profusely from my nose. I decided that running would be even worse.

If I was simply paranoid about the whole thing in my mind, then running away from a cab fare would definitely have the police after me and I wouldn't be able to go back to the housing facility where I was picked up by the taxi. Besides, I had no clue where I was. About ten agonizing minutes later I could see the tops of undulating sailboat masts in the distance and the unmistakable smell of salty air.

When the cab stopped by the pier, I handed the driver a twenty-dollar bill for the seven-dollar fare. Avoiding any contact, I told him to keep the change. My instinct not to run was the right decision and I looked up into the sky and thanked my guardian angel.

It wasn't as easy as I thought to find the "T-Dock" that Cole had directed me to, but I did. Maybe it was because I was looking for a small fishing boat. I never imagined that I had been invited to go out on a 50-foot mega fishing yacht, but as I approached the boat I could see Cole sitting in a captain's chair high on the top of a crow's nest platform waving for me to come aboard.

Just as I stepped upon the stern deck and through the cabin door, I was greeted by Cole's friend Bill who owned the boat. I was so taken by the yacht and the excitement that I introduced myself as Jesse Thorpe and had completely forgotten my alias. Bill then shouted out the window up to Cole,

"Did you invite two guys or one? I thought your friend's name was Pete."

Cole shouted back,

"Yeah so did I."

He climbed down the ladder and approached me with a puzzled and somewhat irritated look. I backed up, raised my palms and looked at him and said,

"I can explain."

Bill interrupted me and jumped between us,

"Hey, hey, no big deal guys," said Bill.

"We're all running from something" he added.

"Forget about it. Come on, let's go fishing."

I apologized again and promised that I would explain it to him, when the time was right.

Bill and Cole were childhood friends that had never really grown up. They came from different backgrounds, but had always shared a passion for fishing. They also shared a dream of someday making the sport they loved become their work, by hosting fishing charters for the out-of-town high rollers who frequently visited the area.

Soon after our somewhat tumultuous introduction, we were heading out into the Gulf of Mexico and preparing bait for our excursion, and all was good again. Cole and the captain had bought live bait and frozen squid for us to use, and my job was to break up the solid frozen blocks and separate the chunks of squid and place them back into the live well. It wasn't the most glamorous of jobs, but neither was sorting hurricane scrap. For now, I wasn't complaining. Watching the mainland slowly fade away had the same effect on my anxiety. It was all good.

I didn't mind cutting the odorous dead bait. It was the least I could do to repay the generous invitation. I wasn't accustomed to making friends so quickly. It must be that Southern hospitality everyone talks about. Back home, I always failed to make a lot of friends despite several years of effort. This was very cool.

I sat on a stool in front of a mounted cutting board facing the stern of the speeding boat. The powerful engines hummed and thrust huge wakes of breaching water in its trail. A lone seagull flew ten feet above the water and struggled to keep pace with the vessel. Her efforts were rewarded with an occasional treat I tossed to her in mid air. I wondered if it was really worth the expended energy for the bird to fly so far and so hard for just the chance of a charitable tidbit.

But I guess that's kind of like life. There are no guarantees or certainties. Most things are by chance, the right place, the right time. But giving up would guarantee the certainty of failure. So, like nature at its very core, we are essentially no different, struggling to chase our own boats in spite of the odds and hoping to be in the right place at the right time.

I had to admire the lone Gull's fortitude, not content to bystand in a fast food restaurant parking lot for welfare birds waiting for a shot at a discarded french-fry handout. Instead, willing to labor for it's rightful position amid Gods' proud chain.

The fishing grounds are about 30 miles out to a shelf, where the bottom of the ocean is filled with growth and vegetation and tons of big fish. There are numerous old shipwrecks, mostly shrimp boats, where the underworld life calls home. The same boat that fish would fear would become an underworld sanctuary for their safety. The death of a shrimp boat captain's dreams would always breed new life in the sea. It was the hunter's final humbled gift to the sacred hunted.

During the excursion out, I kept thinking of Kirk and his penchant for this kind of adventure. He often talked about selling his airplane and getting a boat on Cape Cod, but that never happened. There wasn't any time. I pondered with the thought of how different my decisions in life would be, if I only knew how soon it would all end. If only my own situation was different, I wouldn't waste a minute.

I wondered if Kirk could see me, at that moment, from above. I wished that he could, and somehow I wished he could experience it all through me in the same way that I lived much of my life through him. For now, I would believe he could. Maybe it would inspire me to live like he did. Maybe he knew all along.

Captain Bill came over to me while I was daydreaming, and asked me if I was having a good time. I told him that I really needed this trip and it was the most fun I have had in a long time.

He said,

"Good, because I don't know how much longer I will have this boat. The bank is starting the process of repossession."

Bill had bought the boat for about $800,000 on an investment margin account before the stock market tanked and has been struggling to make the payments ever since. He also lost some uninsured oceanfront property from the hurricane.

Cole was planning on being Bill's first mate for chartered fishing excursions with tourists and big game fishermen. Now he wasn't sure what he'd be doing, so working for some quick FEMA cash, seemed like the best bet for a short term non-commitment.

Bill had plans to build a rustic restaurant & bar on the docks set high upon timbered stilts. The structure still stood half built, but he had no more money to complete it. He was surviving on some old equity for now, but wasn't certain how patient the bank would remain in the months to come. He asked me if I had any money to invest in a partnership and while pulling out my voucher from my shirt pocket, I responded,

"Sure, how about three hundred dollars?"

He laughed.

The only person in this world I knew that could entertain buying a boat like this was Kirk, and Kirk was gone.

After about an hour of full-speed cruising, Cole shouted from the crow's nest that he could see the reef ahead and a few charter boats already in the area. He said we should bait up and get the poles in the water. I was having such a good time; I had completely forgotten that I was a fugitive on the run for my life.

CHAPTER 14

Before pulling into the airport entrance, O'Donnell slowed down and reminded Suzie that the information he had shared with her was top secret and if he was going to have any success catching the guys responsible for Kirk's murder, it would have to stay that way. As the cruiser turned the corner around one of the private hangers, O'Donnell could see Detective Murphy waving at him to stop and not approach any closer. When Murphy came up to the window, he looked briefly at Suzie and then at his boss. O'Donnell, said

"Don't worry about her, she is a witness and is here to observe the scene."

Murphy was out of breath and asked O'Donnell what took him so long to get there? O'Donnell just replied he got hung up and wondered what the big urgency was anyway?

The young detective said that when he opened the door of Kirk's plane he found a pool of blood in the backseat and on the floor. That's when he called O'Donnell on his phone in his office.

Immediately following the phone call, he began to gather evidence and take finger prints, when he was abruptly ordered out of the plane by FBI agent Alden, who said that he would take the investigation from there. O'Donnell was infuriated by this news. He put his police car in park, opened the door, grabbed his hat and started walking directly toward a roped off mini camp that the FBI had set up around Kirk's plane. The Chief focused straight ahead at Alden and charged like a race horse leaving the gate

There were three black Suburban vans with black tinted windows and a large forensics van which blocked any view of the plane from the public. There were also photographers and a team of investigators examining every inch of the plane. When agent Alden saw O'Donnell steaming toward him, he moved away from the crime scene to intercede his aggressive path.

"Damn you, Alden, what are you doing here?" O'Donnell shouted.

"Slow down Chief, back off this is a federal investigation now and you have no jurisdiction here."

Barely able to contain himself, and with his face turning a rutty hue, O'Donnell raised his voice and yelled back at him.

"What the hell are you talking about? Get out of my way, or so help me... This is my case and if you don't get out of here, I will lay you right down in front of your men and I will call Boston and spill your guts."

The agent pointed his finger in O'Donnell's face with an implicitly stern look and suggested that when he calls Boston, he should tell them that it was his recommendation to have Kirk run the sting operation. Alden knew he needed to gain control of the investigation, so when the blood evidence showed up in Kirk's plane and the plane was on the property of a federal air field, he made sure the agency would claim federal jurisdiction. Then the agent looked around, lowered his voice and starred into O'Donnell's face and said,

"You listen to me fatso and you listen good, Boston has no idea about the sting operation and when they find out that you and that idiot Mayor came up with this idea, you are both done, am I clear, Chief?"

O'Donnell backed down slightly, but starred back deep into the agent's eyes and said,

"You son-of-a-bitch, this was your idea from the start and you know it. Sully and I agreed just to get a little help from you guys to clean up our streets. That's what this was to suppose to be about. You aren't going to get away with this," he threatened the agent,

"I'm not through with you yet, Alden. Your hands are stained with Kirk's blood. This is all on you. You know it, I know it and soon, everyone will know it. I can promise you that."

O'Donnell was completely exasperated with Alden's tumultuous power play. The agent's arrogance only furthered embittered the Chief's opinion of him. He was burning on the inside but turned and silently walked away and headed back to his car. When O'Donnell came back to his cruiser he hastily ordered detective Murphy to get back to the station immediately, not talk to anyone, and wait for him in his office. He told him he would be there as soon as he dropped off Suzie at her car.

O'Donnell got in his car. He reached for the glove compartment and grabbed his bottle of nitroglycerin pills and without counting, loosely tossed back several pills in his mouth. He threw the bottle back into the glove box and slammed the compartment door.

Suzie quickly fastened her seatbelt and O'Donnell lit up and squealed his tires as he exited the airport grounds as an exclamation point for Agent Alden's ears. After a few moments, O'Donnell apologized if he had frightened her, but he had to let the FBI agent know that he was not going to just go away quietly.

The car ride back to Springdale was a silent one. Both Suzie and the Chief needed time to sort through their thoughts about everything that had just happened. The silence was broken when Suzie asked why the FBI wasn't just arresting the gang leader who they targeted the sting after in the first place.

O'Donnell explained it was a lot more complicated than that. The FBI agent could never admit they solicited a civilian to do their work and especially one that was killed in the process. If the press ever found out, then Alden would not only be out of a job, but likely would be looking at a lengthy incarceration in a federal penitentiary hotel.

Their lives and freedoms were all at risk for involving Kirk in the elaborate plan to bring down the drug kingpins. He knew he should never have allowed Kirk to be part of the dangerous scheme. It lost Kirk his life and could cost O'Donnell and Mayor Sullivan all they had worked for and could likely land them as permanent residents in the same hotel - not to mention the fact that there was an innocent man, Jesse Thorpe, being blamed for killing Kirk.

A few more moments passed and Suzie asked O'Donnell a straight question.

"Why did you suggest Kirk to the FBI, when you knew it was so dangerous?"

O'Donnell paused for a few seconds and shook his head and said,

"I have asked myself that question every day for the last two weeks and I don't know. It is a question I will suffer with for the rest of my life."

He told Suzie that Kirk had come to his office a few weeks earlier about a Latin King punk that he had a fight with, when he caught him stealing a CD player out of Kirk's prized Corvette.

O'Donnell also told Suzie that Kirk was having some money problems. Suzie remembered her friend Lori, the bank teller, who said that Kirk's trust fund account had been depleted. So, when O'Donnell heard the FBI agent mention bringing down the gang and rewarding some money to someone for helping, he thought that Kirk would be the perfect candidate. Everyone knew him. He appeared to travel with a fast crowd. He needed money and he definitely would never work for the police. He seemed like the perfect fit.

When he approached Kirk about the FBI's secret sting proposition, Kirk replied,

"Hell yeah, I'll do it."

Suzie understood O'Donnell and wasn't mad, she insisted that he not begrudge himself for Kirk's death. It was the gangs and FBI Agent Alden that should be feeling the guilt. The police cruiser pulled into the station's parking lot and before Suzie could get out. O'Donnell thanked her for her support and promised to keep her informed of any developments. Suzie told him to be careful and to call her at any hour, if he needed her or had news to share.

Suzie leaned over and gave the Chief a kiss on the cheek and a supportive look into his eyes. She grabbed his hand and squeezed firmly with hers.

"It's gonna be all right, Chief, they're making Jesse their fall guy for the botched operation. But they don't know who they're up against. Just be careful, the truth will set him free. I have faith."

CHAPTER 15

The first time Kirk had ever spoken to Agent Alden was at an arranged meeting at the Meadows' High School track. The track surrounded the school's football field, where Kirk had lived out his glory years, amid scouts from Division I colleges and even the NFL. Both Kirk and Alden were dressed in running suits and running shoes and blended in with the several town residents who routinely used the soft- surface synthetic track to get their daily dose of exercise.

Agent Alden was in good physical condition, but wasn't a regular runner. You could tell he had just bought new running shoes and a new black sweat suit, just for his encounter with Kirk. The black pants had a red stripe down the side, and still had a tag from the sports store, hanging from one of the back pockets.

Kirk had already been running for about an hour when Alden jogged up next to him and introduced himself as a friend of Chief O'Donnell. After a few more turns around the track, Kirk stopped running and walked over to the fence to grab his bottle of water and wrapped a towel around the back of his neck. Out of breath, he pointed to the stands and said to Alden,

"Ya know, I've always wondered what it would be like to sit in those stands and look out over this field, instead of always being on it, come on, let's talk."

He led the way to the top of the metal bleacher stands and sat down against the plywood wall of the empty and enclosed announcer's booth. After several minutes of small talk about the New England Patriots, Kirk cut to the chase and said,

"O.K. what's the deal? What do you want from me?"

Alden appreciated Kirk's straight-talking attitude and without hesitation laid out his plan to bring down the drug trade network of the Northeast and what Kirk's role would be in making it happen. He made sure that Kirk understood the level of secrecy that would be required in order to protect him during the operation. Kirk remained his cool self and encouraged Alden to move along with his proposition and get to the good stuff.

The operation itself had been well thought out and would take place over the course of three months. Kirk would begin by making contact with some of the street dealers and eventually move up the ranks of the distribution levels to some of the key players in the drug trade. The strategy would be to gain their trust slowly and gradually entice them with a new source for their drug supply. Supply was never a problem to the street gangs; it was safely moving the drugs around the chain of cities in the region that created the greatest threat to them.

The gangs owned the streets. They were born there, they lived there and in most cases they died there. When it came to driving up the interstates, crossing borders, or entering other neighborhoods, they were like fish out of water and never survived for very long.

The agent was sure that the gang leaders would recognize that Kirk represented a good opportunity for their drug business. Kirk could go anywhere and not be bothered by authorities and that would be his selling point to the gang leaders, after first gaining their trust. Agent Alden even suggested that Kirk might consider offering his plane to pick up and move large quantities of street drugs from city to city. He knew that the gangs wouldn't be able to resist a sure-proof way of moving the supply around the Northeast.

Every detail of the operation had been worked out by Alden and he would guide Kirk through every move he would have to make. Kirk was ready to agree but needed to know if it was worth it for him, given the risk.

"All right, I know what your incentive is, but what's mine? I'm the one out front here."

Again, the Agent admired his business demeanor and responded, *"Fifty thousand- if we're successful"* he answered.

Kirk laughed at him and stood up from his seat.

"Fifty-thousand for risking my life?

Kirk began to walk down the stands. The agent quickly followed him and stopped him,

"Whoa, whoa, hey wait a minute, I'm sure there is something we can work out. I don't have a lot of money at my disposal, but maybe we can attract some dirty money in the process of the operation."

Kirk looked at him, smiled and said,

"Why don't you work on that part of the plan and get back to me."

Then Kirk turned and pointed his finger at the agent with his hand in the shape of a pistol, he winked at the agent with a lackadaisical and devilish smirk and then pointed his index finger to his mouth and blew at the smoking barrel of his make believe gun, just like an old western gunslinger. In his own je ne sais quoi manor, Kirk slowly turned away and resumed his running back around the high school track, among a group of admiring young ladies. As always, Kirk was in the driver's seat.

Agent Alden was now even more convinced than ever that Kirk was the man for the job. Kirk oozed confidence and charisma. Alden was enamored. He yelled to him as Kirk ran away,

"I'll call you."

Kirk just ignored him, played it Newman-cool and never looked back.

CHAPTER 16

Chief O'Donnell's office had turned into a crowded waiting room while he was away. Detective Murphy, as instructed, was sitting to the side of the office waiting for his boss to return from the airport. He was joined by the Mayor, the district attorney and a federal agent from the FAA.

When O'Donnell entered the room, he paused for a moment, looked around at the room at the gloom of eye-evading faces and asked his old friend, what the hell this was all about. The Chief felt as though he had been ambushed like a surprise family intervention and demanded to know why they entered his sanctum without notice.

Mayor Sullivan quickly spoke up telling O'Donnell to take a seat and just relax and he would explain everything. O'Donnell was no dummy, he knew that a gathering of uninvited guests like this, spelled trouble with a bold capital **T**.

He looked over at Detective Murphy and told him he could leave and take his "things" with him home. Murphy interpreted his boss's gesticulating eyebrow to mean; take the evidence he had just collected and bring it to his house. The detective did exactly that. When the door shut behind Murphy, O'Donnell slowly walked around his desk and took a seat in his high-back leather chair.

The federal agent spoke up first, but was stopped by the Mayor, O'Donnell's long time friend.

"Excuse me; I will conduct this meeting, thank you very much."

He looked at O'Donnell and told him that he was sorry to be so blunt, but he knew the Chief was a straight shooter and he wasn't about to beat around the bush to his old friend. He told the Chief he was no longer going to be working on the case and, in fact, a recommendation had been made, due to health and stress, that he takes a leave of absence from active duty on the force.

O'Donnell knew exactly what that statement meant. Just like that, he was officially relieved of his duties as a police officer. Mayor Sullivan added that the recommendation had come from the federal level and that he had little authority to override the high ranking decision.

"I'm sorry, Tommy, but it's for the best" added the district attorney. *"This Preston thing has gotten too big and you know with your heart and all, I just think you should think about slowing down."*

O'Donnell sat silently in his chair and didn't say a word. He showed no reaction to anyone's words. He took a long deep breath, pushed back his chair and stood up and in a clam laconic way said,

"Very well then. If you will excuse me, gentlemen, I will get my things."

The Mayor and district attorney couldn't bear to watch the proud O'Donnell stand up and leave his chair. They looked down as he walked around the desk and grabbed his hat and jacket from an old wooden coat rack. He turned and stepped back to his desk, removed his badge and his service revolver and placed it on top. He reached for and picked up the framed picture of his wife which had stood on his desk for more than 35 years, and looked at it for a few seconds and forced a smile. As he turned toward the door, and began to walk away, the ambivalent federal agent spoke up,

"Oh and uhhh... we are going to need your lap top, and all of the evidence, notes, and files that you have collected pursuant to the Preston case."

O'Donnell stopped in his tracks with his back to the others, and stood still, he took another deep breath, bit his lip and then silently walked out the door of his office for the last time, without looking back, without saying a word.

When the door closed, the Mayor wiped his eyes with the back of his hand and muttered,

"God damn it, God damn it all."

He looked over at the FAA agent and shook his head at the man's audacity.

"Don't you guys have any heart?"

It was one of the most difficult gut-wrenching things the Mayor had ever been asked to do. He felt like he had just lost a part of himself and had never felt so low in all of his years of public service.

The federal agent walked out the door and left the two men alone in O'Donnell's now former office. The Mayor asked the younger prosecutor,

"What's it all about? You spend your whole life doing the best you can and what do you get... kicked in the teeth. I don't know, Maybe it's time for me to get out too, it's just not worth it anymore. Nobody ever appreciates the work you do. There's always someone who wants your job or someone else who wants your influence. You've really got to hold close to your friends and your family, because in the end, that really is all you've got in life, family and friends, and in this business, you lose a lot of your friends, too. Most people are just too blind to see life's real meaning and when they do, it's too late. Let's get the hell out of here."

CHAPTER 17

We had spent all day fishing on Captain Bill's gorgeous boat and must have hauled in about 1000 lbs. of Amber Jack, Red Snapper and Grouper. It was a great day. The weather out in the Gulf of Mexico was perfect, not a cloud in the sky. The sun had about another hour of shining on the rippled water over the horizon before setting and it was time to head back to the docks. Bill entered our coordinates into the boat's navigation computer and started the auto pilot function.

With the unmanned yacht speeding smoothly back to land, Bill, Cole and I sat down in the suede couches of the luxurious cabin, smoked cigars and opened a couple of cold beers. We talked about all the "big ones" that had gotten away and laughed about my struggle to land the biggest rubber tire I had ever seen.

I felt like I had known these guys forever and I began to think about never going home. Soon the boat was close enough to see land and the same dark rain clouds that we had escaped for the day. The sky over the land was churning with dark grey layers of fragmented doom. The ominous look of the weather brought with it the same unsettling feelings I had left behind, the uncertainty of my fate. My stomach began to gurgle like the water in a clogged sink reacting to an added crystal solvent. For the next twenty minutes, the shifting winds carried directly through me, constricting my temporary freedom.

Being on the open ocean, away from land and everything it brings, was a welcomed exercise in futility, nothing to think about, nothing to worry about, just a one-on-one spiritual session with God's most mysterious and powerful creation. It is a stark contrast between the sea's cleansing water and the land's staining soil, nature's selective purpose and man's chosen greed. Someday, someday I will return and never leave.

Bill asked me to walk up on the bow of the boat and prepare the lines for docking, and he would release the auto pilot and manually maneuver the boat into the slip. I hopped up on the front of the boat and tossed out the large hanging rubber bumpers, and coiled one of the lines in my hand so I could throw it to the waiting dock hand.

As the yacht approached the T dock, the dockhands came into focus and I waived to them with my intent to toss the line. I was a little nervous about my responsibility, but everything went perfectly fine and just as planned. As I walked back around the boat deck to see what else I could do to help secure the boat, I heard the loud and forceful voice of a Louisiana State Police Captain,

"Get down on the floor and put your hands on the back of your head, NOW!!!!!"

Needless to say, I did exactly as he commanded. Three officers jumped onto Bill's boat with their guns drawn and pointed them directly at my back. One of the three grabbed his handcuffs with one hand and clamped the cold steel on my wrists, while one of the other troopers frisked my entire body and read me my Miranda rights. Then they ordered me to my feet, as if I could just spring up like a gymnast from a floor exercise. I must have looked pathetic and to compound the show…right on que, with my hands behind my back, I could not stop my bleeding nose from drenching the front of my white t-shirt. The blood dripped down my chin and down my neck and all over me.

When I stood up, I saw the confused and bewildered faces of my new friends in shock for what they were witnessing. I was escorted off the boat and through a crowd of curious onlookers that had gathered on the main dock area and a couple of shoulder mounted news cameras with bright lights blinding my vision.

Among the many faces I saw starring at me through my squinting eyes, was the taxi driver who had likely tipped the police of my location. He was being interviewed by a TV reporter as a brave hero for what he had done. I can't believe I tipped him twenty bucks.

It's bad enough having the government against you, but combine that with the media's influence on public opinion and you are presumed guilty until proven innocent, and even if you are proven innocent, well, the damage is still permanently done, the food is just better.

I was more embarrassed than I was concerned about my situation. I did have some faith in the system and I knew that my innocence would eventually prevail. I just hoped that Bill and Cole could forgive me for not being honest with them up front. I was placed in the back of squad car and whisked away with sirens blaring and lights flashing, with a motorcycle escort through the busy streets. I asked the cop if the high speed and the siren were really necessary, since it was hardly an emergency and he looked in his rear view mirror and answered, "*shut-up*." Okay…. I guess some of these guys are just kids that never grew up.

The police had made it very clear of my right to remain silent and now they made it clear of my right to speak, too. I wanted to ask if they still allowed the accused one phone call, but instead I heeded his professional advice and kept quiet for the rest of the "French Connection" ride to my knew residence, the state police barracks.

CHAPTER 18

When O'Donnell left the police station to go home, he had never felt emptier in his entire life. After his wife passed away, his work had become his comfort and his co-workers had become his family. It was hard for him to imagine a life without it or without them. The Chief had often dreamed about his retirement, but somehow the thought of it was always far off in the distance. His sudden dismissal was met with an overwhelming feeling of loneliness.

O'Donnell got into his car and pulled out of the municipal parking lot. He was completely oblivious to his surroundings and could barely operate his car with full attention. Every sight was a dazed tunnel vision stare through surface layers and beyond reality. He was depressed. He was mad. He was alone. On auto-drive and without a blink, the Chief drove all the way home and into his driveway, opened his automatic garage door, pulled in and closed the door behind him.

Before he turned off the car, he glanced at his wife's picture that he had just removed from his desk and sat still in the driver's seat. For the next several minutes, his consciousness had slipped into a complete auto biographical replay of his life. He never expected that this chapter of his story would close with such a feeling of emptiness.

He closed his eyes and saw black and white images of himself projected on a home movie screen, by an old crickety 8 mm film projector. He watched the silent events of his life unfold and pass before him, like he was in the spirit of an audience. He watched his parents helping him to build a sand castle on a Cape Cod beach, his first day of school, his wedding day and the graduation ceremony at the police academy. He saw his mother, wearing a cooking apron, smiling and standing next to his father as he carved a Thanksgiving turkey at the family dinner table. They were beautiful memories of a life well lived. The movie began to slow and move in a different dimension. He was now watching from above, the graveside service of his beloved wife's funeral, but did not see himself among the mourners. He felt warmth, a glowing light and heard his wife's voice. He called out to her and her image turned toward him from amidst the crowd of mourners. She smiled and gestured for him to come along.

While the Chief sat idly in the driver's seat with his eyes closed, the closed garage had filled with carbon monoxide fumes from the running car. He didn't plan on taking his life, but at the time, it seemed like an easy way to just fall asleep. He opened his eyes briefly, kissed the picture of his wife & reclined his seat back.

His next vision was a conscious one, the faces of a doctor and an emergency nurse hovering over his body in the ER of Mercy Hospital in Springdale. He had been discovered and saved by Detective Murphy, who had stopped by his house after learning of his police department dismissal. O'Donnell's car had fortunately run out of gas and the detective had arrived just in time to smell the fumes escaping from the garage. Hearing the car running inside, he broke through a window, and hastily called for an ambulance.

Thanks to the quick actions of Murphy, the Chief's outlook for a full recovery was very good. He would remain at Mercy Hospital for several days to determine if any permanent damage had been sustained from the prolonged lack of oxygen. He also needed to be properly screened for depression and a full psychological analysis before he could be released, particularly because he lived alone.

O'Donnell was depressed and had little will for life, although suicide was never really an option, it just happened that way. It was a difficult time for the Chief. The career to which he dedicated such purpose had been taken away in an instant, as if it had no meaning. All those years, he thought, for nothing, just a lousy paycheck.

His private hospital room was adorned with bouquets of flowers, balloons, and baskets and a steady stream of visitors was allowed to enter the room for short visits. They all made him feel better, but didn't change the void that he felt deep inside. I never understood the tradition of cutting and killing beautiful flowers to give to a sick or grieving friend.

Personally, I preferred the planting of a tree or just a warm supportive hug. Dying flowers didn't devalue their thoughtful intent, they're just so temporary, and in a few days the Chief would be all alone, once again.

One of his many well-wishers was the emergency room physician that had acted so quickly to save him, when his seemingly lifeless body had arrived by ambulance to the hospital. His name was Dr. Seaver. The doctor entered the room, during his nightly rounds, to check on O'Donnell and see how he was doing. He also wanted to share a story with the Chief about a personal experience that had changed his life many years earlier.

The doctor closed the door, pulled up a chair along side the bed and placed his clipboard on the side table and removed his bi-focal glasses. Seaver wanted to be certain he had the Chief's full attention. He told O'Donnell that he was 16 years old at the time and had been caught shoplifting an expensive watch by a store clerk at the mall. He was pressured by his friends to steal the watch and then return it to another store for a cash refund. They would take the cash and buy beer and cigarettes with it. Then they would skip school and hang out down by the river all day. O'Donnell listened to Dr. Seaver tell his story and was surprised to see what a fine man the doctor had turned out to be, in spite of his troubled childhood.

He asked the doctor,

"What did you do to turn your life around?"

The doctor looked back at him and answered,

"It's not what I did. It's what you did. When you responded to the call from the security department at the mall, you took me out to your police car and we took a long ride, before you dropped me off at my house. You talked to me about life, how precious it was and how I was wasting my life away by hanging out with my delinquent friends. For two weeks I saw your cruiser down the street from my house every

morning making sure I went straight to school. Isn't it ironic that by that twist of fate, you saved my life and now, I had a part in saving yours? Thank you, Mr. O'Donnell, you will never know the differences you have made to people around you, thank you."

The doctor stayed in the room for several more minutes and talked with the Chief before continuing his late night rounds. When he left, O'Donnell reflected on the doctor's words and thought about all of the people who had visited him and who cared so much about him.

The doctor's visit had been a much needed catharsis for O'Donnell. He felt better about life and comforted in knowing that he had made a difference, after all. He dimmed the light, lowered the back of his bed, and fell asleep, with a peaceful and contented look upon his face.

CHAPTER 19

Suzie Dillon had just returned from a jog with Casey, her adopted beagle, when the phone rang in her apartment. The call was from Detective Murphy, who Suzie had recently met and gotten to know at the hospital while they were both visiting O'Donnell. Murphy knew that she was very close to the case and wondered if she had seen the news reports that an arrest had been made down in New Orleans in the Preston murder case.

It was "breaking news" all over the cable networks and the FBI was scheduled to conduct a press conference and announce that they had their man. Suzie had not heard the news and couldn't believe that the FBI was so convinced their case was closed, after what the Chief had shared with her in the police car about Agent Alden and his deal with Kirk.

Suzie asked if Murphy could come by her apartment and they would talk about it. He said he would be right over and hung up the phone. Suzie turned on the television set, put a fresh pot of water on the stove for tea and quickly changed out of her running clothes, before Murphy would arrive and see her.

Every channel was reporting there had been a break in the case. All the news anchors were recapping the events of the murder as they awaited a press conference from New Orleans. A video of the arrest scene on Bill's boat was on an endless loop tape and played continuously, over and over again. My bloodied image only contributed to everyone's conclusion that I was no doubt guilty and would not be proven innocent. Suzie sat on her sofa, glued to the coverage of the story, when her phone rang again.

The news was spreading quickly through town and she wasn't surprised to be getting more calls. She was surprised, however, to hear the voice of Chief O'Donnell on the other end of the line. He too, was watching the press coverage from his hospital bed and wondered if Suzie was watching. She told him she was, and that she was getting very angry and didn't know what to do. The thought of her friend going to jail had first seemed impossible, then improbable, and now it was inevitable.

"My god, poor Jesse," Suzie said into the phone. *"He looks so helpless"*

"We'll make this right Suzie, don't give up hope," O'Donnell was trying to comfort her and convince himself at the same time.

O'Donnell said he was being discharged later in the day and he thought it would be a good idea if they talked some more. The intercom buzzer sounded from the lobby of the apartment building and Suzie told O'Donnell to call her later and that she was thrilled he was going home. Suzie buzzed-in Murphy to the apartment complex and walked over to unlock her door, all the while looking over her shoulder at her television set.

Murphy knocked on the door and Suzie welcomed him in. It was Murphy's day off. He entered the apartment and Suzie invited him into the living room to watch the press conference with her and offered him a cup of tea. They exchanged some small talk about the Chief and his recovery and both agreed they would stop over to O'Donnell's house in the morning to check on him.

Murphy wandered around the living room a bit as Suzie prepared two cups of tea. He noticed a picture of Suzie in a cheerleading outfit next to Kirk, taken after the New England Championships. She walked up behind him and said,

"Did you know Kirk?"

Murphy answered,

"No, no I didn't. I grew up in Boston, but I feel connected to him now. I think about the people who killed him. It's weird, but when you're a cop, it's hard to not get personal. Sometimes ya feel like you're all the victims got."

Suzie handed Murphy the cup of tea, and wondered what he meant by the statement.

"Do you think you know who killed him?"

"I am pretty sure I know, but I don't know how I can prove it," Murphy added.

The news anchors on television alerted their audiences that the press conference in New Orleans was about to begin. Suzie and Murphy quickly sat down on the couch and Suzie grabbed the remote control pointed it at the television and increased the volume. The scene of the conference was set up outside the main entrance and on the steps of the Louisiana State Police Barracks.

There was a podium with the state seal, surrounded by flags and about twenty microphones standing like a large bouquet of black metal tulips waiting for the first public statements on the arrest. Behind the podium stood five men from various branches of law enforcement and elected officials seeking their moment in the national spotlight. In front of them stood an onslaught of reporters and a spattering of live transmitting satellite dish trucks.

The conference and the statement were clearly being handled solely by the FBI and others would only speak if a reporter poised a question in their respective line of expertise. The FBI agent stated and spelled his name for the reporters and read a short prepared statement.

"At 7:35 P.M. Eastern Standard Time, New Orleans's local law enforcement agency in conjunction with state and federal authorities, apprehended Jesse Thorpe and charged him with the murder of Kirk Preston. He was taken into custody without incident and will remain in Louisiana for the next several days until the extradition process to Massachusetts can begin. We would like to thank the local police for their excellent work for following up on several tips from witness

sightings of Mr. Thorpe in the New Orleans area . . . I will now take your questions."

After several minutes of unanswered questions, the news networks left the coverage of the conference and resumed their regular programming.

Suzie's eyes had welled up with tears while watching the news coverage. She was so confused over everyone's rush to judgment. She began to cry. Murphy consoled her with a reassuring hug and promised to help prove that they had the wrong man. He knew however that he would have to pursue his theories outside of the police station, since the investigation was now in the hands of the FBI.

Before Murphy left, he asked if she could let him into my apartment, so he could take a look around. She said that would be okay with her, anything to help. She did not know who else to turn to. Suzie shut off the TV and put Casey in the back bedroom and they went down the hall to apartment 619.

When Suzie put the key in the lock and opened the door, she immediately sensed that something was not right. When she locked the door the last time she was there, she locked both the deadbolt and the lock in the knob. Now, only the deadbolt was locked.

Her intuition was right, someone had been in the apartment and had stolen the computer off of the desk in the den and had emptied a file cabinet and left the drawer open. Suzie was afraid to take another step and asked Murphy to check the other rooms while she waited outside. After a few minutes, he came out and told her that everything was clear and she should come back in and see if anything else looked out of place. She wondered if they should call the police. Murphy just looked at her with a smirk and answered,

"Hello? Remember me?"

Suzie smiled a little and responded,

"I'm sorry. I'm just scared."

Murphy understood, and told her that they should definitely not call anyone, except maybe the Chief and get his opinion on what to do.

Suzie did not want to be alone, and asked the young detective if he would stay with her for a little while longer. He welcomed the request wholeheartedly. He sensed a personal connection with Suzie and wanted to spend more time with her anyway. They locked up the apartment and decided to take a walk in a park across from the apartment complex.

Suzie didn't want to breach Chief O'Donnell's trust, but was dying to know if Murphy knew about Kirk's involvement with the FBI and the sting operation. She thought a long walk in the park might give her the opportunity to find out what he knew and what his theory was behind Kirk's murder.

Murphy waited for Suzie at the front door of the complex while she went back to her apartment to grab a sweatshirt. While waiting he noticed a hidden security camera above the door directly toward the buzzer panel. He took a small notebook out of his back pocket and made a note to follow up with the security company that monitored the building. When she came out the door, he put his notebook away and they walked together across the street to a leaf-covered path leading into a beautiful wooded park.

Suzie thanked him for being there and repeated her disbelief of everything that was happening. He assured her that everything would be all right and briefly held her hand as they walked. She asked him who he thought was responsible for Kirk's death. He wasn't sure, but his instinct was that it was gang-related and that Kirk was in the wrong place at the wrong time. He went on to tell her that he suspected a nefarious thug named Lopez, a Latin King.

He told Suzie that he was already in custody on a stolen car and drug charge which took place on the same weekend of Kirk's murder. He and O'Donnell had been chasing this theory since the day of the murder, but didn't have enough evidence to charge Lopez, at least not yet.

The gang leader was bad news. He had killed before when he was just fourteen, but was released from prison on his 21st birthday.

Since his release, Lopez was known to law enforcement as a key figure in the drug trade, a profession he had learned in detention, courtesy of the taxpayers of the Commonwealth of Massachusetts.

Murphy told Suzie he hadn't given up on the Lopez theory. But it would be hard to prove, now that he was off the case. But he wasn't done. He had some ideas and planned on following up on them during off-duty hours.

CHAPTER 20

Chief O'Donnell came home after his hospital stay to a dark and lonely house. He had been transported by an old and retired friend who now volunteered for the hospital. They both entered the house and sat down for a few minutes and reminisced about the good ol days in Springdale and how different things had become. O'Donnell shook his head and said he would probably be heading down south soon, but first he had some more business to attend.

O'Donnell thanked his friend for driving him home and, in a subtle way, asked him to leave at the same time. The Chief was exhausted from his hospital stay, and just wanted to change into his flannels, make some hot chocolate, and relax for a while.

After about an hour of sifting through cards that he had received and watering all of his plants, he went into his guests' bedroom which had been converted into a home office and logged onto his computer. He had received dozens of e-mails from friends and co-workers sending their best wishes and thoughts to him.

Among the e-mails was one that stood out from all of the others. It had been sent from Nicky Cardoni @Cash-Go-Pawnshop, in Miami, Florida.

O'Donnell remembered speaking to Nicky, the owner of the pawn shop, about a ring belonging to Kirk that a patron had brought into the shop. The Chief recalled that Cardoni was going to have his daughter send the surveillance image of the guy who left the ring that Kirk always wore. O'Donnell positioned the computer mouse over the attachment file and opened up a picture of me, Jesse Thorpe.

The e-mail had also been copied to the police station's info e-mail address. O'Donnell could not believe his eyes. He knew that this was extremely incrementing evidence. It didn't make any sense. For several minutes, he sat motionlessly in his chair. He was certain that the FBI would exploit this evidence and use it to convict an innocent man. He questioned why anyone would be so careless as to try and pawn a stolen ring. The Chief also knew it couldn't possibly be true.

The Chief was an excellent cop and had decades of street experience and instinct in investigating odd and hard to solve cases. To him, the whole ordeal was beginning to look like a set-up and the pieces of the puzzle were coming together to reveal a picture of corruption, greed, deception, power and influence at the most dangerous level. It was all becoming very clear. He didn't get relieved of his duty because of health, it was to get him out of the way, so the FBI could take the case in a different direction, its own, and shine the spotlight of incrimination off of the agency.

The Chief felt powerless to do anything, but wasn't about to roll over and watch justice be swept away, not after dedicating his entire life advocating for victims of crime and protecting the "little guy." He thought about the first meeting that took place in Mayor Sully's office with Agent Alden and wondered how much of this dirt came from Alden's soiled hands.

O'Donnell decided he would pay the Mayor a visit in the morning and share his thoughts over a coffee and a couple of doughnuts and get his take on it. Before logging off, O'Donnell picked up his phone and called detective Murphy on his cell phone. When Murphy answered, he told the Chief that he had just left Suzie's apartment and wanted to tell him something.

The Chief interrupted the young detective before he had a chance to say anything more and asked him if he wasn't doing anything if he could come by for a few minutes on his way home. If O'Donnell's theory was right about the FBI's role in covering up Kirk's murder, then no one connected to the investigation was safe and even a simple phone line could not be trusted.

Murphy said he would be right over and asked if he could bring his former boss anything from the convenience store. O'Donnell thanked him for asking and requested some cream for his coffee.

Although he was very tired, he knew he wasn't going to be able to sleep and decided not to fight it.

While waiting for Murphy to arrive, O'Donnell attempted to log onto his e-mail at the police station and see if he could catch up on any developments. He wasn't completely surprised to learn that his username access had been denied, but was nonetheless aggravated. It was quite clear to him that he was never going back to the force in any capacity whatsoever.

O'Donnell went back to the e-mail picture sent from Nicky Cardoni's daughter in Miami. He left it on the screen to show Murphy when he arrived. O'Donnell went into his small kitchen and put a pot of coffee on and grabbed a couple of cups from the cupboard and brought them into his computer room.

On the wall of the room he could see the light and shadows of a car pulling into the driveway and knew that Murphy had arrived. O'Donnell quickly ran to the kitchen and pressed the wall mounted, garage door opener. He opened the kitchen door, which lead to the garage, and instructed the young detective to pull right in next to his car and wait for him to close the double overhead door.

"Stay in your car. Don't get out yet," the Chief blurted out.

When the door came to a closed stop, Murphy got out of his car, he asked the Chief why he was acting so paranoid. O'Donnell said he would explain inside the house. O'Donnell reached out to shake his hand with his right hand and reached for the bag with the coffee creamer with his left. Then he invited him to come inside. As they passed through the kitchen, O'Donnell picked up the coffee pot and led the way into the computer room asking Murphy to follow.

Chief O'Donnell knew that his only access to police records and evidence would now have to be through a first year rookie detective. He also knew that if he was going to make any progress in exposing Agent Alden, he would need to explain to Murphy all about the FBI sting operation that involved Kirk and lay out everything he knew. O'Donnell was very aware of the potential danger that Murphy could face once the FBI made a connection between the two of them, but he had no choice.

The detective was a very smart investigator, he had actually worked for a short while as a public defender in Boston, until he helped exonerate one of his criminal clients over a technicality, only to see him return to the streets and commit a deadly assault on an elderly man. After the realization that he had contributed to the crime problem, he moved to Springdale, entered the police academy to make right what he felt was a system gone wrong. The pair had the makings of a great team. O'Donnell's years of experience combined with Murphy's intelligence and detective skills.

The two cops sat down in front of the computer and O'Donnell poured some coffee. He pointed to the picture on the screen and asked Murphy,

"See that guy? That's a picture of Jesse Thorpe. This guy in Miami sent it to me. The guy owns a pawn shop and says that Jesse brought in Kirk's high school football ring to pawn for some quick cash. I don't believe any of it. I think he's being set up. There's something sinister going on here."

Murphy looked back at O'Donnell and asked,

"What are you talking about, set-up? Why would anybody try to frame Jesse for Kirk's murder?"

O'Donnell looked back at him and proceeded to tell him everything about the case, including why he felt he was no longer the Springdale Police Chief.

Detective Murphy sat in disbelief as O'Donnell detailed the initial meeting and the severe problem that FBI Agent Alden had created for himself when Kirk showed up dead on the mountain side in Holyville. Murphy was speechless and sat squinting his eyes, as if he realized that his life had just taken a very interesting turn.

While O'Donnell continued to share his theory of FBI involvement, Murphy was thinking about the break-in he and Suzie discovered at the apartment complex. He remembered how the Chief, days after the murder, had encouraged the detective squad to look toward gang activity. He also recalled the arrest of Angel Lopez in a stolen car with Cocaine in Holyville the night before Kirk's body was discovered.

Murphy asked O'Donnell,

"Do you think Lopez killed Kirk as a result of the FBI sting? O'Donnell replied,

"I have no doubt. Agent Alden likely set up Lopez, using Kirk as the bait, and when Lopez figured it out, he strangled Kirk and somebody dumped his body."

Murphy scratched his head and asked,

"If that's true, isn't it too coincidental that Lopez dumped Kirk's body at the climbing mountain where he and Jesse were supposed to be climbing together?"

O'Donnell, lowered his bifocal glasses to the end of his nose and looked at Murphy directly in the eyes and said,

"Who said anything about Lopez dumping the body at the mountain? Maybe it was Alden covering up a murder and trying to pin Jesse for committing it. Why else would they continue to impugn Jesse to the media every chance?"

CHAPTER 21

The jail cell where I was being held was a four by six concrete room with an exposed and seat-less metal toilet and a cot without a pillow. Just two weeks earlier, I was lounging on my soft couch watching a special on television called "Real Life Cells" a reality show about life inside prison walls. I had taken my fascination with reality shows a bit too far this time.

The reality was spending my days starring up at a paint chipped ceiling covered with dried toilet paper balls and listening to the sounds of mentally disturbed inmates, yelling and rapping the heavily painted metal bars with any possession they could find. There was no escaping the insanity. It truly was a "living hell." The solitary experience vacuumed my soul from my being and left my thoughts blank and void of any substance. For one hour each day, I was released from my crypt and required to go outside to the central yard of the complex for recreation time. I am not sure which was worse; the non-ventilated, urine-stanched crypt or the vulnerably exposed playground, with prison veterans sampling up the fresh meat for either a fight or a kiss.

Taking a Darwinian approach would prove to be my only means of survival in this strange world. It is never the strongest or the smartest who endure the challenges in life, but those who best adapt. So this culture, this jail, would now be my own concrete and steel Galapagos Island.

It was hard for me to believe that only days earlier, I had been "living large" on a luxury yacht angling game fish in the Gulf of Mexico, and now, I was trying to survive by avoiding eye contact with murderers, rapists and thugs. A friend once advised me to *never underestimate the fundamental randomness of life*. Yikes, he was right.

Today, however, my routine would be different. I was scheduled to have a meeting in the jail library with a court appointed lawyer explaining to me the extradition process and what I might expect in terms of my travel back to Massachusetts.

I also wanted to know why I had not been allowed to call anyone and let them know I was all right. I knew Suzie would be wondering how I was doing and I really needed to hear her sweet voice.

Ironically, the only friend I had made while I was in jail was the prostitute that I had solicited my first night in the New Orleans "house of ill repute." I decided that it was a thousand dollars definitely well spent and my decision not to engage in any sex that night was a fortunate one, since it turned out that my friend was actually a guy. No wonder the madam thought I was kinky. And I thought it had to do with the bath tub. He/she was well versed in the culture of incarceration though and kept an eye on me when I was out in the yard.

My meeting in the library was not what I had expected. I pictured a middle-aged, over weight scruffy lawyer with excess dandruff on the shoulders of his grey nylon suit carrying a battered double compartment briefcase and a bursting legal file. Instead, I was met by a gorgeous 22 year old law intern, who reminded me a lot of Suzie when I had first met her.

She had long strawberry blonde hair, deep green eyes and a sultry tan. She wore a professional blue business suit jacket with brass buttons and a knee length skirt, with feminine high heeled black stiletto shoes. She was a pampered poodle among chained junkyard dogs. I found myself making an extra effort to analyze her every inch and smell her perfume so as to savor it in my memory to be recalled later back in my disgusting open toilet cell. I realized how I had changed in just a few short days to feel and act more like a caged animal, than an innocent victim of circumstance.

I completely missed her first few sentences when I became entranced in her eyes, but snapped out of it when she handed me her card and asked if I had any questions. I asked her when I would be leaving, and she informed me that the process had gotten complicated, due to multiple jurisdictions being involved, and that it may take up to a month.

I also inquired about making a phone call. She said she would stop at the warden's office on her way out and arrange for a communication officer to escort me to the phone bank area of the jail.

The meeting was less than five minutes old and suddenly over. When she stood up to leave, I reached out my hand in anticipation of touching hers. She looked at my hand and then up to my eyes, smiled and turned away, signaling for the guard to open the conference room door and let her out. Just before she exited the room, she looked back and said,

"Call me if you need anything."

I could tell, by her voice, that she really was sincere and I hoped that she could see beyond my embarrassing orange jumpsuit and my cuffed wrists and shackled ankles. Truthfully? I think she liked me. Wishful thinking anyway. I quickly uttered,

"You know, I don't really belong here. It's all just a big misunderstanding. I am pretty sure I'm being set up. Kirk was my best friend."

Continuing to look down, signing and checking off papers, she replied,

"Yes, I'm sure you are innocent. Everyone in here is."

I thanked her for her help and she was gone.

After several minutes of waiting for my escort to arrive and bring me back to my cell, an assistant to the warden unlocked the library door and told me to follow him to the visitor's center where I could make one three minute supervised phone call. The phone center looked like a Hollywood set, complete with inmates talking with their spouses on handsets and looking through 2 inch, handprint-smeared Plexiglas partitions, while under the watch of stone-like guards.

I had seen it dozens of times on television, but without the personal emotion of so many small children crying at the sight of their daddies behind glass and just wanting a simple touch. It was bad enough to be in jail, but seeing children affected in that way, was so senseless. They did not deserve it.

They'll likely grow up with broken values to hate law enforcement, believing it was the police who unjustly took their dads away. With no respect for the law, they'll grow to become criminals themselves. And so here, in this harvesting room – the seed is planted in these innocent children for the endless cycle of crime to bloom and spread. I was never this cynical about life before I entered these walls, it just happens here.

My thoughts were interrupted when I was directed over to a vacant booth where I was allowed to make my one phone call. I quickly dialed Suzie and prayed that she would be home to pick up the phone, but that was not to be. Rather than leave a message I quickly hung up and asked the guard if I could re-dial, because something had gone wrong with the line. The guard agreed to let me re-dial, but informed that now I only had a few minutes. I dialed the Spa where Suzie worked faster than a radio contestant trying to win Rolling Stone tickets.

When the receptionist answered I said,

"Hello, may I please speak to Suzie Dillon?"

The voice at the Spa, responded,

"Suzie is with a client, may I take a message?"

"This is Jesse Thorpe. I need to speak with her immediately, please."

The attendant, who could hear the urgent tone of my voice, transferred me to Suzie's station and she picked up the phone.

"Jesse? Jesse? Thank god. It's you . . . how are you? Are you Okay? I've been so worried about you."

"I'm all right I won't be out of here for at least a month though. Did you call that FBI guy, Alden, I told you about?" I asked.

Suzie replied,

"Don't worry about that. Everything's going to be all right. Do you want me to come down there and see you?"

Before I could answer her, the auto timer disconnected the call at the three minute limit. I had lost at least a minute on that first call. The guard tapped me on the shoulder and told me my time was up, and to get up and head back to the cell block.

CHAPTER 22

Kirk Preston met several more times with FBI Agent Alden at the high school track and each time they would routinely sit and chat, atop the bleacher stands, against the announcer's booth. Each meeting brought Kirk a little closer to beginning the sting operation and the hopeful dismantling of the illegal drug trade network in the Northeast. Agent Alden did most of the talking and Kirk did most of the yawning. Kirk was a doer and was getting very impatient with Alden's long stretched focus to detail.

Kirk's competitive nature looked at this sting operation as more of an adventurous game, not fully acknowledging the very real danger he was about to put on his life. Alden was confident that the time had come for Kirk to make his first connection. He also sensed Kirk's lack of attention and did not want to risk losing his anxious excitement about being an undercover operative for the FBI. Kirk had "done it all" and was easily bored with his mundane life.

He loved the prospects of a covert operation involving danger, money, and drugs, while being protected by the FBI. To Kirk, that was "too cool." Kirk also needed the money, but didn't want anyone to know.

Alden instructed Kirk to make a visit to a pool hall in downtown Springdale. He told him that his first contact would be there with two or three other guys playing pool. Alden knew exactly when Kirk should arrive and described exactly what the guy looked like. The plan would be for Kirk to walk in and order a bottle of beer and stand at the bar amidst the circum ambient scum, playing it cool and not looking at anyone. Then walk over to the pool table and lay a hundred-dollar bill on the side rail and walk away.

Alden was sure this would get the attention of a street thug known as "Sonny." Placing money on the rail was a way of reserving the next game, and a hundred dollar bill meant he wanted to play some serious pool. Kirk was to lose the first game on a "scratch ball" and calmly reach into his pocket and reveal a wad of bills. Then wet his thumb and peel off another "Ben Franklin" and place it on the rail. The plan would be to win a few and lose a few, but to be sure and leave about a thousand dollars in Sonny's pocket before it was all over. Kirk would then grab his leather jacket, nod his head at Sonny and walk away.

The carefully choreographed operation worked flawlessly and in a couple of days Kirk returned to repeat the performance, with even more money. This time, however, his entrance to the hall did not go unnoticed and Sonny gave a signal to his guys to clear the table and immediately buy Kirk a beer.

It was the middle of the day and the middle of the week. The only patrons who would frequent a pool hall in Springdale during the day are guys who didn't work or are looking for a hustle. There were four beat up pool tables with beer stained felt and cigarette burned wood. Above each table dangled a naked 40 watt light bulb hanging by a single cord, spliced and covered by electrical tape. A musty stale smell permeated the room. Old half filled beer bottles housing floating cigarette butts lined the dusty window sills and flies buzzed around the room hopelessly searching for a way out.

It was a dark room and it took several seconds for your eyes to adjust after coming in from the bright city street. The only luminary in the room came from rays of sunlight entering through a wire caged window, cutting through the dusty, smoky haze of the bar room air. With every movement in the room the dust particulars would move through the sun rays like an underwater school of tiny plankton in the changing tidal movements of the ocean.

Along one side of the bar was a scruffy middle-aged bartender wearing an old sweat stained Smith & Wesson jersey and sitting behind the bar, reading a porn magazine, oblivious to his surroundings. He had a cigar hanging from one side of his crusty chapped mouth while coughing through the other.

Everything was going as planned and Kirk began to double his wagers and, of course, losing more than he won. After enriching Sonny again, he grabbed his jacket and started heading toward the door. This time he was stopped by Sonny who asked him,

"Hey what's your hurry my friend?" Why don't you stay a while?"

Kirk looked back and said,

"I'll see you next week, man."

He then turned away and left.

As promised, a week later, Kirk returned. When he came through the doors, Sonny was ready for him and suggested that they raise the stakes of their little game to a thousand dollars a rack. Kirk agreed, but told him he didn't have a lot of cash with him. Sonny didn't care and said he would take a marker if Kirk lost.

This was an entrusting sign of respect for Kirk and exactly what Alden had predicted would happen. About an hour had past and Kirk was intentionally down six thousand dollars when he told Sonny that he was having a bad day and thought he had better quit. Kirk gave him five thousand dollars in cash rolled in a ball and held together by a rubber band. He said he would have to owe him the rest.

Before Kirk left, he grabbed a vial from the inside sleeve of his leather jacket, walked over to Sonny and discretely put it in his shirt pocket and walked away.

The vial had been provided by Alden as part of the operation. It was a quarter ounce of pure uncut Cocaine and packed inside a 35mm film roll plastic container. Kirk never asked Alden where he got it from, but assumed it had come from some evidence collected by the FBI. Alden was certain that Sonny had never seen Cocaine in this pure form before and would likely get the attention of the gang's leaders.

Now that the alluring seed had been planted, the tease would be for Kirk to not go back to the pool hall for another three weeks, keeping Sonny and company wondering if they would ever see him again, and more importantly, wondering where Kirk had gotten the pure white gold.

CHAPTER 23

Chief O'Donnell woke up to the honking sounds of geese as they flew over his house heading toward their warmer winter home. Lying in his bed, he had a direct view, through his bedroom window, of their perfect flying formation. He starred at the lead bird that instinctively formed the apex of the flowing disjointed triangle. The leader was propelled by thousands of years of selection and driven by the thirst of others for the position of his directive role.

For a moment, the Chief felt connected to the struggling lead bird and then, in the blink of an eye, the formation randomly peeled off in another direction and the once proud pilot was demoted to a vanishing blend among the flock. The Chief closed his eyes and listened as their distinctive sound faded into a silent emptiness.

It was beginning to get colder in New England and the foliage season was passing its peak. It was a strange morning for O'Donnell. For the first time in decades, he did not set his alarm clock. He didn't have an office to go to or a time schedule to follow. His own season had also changed. But that, by no means, meant he had nothing to do.

Like the geese, he, too, had a long and arduous journey. His flight was just beginning in the search for Kirk's killer.

The Chief had not slept well, bitterly thinking of how he had been ousted by the feds and how they were protecting themselves at the cost of an innocent man. The only part of his routine that he would not change was his visit to his old buddy Mayor Sullivan to talk about this horrific injustice.

Before he left, he called Detective Murphy to tell him where he was going. Murphy wanted to tag along, but agreed that it would not be a good idea to be seen with the Chief, particularly at city hall.

Murphy insisted, however that O'Donnell call him immediately after his meeting with the Mayor.

O'Donnell had no gas in his car after it had, fortunately for the Chief, run out in the garage while he fell asleep on the driver's seat. So, he decided to fire up his Indian Motorcycle and take it for a spin to Springdale City Hall, while the weather would still allow him to ride.

He would skip the doughnuts this time and head directly to Sully's office. He had to park his classic motorcycle two blocks away from his usual designated "police and city vehicle" spot outside the front entrance, but he welcomed the chance to take a brisk walk after being trapped indoors during his three-day hospital stay.

Along his walk he was greeted by numerous well wishers and friends. Everyone loved the charismatic old Chief, especially when he rode his Indian in the city. He wore a pale yellow leather jacket with Indian fringes hanging from the sleeves and black leather chaps over his blue jeans and he walked with bow-legged gimp that couldn't stop a hog in a two foot alley.

O'Donnell stood at the receptionist's desk outside of the Mayor's office door and spoke to his secretary. She said he was on an important phone call with a U.S. Senator and that he would have to wait until the Mayor was free before he could go inside. The Mayor could see O'Donnell standing outside through a slightly opened door. He put the senator on hold and called in his old friend. O'Donnell walked in and was greeted with a bear hug from the Mayor.

"Tommy you son-of-a-gun, you had us all worried, why didn't you call before doing something like that?" the Mayor asked in a mildly angry, but loving tone.

"I'm sorry Sully, I don't remember what came over me, don't worry, everything is all right. Shouldn't you be taking your phone call?"
The Mayor looked down at his phone and answered,

"Uhh, he can wait; the only time he ever calls is when he wants an endorsement in an election year. Sit down, sit down, I can talk to him later."

The Mayor got back on the phone with the senator who proceeded to invite the Mayor to attend a public function he was planning in Meadows the following week. He also asked him for his support and requested that he perhaps could say a few words of endorsement during the event. The Mayor agreed and the senator, as he customarily had done every election year, thanked him and offered his assistance anytime for anything he needed.

Western Massachusetts rarely received visits from its U.S. Senators, unless it was leading up to an election. In fact, Western Mass felt so removed from Boston and the rest of the state that there had actually been a movement for the Western part of the State to secede from the Commonwealth and join Vermont. The idea never got any steam. The backers were typically a group of tax-evaders still living in the memory of Woodstock and for historians who were wishing to relive Shays rebellion. The Mayor hung up the phone with the senator and apologized to O'Donnell for the interruption.

"So I see you took out the bike for a spin, how's she running?" asked the Mayor.

"Oh pretty good, I'm gonna have to winterize her soon. I'm hoping maybe there will be an Indian summer first though," answered O'Donnell.

The Chief had always contended that the origin of the term "Indian summer" came from a group of Springdale Indian Motorcycle enthusiasts who held out every year for just one more ride. After chatting for a while, O'Donnell got serious and asked the Mayor if it would be all right if he shut the door. The Mayor said,

"Sure of course you can. Is it about the Kirk Preston murder? Look, Tommy, maybe you should back off a little. The Feds are handling it now," almost showing his relief that the city was no longer handling the high profile murder.

"They've been updating me everyday," the Mayor added.

"I know. That's the problem Sully," said O'Donnell.

"I can't stand by and watch what they're doing to this Jesse Thorpe guy. It's not right," insisted O'Donnell.

"I know, I know, but there's nothing we can do about agent Alden now, it's too late and it's gone beyond my local authority," said the Mayor.

"Agent Alden has to be exposed for what he's done, he has Kirk's blood all over him, and we can't let him get away with it, come on Sully you know me, I don't always say what I believe, but I always believe what I say, Alden's a bad egg and wouldn't hesitate to take us down too," argued O'Donnell.

"Believe me, I feel sick over it, but what can I do? Does Jesse need a good lawyer? Maybe I can pull some strings," said the Mayor in empathy over the sitituation.

"This isn't just about Jesse, it's about Alden" said O'Donnell. *"I want to nail Alden to the wall and I need your help to do it."*

O'Donnell reminded the Mayor that there was also another reason to take action. There was some drug dealer out there who was going to get away with murder, if Alden had his way. Sully looked back at his friend and pressed the intercom button, requesting that his secretary call and get the senator in Boston back on the phone line. He looked back at O'Donnell, and said,

"You're right Tommy. Let's see how badly he wants the support of Western Massachusetts. A little tête-à-tête can't hurt during his visit."

"Sully, you mean you would ask the senator for his help on this?"

"That's exactly what I'm going to do. You don't bring a knife to a gun fight, do you?"

CHAPTER 24

When O'Donnell came back home, he called detective Murphy and then returned a phone message that he had received from Suzie. He asked both of them to come over to his house as soon as possible. He told them it was time to get to work. Before they would arrive, O'Donnell cleared off his dining room table and began to systematically organize a strategic "war room" staging area to gather the facts and evidence needed to bring down FBI Agent Wayne Alden.

Time was of the utmost importance and there was none to waste. The Chief would do what he knew how to do best, lead an investigation and organize a team. He had already begun to categorize in his mind the responsibilities he would delegate to Suzie and Murphy in order to get the job done.

Murphy arrived first. Again, he would drive directly into O'Donnell's garage and wait for the door to close before getting out.

When he entered the house, he anxiously asked O'Donnell what the Mayor had said at the city hall meeting earlier in the day. O'Donnell told Murphy that the Mayor shared his sentiment and agreed that Alden had to be exposed.

O'Donnell went on to say the Mayor was planning on disclosing everything he knew to US Senator Kerrigan when they meet at an upcoming event in Meadows. He wanted to talk to him in private and in person. He added that the Mayor wanted to give the senator as much information about Alden as possible, including the sting operation that he involved Kirk in, giving him a part to play in the dangerous world of modern day gangs. Murphy appeared excited about the news and was ready to do whatever was necessary.

O'Donnell brought Murphy into his dining room and showed him how he was planning on moving forward. Just as he was beginning to give Murphy his list of objectives, the doorbell rang. O'Donnell went down the hall and into the front living room to answer the door and let Suzie inside. O'Donnell embraced her in the foyer as if she was a long lost daughter and thanked her for being so kind and spending so much time at his bedside at the hospital. He told her he was very touched and would never forget her thoughtfulness.

Suzie and O'Donnell walked down the hall to the dining room where Murphy quickly stood up from his chair and also affectionately welcomed Suzie. O'Donnell was a bit surprised to see how close the couple had become, but was delighted. He felt the new found friendships that had been made during the entire tragedy were like rainbows through storm clouds and he was comforted by them being there, his new team.

The three of them sat down and O'Donnell began the informal meeting by sharing with Suzie the same news he had just told Murphy about the Mayor's intention to talk to the Senator. O'Donnell started with Suzie and asked if she could take a few more days off from the spa and fly down to talk to Jesse.

Suzie responded by saying,

"If the spa doesn't let me, then I'll quit."

"Great," said O'Donnell. *"I have a list of questions that you need to ask him about evidence the FBI is holding against him. I'll go over all of that with you before you leave."*

O'Donnell then turned toward the young detective,

"Murphy, I want you to bring me all the evidence that you collected from Kirk's plane before the FBI took over the case. Also, try and get access to the latest developments and what leads they're currently working on. Any questions?"

"Yes, I was wondering if I could get a key to Jesse's apartment?" asked Murphy.

"I want to snoop around a little more and find out who was in that apartment and stole his computer and why?"

"Excellent," exclaimed O'Donnell.

"Suzie, give Murph the key and please, please, please be careful when you go in there. If these guys get wind of what we're up to,

Jesse won't be the only one in trouble."

"No problem Chief," Murphy said.

O'Donnell continued to review all of the areas that needed attention and questions that needed to be answered. He handed Suzie and Murphy each a new untraceable cell phone and told them from now on to call only on these cell phones and instructed them to never leave any messages. He issued a caveat for them to be extra vigilant and cognizant of their surroundings at all times.

"We have to get busy. The Mayor needs all this information by next week," the Chief reminded his new detective team.

"I'm going to pay a visit to some old friends in the Holyville Police Department and see what they got on Lopez," said O'Donnell.

"All right guys, let's meet back here tonight around nine and we'll take the next step. Murphy, why don't you leave first, I don't want you guys to be seen together."

With that advice, Murphy stood up and gathered his notes together and headed to his car and back to the police station. O'Donnell asked Suzie to stay for a few more minutes until Murphy was clear of the neighborhood.

Suzie asked O'Donnell,

"When do you want me to fly to Louisiana?"

O'Donnell answered in a fatherly toned voice to Suzie mixed with a splash of authoritative detail, in the manner he would address his former rank and file officers,

"Try to get on a flight tomorrow. Take this cash," O'Donnell handed her an envelope, *"And don't use any credit cards during your trip. After you have left Jesse, I want you to make a quick detour to Miami and visit a pawn shop before you come home."*

"A pawn shop? The pawn shop that was on the news? Why?" asked Suzie.

"Come here I'll show you something in my bedroom."

O'Donnell walked down the hall and into his bedroom with Suzie following behind. She was amazed at how clean and orderly he kept his house, without a woman's touch to keep it organized. Walking into the bedroom, she saw a framed picture of the O'Donnell's on his nightstand, next to his bed. She couldn't remember if it had been five or six years since his wife had passed away.

O'Donnell opened the top drawer of his dresser and took out a pair of socks that had been rolled up. He turned and looked at Suzie and reached inside one of the socks and pulled out his hidden ace. Holding it out as if it was some kind of elementary school show and tell game,

"Do you know what this is? This is Kirk's football ring," he said.

"Oh my God. Where did you get it?" Suzie asked.

"I've had it all along. Kirk gave it to me for safe keeping during his sting operation. He knew one of the cockroaches had stolen his gold chain and he wasn't about to take any chances with his most precious possession." He continued to display the clunky gold ring in the palm of his hand.

"But, then, why did the pawn shop claim that Jesse brought it to them?" asked Suzie.

"That's a question for you to find out," he said as he securely re-concealed the ring back in his sock, placing it back in his dresser drawer. *"It's also one of the most damning pieces of evidence*

against Jesse and now we know it is a lie. I got a hunch the answers you find in that pawn shop will help lead us where we need to go."

It was now abundantly clear to both of them, that somebody was going to a lot of trouble to frame me as Kirk's last vision.

CHAPTER 25

FBI Agent Alden had reviewed every scenario with Kirk before he went back to the pool hall. He was certain that the "little appetizer" Kirk gave to his pool partner would serve as the first course for a much larger main meal yet to be served. This time when Kirk entered the dark pool hall, he went straight up to the bar and took a seat. He was very aware of the attention his presence had stirred among the small crowd, but blended in like the master chameleon he was.

In his peripheral sight, he could see the guys at the pool table pointing over to him and whispering. He also saw his contact, immediately pick up his cell phone and make a call while looking over at him the whole time. After completing the call he handed the phone and his pool cue to one of his friends and started walking over to Kirk at the bar.

"Hey, hey, where you been, friend?" he asked with a Latino accent as he approached Kirk. Kirk slowly sipped a long swell from his beer bottle, curled his lips tightly inward as he swallowed and placed the bottle on the bar. He looked over his shoulder at him and smiled, giving him a hearty street pumping hand shake. Kirk responded,

"Hey I've been out of town on business. How you doing? Kirk joked, *"Hustle anybody today on that pool table?"*

"Nah, not till now anyway, you gonna play or what?" the man said in an enthusiastic voice.

"Are you kidding man, you're out of my league," Kirk answered.

"Today I'm just having a couple of beers and then I got to get out of here."

"Relax friend, there's somebody I want you to meet, he's on his way over. Hey, thanks for dat blow last time I see you. Dat was really sweet man." He rubbed his nose with his fingers and smiled with a look of ecstasy, just remembering the buzz.

"Hey no problem, oh and here's the other thousand I owed." Kirk reached into his jacket and flipped open his money clip and paid his debt with ten crisp one hundred dollar bills.

"Hey man, you all right, I forgot about it, thanks, man."

Just then the front door opened and three dark figures appeared silhouetted against the bright sunlight from the outside. The dust particles and smoke from the room filtered the rays and added to the cinematic entrance of a clear ranking street hood. It was like a feared gunslinger's entrance through a pair of batwing doors in an old western saloon.

The man in the middle was tall, more than six foot six and slender with long dread lock hair hanging over the front of his shoulders. He was framed by two shorter, but stocky, figures, both wearing baseball caps with a cloth tail hanging behind their heads, like some urban style French Legionnaire's hat.

Trying to remain cool, Kirk acted as if he had not noticed their presence, but it was difficult to ignore the change in the room. The two guys were definitely serving as tutelary body guards and were quick to take their boss's jacket and gloves, as he slowly and methodically peeled them off.

"Hey there's my friend now, let me introduce you."

He walked over to the front door, whispered something to him and pointed back toward the bar. Together they slithered like snakes over to Kirk who was still sitting with his back to the men and drinking his beer. Kirk thought to himself, this is exactly what Alden said would happen and Kirk didn't flinch, remaining James Dean cool. The old bartender, stood up and looked at the ominous arrival and raised his voice,

"Angel . . . I don't want no trouble here."

"Relax Pop relax, I just want to meet this fine patron and buy him a beverage," he said.

"Hi, I'm Angel Lopez and you are . . . ?"

"My name is Kirk, Kirk Preston," Kirk said with attitude, as not to appear nervous on this introduction to a high ranking gang member.

"Nice to make your acquaintance Mr. Preston, pardon my curiosity but we don't often see folks like you in this establishment. My friend Chico here, say that you are a high class kinda guy," Angel said looking down at Kirk.

Lopez didn't waste any time letting Kirk know that he was in control. Lopez slid his sunglasses to the end of his nose, lowered his chin and looked over them into Kirk's eyes,

"My associates tell me that you drive that Corvette outside. Nice ride. I would love to take a ride in it someday. Maybe even right now," Angel suggested, lifting one eye brow.

Kirk looked up at Angel and responded with a snicker,

"Who wouldn't want a ride? Maybe someday dude," said Kirk.

It was obvious that Angel was accustomed to getting his way and he was quite agitated by Kirk's smug response. Kirk had never been cooler. He remained impervious to Angel's performance of bravado and ordered himself another beer.

Angel petulantly shrugged his shoulders and pulled his collar away from his neck. He took a big breath and with a lured sneer, bit the bottom of his lower lip. Angel turned and walked away without saying a word. Angel never let anyone bother him…more than once. He gestured to Chico to come over to him, which he did. After a few minutes' Chico came up to Kirk and asked him if he would play a round of pool with Angel, but not for money. Kirk told him that he might, when he finished his beer.

Angel impatiently waited for Kirk to acknowledge him and fought back the urge to rush Kirk and thrust a switchblade into his back. After about ten minutes of agonizing disrespect, Kirk stood up and strolled toward the pool table and walked right by Angel on his way to the bathroom. Angel kept his cool and told Chico to rack-em up.

When Kirk came out of the bathroom, Angel handed him a cue stick and said,

"Let's play, Mr. Preston."

"I'm not playing for money and I'm not taking a marker," Kirk announced.

"How about we play for a ride in your car?" Angel suggested.

"And if I win?" asked Kirk.

"I will buy you another beer," said Angel.

Kirk just stared back at him for what seemed like an eternity and said,

"You break."

When it was Kirk's turn, he proceeded to clear the table, like a pro. He banked; combo'd and sliced shots with the confident authority of a seasoned hustler, never once looking at Lopez.

When he made his final winning shot at the eight ball, he looked up and handed the cue stick back to him, and said,

"Maybe we should've played for money."

Angel was not happy about being upstaged in front of his cohorts and the protruding vein in his forehead made it obvious. Kirk was fearful that he may have pushed Lopez too far and could jeopardize the whole plan. So, when he walked away from the pool table and headed back to his bar stool, threw down the rest of his beer turned to Lopez and said,

"Come on, let's take a ride."

Kirk and Angel grabbed their jackets, put on their sunglasses and left the pool hall together. This was Kirk's chance to break through the street level gang and make inroads with the real players. Getting to Angel Lopez was agent Alden's strategy from the very beginning. Alden had good information that Lopez was the "lieutenant" that directed the movement of drugs through Springdale and the Northeast corridor.

As they approached Kirk's vintage Corvette Stingray, Kirk extended his arm out with keys in hand, and unlocked the alarm mechanism. Then, to Angel's surprise, Kirk tossed him the keys in a high and slow floating arch and suggested that he drive. Angel smiled like a kid on Christmas morning and jumped in the driver's seat and then started up the 300 horse power engine. This was not exactly what Alden's plan had called for, but Kirk was always over confident and felt he needed to "play" Lopez a little if he was going to gain his trust and move closer to the big sting.

Angel asked Kirk where they should head. Kirk suggested they get out of the city and head toward the countryside where Angel could better test drive Kirk's Corvette.

"This city strangles me sometimes, you know what I mean? Buildings, stop signs, lights, cops, I feel like I can't breath. Like I'm buried alive banging on a coffin ceiling five feet under, in the middle of a barren desert. Sometimes I'm so trapped; I just have to get out in the open, drive, fly and breathe. What do you say we escape for a little bit?"

Angel loved the idea,

"Sounds cool to me man. I got no wheres to be and I ain't got no one to see."

After several miles of twisting country roads, Kirk asked Angel to pull over at an old country store where Kirk would always stop to buy cigars. The owner of the store usually kept a box of Cubans under the counter for his special customers.

Angel pulled the car into the parking lot and Kirk hopped out leaving Angel in the priceless car by himself. Angel could not believe that Kirk trusted him and was dumfounded by his actions. It was a small gesture but a huge step in their new found relationship. Angel was not accustomed to anyone trusting him, not even family. He was quite impressed with his new friend.

When Kirk came out of the store, he jumped in the car and gave Angel a fresh Havana cigar and said,

"You wanna have some real fun?"

Angel put the car in gear, and replied,

"What do you have in mind?"

Kirk told him to head down the road about another 4-miles and turn into the Westford Airport. Angel had no idea why, but couldn't remember ever having a better time. He welcomed any ideas Kirk offered.

Kirk opened the glove compartment and grabbed a gold cigar cutter and snipped the end of one of the smokes and handed it to Angel. Then Kirk struck a wooden match against the dashboard and raised the flame to Angel's face. Kirk lowered his window and tossed the match.

"Come on are you going to drive this thing or what?" Kirk asked the now timid Angel. Angel looked over and smiled and floored the pedal. The Vette popped into a thrusting higher gear and both could feel their backs receding into the sleek black leather seats. The fall leaves scattered from the roadside in the wake of the powerful speeding sports car.

Angel pulled through the main entrance of the airport and Kirk activated the gated private area of the runway where he kept his plane. Angel asked what this was all about and Kirk said,

"Come with me, it's time for me to drive"

Angel looked at him with astonishment and yelled,

"No way, man! Are you serious? I've never been in a plane in my life"

Kirk then said, in a friendly voice with a touch of bravado arrogance,

"Well, prepare yourself to touch the hand of God, let's go,"

CHAPTER 26

It was 9:00 P.M. and Chief O'Donnell was sitting at his dining room table preparing for Suzie and detective Murphy to arrive and report their findings to him. He had a thermos of coffee and a tray with some warmed cinnamon rolls on the table. O'Donnell had also placed a clean pad of paper and a pen on the table in front of each chair. He lowered all of the window shades and closed the curtains to insure privacy.

While he was placing the cups and napkins on the table, his new cell phone rang. It was Murphy on his new phone telling the Chief that he had picked up Suzie and they were on their way and for him to be ready to open the garage door when they were in the driveway.

Suzie brought little Casey, Jesse's Beagle, over with her to get familiar with O'Donnell and his house. O'Donnell had already agreed to dog-sit while she flew down to Louisiana. When they came through the door, Casey was excited to have an entire house to run around and explore. Suzie was thrilled to see the dog jump up on the Chief and run right over to his couch and jumped over the backrest. Casey was feeling right at home and Suzie felt comfortable with asking O'Donnell to watch him for a few days, while she traveled down south to Louisiana to visit with me.

O'Donnell offered a cup of coffee to Suzie and Murphy and they sat down at the converted dining room table. Little Casey ran under the table and sat at O'Donnell's feet and barked until he handed the dog a small piece of a cinnamon roll and only then he stopped. Suzie laughed and warned O'Donnell,

"Oh great, now you've done it. I've trained that dog for two weeks not to beg. He's been with you for ten minutes and it's all over. You're an old softy Chief."

"I can't help it, just look at those sad little brown eyes," O'Donnell explained.

"We're gonna get along just fine," O'Donnell said, as he gave Casey a loving pat on the head and a scratch behind the ear.

Suzie shook her head at him and wondered if she would ever get Casey back again.

"All right already, let's get to work, what cha got Murph?" asked O'Donnell.

"Well it's not good," Murphy warned, as he reached down to the floor and picked up an expandable legal file and put it on the table. He untied the string and opened a compartment and presented a copy of the lab results from the forensic team in Boston.

"Wow, great, how did you get them?" O'Donnell inquired.
"Well . . . ," Murphy said,

"I still know a few guys from my days in Boston," he proudly aggrandized.

It was apparent that he wanted to impress Suzie with his influence. Suzie smiled at him, as he boasted.

"It's not good," he handed O'Donnell and Suzie each a narrative copy of the scientific conclusion which explained the technical data.

"They only found two sets of finger prints in the plane, Kirk's and Jesse's."

Suzie quickly interjected,

"Well that doesn't mean anything; Jesse took rides in Kirk's plane all the time."

"Yeah I know, keep reading . . . They also found blood in the plane." O'Donnell looked at the paper and sat quietly twirling the end of his handlebar mustache, between his two fingers.

Again, Suzie interrupted,

"Didn't you already know there was blood?"

"Yeah we knew, we just never expected to find Kirk's and Jesse's."
"Jesse's? Are you sure?" asked Suzie.

"It's not my conclusion. It's the state's," replied Murphy.

"All right never mind about that, what else ya got?" O'Donnell wanted to know.

"Well, it gets worse. The FBI found evidence that suggests that Jesse was to be the beneficiary of Kirk's life insurance policy, a whopping million dollars. It was a policy so new that the ink hadn't even dried before they found Kirk's body."

The report was disconcerting to O'Donnell, to say the least; he took a deep breath and slowly exhaled, then sat idle, again twisting his mustache in a trance like state. He felt like a one-armed man in a row boat and was frustrated by the mounting piles of incriminating evidence against Jesse. The hurdles facing their progress were daunting. Then he blinked his eyes several times and looked at up at the ceiling and blurted out,

"Damn it all! Suzie, did you book your flight yet? We need some answers from your friend, and they better be good ones."

Suzie answered,

"I have a 7:00 AM flight. I should get there around 10:00. I checked with the Jail and they have visiting hours at 11:00."

"Good, I'll drive you to the airport in the morning and we'll have a little time to review the questions I have for Jesse. Please tell me again, how well do you know Jesse?" asked the Chief.

Suzie put her hand on top of O'Donnell's and squeezed.

"He didn't do it. I know he didn't do it," she said.

The three of them felt very dejected from the news that Murphy had reported. For the first time, they questioned whether or not they could do anything to discredit the FBI's strong evidence in the case against me.

O'Donnell made a copy of Murphy's evidence on his personal desktop scanner and handed back the originals to Murphy. The rookie detective placed them back in his binder and asked O'Donnell,

"Did you have a chance to talk to your buddies in Holyville about the Lopez arrest?" asked Murphy.

O'Donnell responded,

"No, I thought I would head up there after I drop Suzie at the airport. I'll let you know what I find out tomorrow night. Can you get any more info on that life insurance thing? That seems awfully obvious. It doesn't make any sense why Jesse would try to get away with that."

Murphy answered,

"The FBI thinks that Jesse was trying to make Kirk's death look accidental and that's why he left town, as an alibi."

"Hmmmm, I don't know . . . that's quite a stretch," responded O'Donnell.

O'Donnell didn't see any point in proceeding until Suzie had a chance to get some answers. Again, little Casey began to bark at O'Donnell's feet. This time he continued to bark even after the Chief gave him a treat under the table.

O'Donnell remarked that Casey was so smart, that even he was bothered by the fact that his owner was in big trouble. So after only 20 minutes of discussing the new evidence, O'Donnell offered a 2nd cup of coffee to Suzie and Murphy, and Suzie accepted,

"Just half a cup, I got to pack for my flight in the morning."

They all sat at the table and talked for a while. Suzie and the Chief reminisced about Kirk and his football days and what a great person he was. They wanted Murphy to know all about Kirk and loved sharing their memories about his crazy antics and wild stunts.

O'Donnell asked Suzie,

"Didn't you and he have a little thing going?"

Suzie blushed,

"Me and Kirk?" she laughed, looking over at Murphy.

Suzie picked up little Casey and gave her a hug and a kiss on the forehead and then put her back down, telling her to be a good little girl and behave for the Chief.

Both Murphy and Suzie picked up their empty coffee cups and saucers and walked into the kitchen to place them in the sink. They threw their paper napkins in the basket under the counter top and thanked the Chief for his hospitality. Murphy commented on the fact that now that the Chief was semi-retired, he was buying fancy breakfast rolls and muffins instead of his standard doughnuts. The Chief insisted he was still a paper cup and doughnut kinda guy.

O'Donnell thanked them both for coming and told them that they might as well wait to meet again after Suzie got back from New Orleans. In the meantime, he asked Murphy to keep an eye on the feds and see what they're up to. He reminded them again, to keep their new untraceable cell phones with them at all times, in case he needed to reach either one of them, or they needed to call the Chief.

After a few more minutes of small talk, Suzie and Murphy left O'Donnell's house and headed to Suzie's apartment, where Murphy would drop her off before heading to his own house. It was a full-moon night and there was a chill in the air from a steady Canadian wind, a precursor of the season to come. Suzie snuggled up to Murphy in the car while he was driving, until the heater vents began to blow warm air.

She wasn't prepared for the cold weather and her need for coziness suited Murphy just fine. He thought about putting his arm around her, but decided to wait until he pulled into the parking lot of the apartment complex, where he planned on giving her an innocent and non threatening "bon-voyage" kiss, instead.

O'Donnell was standing at his sink rinsing off the plates and cups and placing them in the plastic plate tray for them to dry. Whenever, he performed this chore he would think of his late wife. It was a routine that they had shared for years and he would still find himself talking to her years after she had passed, while he cleaned dishes. When he turned the water off, he could hear little Casey barking from the dining room. O'Donnell walked from the kitchen and into the dining room,

> "*Hey, hey, little girl what's going on out here? There are no more goodies on the table for you,*" he lovingly informed the beagle who was still under the table.

O'Donnell moved one of the chairs out of the way and kneeled down in front of Casey.

> "*What are you so upset about my little friend? Come to daddy.*" Casey stayed underneath and starred up at the underside of the table and continued to bark. O'Donnell wasn't familiar with Casey's personality, but figured either the dog was crazy or she was trying to tell him something. So, he crawled under the table and sat next to the dog, to determine what she wanted. O'Donnell followed the dog's line of sight and discovered a small listening device with a blinking green light. O'Donnell sat motionless as he came to the realization that his house had been bugged.

He had seen them before and he knew that it was not your typical Radio Shack rig. This was a top of the line remote transmitter, similar to the government issued specifications used by the FBI. O'Donnell did not tamper with it; instead, he grabbed the dog, and said,

> "*O.K. my little friend you're going to have stay in the bedroom if you can't behave around food.*"

He got back up and moved the chair back into its position.

O'Donnell had spent most of his life investigating crime, gathering evidence and he found himself on the other side of the law. He was agitated at the thought that someone had unlawfully entered his home and was listening to his private conversations. Although he had no idea how long the bug had been under the dining room table, he was fairly certain it had been planted while he was in the hospital.

What he did know, however, was that if someone was listening in, then Suzie and Murphy were in danger. Now the Feds knew that they were working on the case to undermine the investigation and that they were on to the fact that Alden somehow was deeply involved. But O'Donnell's years of experience would not be wasted; he left the bug in its place under the table, fully operating and began to plot how he could perhaps use the device to his advantage.

CHAPTER 27

Angel Lopez was sitting in the copilot's seat in the cockpit of Kirk's plane as Kirk finished his pre-flight check of the prop, the wings, ailerons and fuel sensors. Angel was afraid to touch anything. He sat with his hands under his thighs and looked at the array of dials, buttons and levers. His seat had a duplicate yoke and throttle, just like the pilot's side of the plane. Clipped to the upper sun visor were several pictures of women with phone numbers and stars next to their first names, some sort of rating system Kirk associated with each of his heavenly airborne conquests.

Angel could not believe that he was actually going to fly in a plane. His heart was thumping and his sweaty hands were trembling in anticipation of taking flight. His stomach had not felt this nauseous since the day he was paraded in a line up in front of a one-way mirror on display for the victim and witnesses of a gang beating. He considered bailing out of the plane just as Kirk climbed into the pilot's seat, but he, the hard line gang member, didn't want to appear nervous to his new friend. Kirk made a log entry in his flight book, placed the book back under his seat and shouted "clear" out his window.

Kirk started the plane and began to taxi to the runway. In route, Kirk called flight control to request permission for take off and was notified to hold on the tarmac for incoming approach of four A-10 fighter jets landing. The municipal airport shared its runway space with the Air National Guard and a squadron of A-10 Tank Buster Attack Jets.

Angel looked at Kirk and said,

"What's going on man?"

Kirk pointed to the right of Angel and responded,

"Check it out...you think your friends are tough? Get a load of these guys," moving Angel's attention to the incoming aircraft.

The fighter planes touched down within 100 feet of Kirk's plane at more than 150 miles per hour, with missile attachments under each wing. The force of the jets could be felt inside Kirk's plane, with strong vibrations of the instrument panel and the entire plane teetering to the side.

"Wow!" screamed Angel. *"That's amazing, man."*

"You bet your ass they're amazing," said Kirk. *"You can thank those guys you're a free man to think, say, and do what you want. When you're sleeping or out partying, these guys got your back 24/7 right in your backyard. Next time you hear that thunderous sound of power, just remember...that's the sound of peace, my friend."*

Kirk looked over at Angel and smiled. Kirk had Angel completely in awe of him, exactly what he and Agent Alden wanted. Kirk, however, never let himself forget that Angel was still a punk, a punk who got away with murder, thanks to a rookie cop's Miranda rights screw up. He knew everything about Angel. Alden had access to all of the gang's member's records, even the juvenile records that were often sealed upon the offenders turning adult.

Angel was definitely a punk. He stabbed and killed a guy over a bad loan debt, just to set an example on the street. He was only fifteen years old at the time. Later in life, when he was twenty, he was involved in another slaying. The court appointed attorney had the case thrown out before making it in front of the judge due to a violation of due process and the absence of proper notification of his constitutional rights.

The extent to which society will go in order to insure that a single innocent person is not wrongly accused, has paved the freedom road to thousands of repeating offenders among us and ignored the responsibility to account for the victims constitutional rights, imprisoning them in a life without retribution, protection or justification. And yet the very same system has locked its doors on me, silencing my innocent voice to the world.

Kirk knew that Angel would get what was coming to him, eventually. It was only a matter of time. When the fighter jets cleared the runway, Kirk was given permission from the tower to take off. He completed the taxi and took position on the center line of the runway and instructed Angel,

"Go ahead push the throttle lever forward slowly and smoothly."

Angel grabbed the control and followed Kirk's instruction. When the plane reached take-off speed, Kirk pulled back on the yoke and the plane gently lifted off the ground. Angel looked out the window, and just screamed. It was odd to Kirk knowing he had a hardened criminal sitting next to him who had been reduced to a wide-eyed child, giddy with excitement. Kirk, an experienced pilot with thousands of flying hours, took a steep bank to the right and then leveled off and headed southeast toward the Long Island Sound and the Atlantic Ocean, just a short 30 minute fight away.

Kirk notified Hartford International Airport of his flight path through the larger airport's airspace and then leaned back and gave the controls to Angel to fly. The plane was actually already in an autopilot mode; Kirk knew that Angel would be impressed with his level of trust after only knowing him for a few short hours. Kirk loved the plane's autopilot. He usually referred to it as his "Mile-High Club Chauffeur."

With Angel occupied scanning the horizon for air traffic, Kirk made a staged phone call to Agent Alden to set up the next move in the sting operation. The voice on the other end answered,

"Hello. This is Alden."

"Hey, this is Preston, how are ya?"

Alden immediately knew that Kirk was around Angel. They had preplanned a signal that he would use his last name only when he called if he was with any gang members at the time.

Preston then continued the conversation,

"Good, good, I'm in my plane with a friend, it's a gorgeous day, the air is really smooth. Hey listen, I was wondering if I could stop and see the man in about an hour."

He paused for a moment, as if he was listening to an answer and then continued,

"Great, great, that sounds good. I'll give you a buzz later, thanks."

Agent Alden was surprised to learn how quickly Kirk was moving the plan along, he never imagined that Kirk could get the area's gang leader isolated and in his control in such a short period of time. The plan was for Kirk to land his plane in White Plains, NY and leave Angel in the plane waiting, as he pretended to meet someone inside a storage hanger facility on the airport campus and then return to the plane.

Kirk closed his phone and placed it in his inside pocket of his leather jacket and grabbed two of his Cuban Cigars out of his other pocket.

He handed one to Angel.

"Are you havin' fun?" he said to Angel.

Angel looked over and smiled at him and answered,

"You are a pretty cool dude man, where'd you get all your money, anyway?"

Kirk cut the end off of his cigar and struck a match off the side of the cockpit door and lit his cigar,

"Oh . . . a little bit here and little bit there, I got a lot of important friends I do business with."

Angel looked at him and asked,

"Oh yeah? What kind a business, man?"

Kirk wasn't about to open up to Angel that easily, so he responded,

"Mostly importing."

Angels pushed on,

"Importin' what?"

Kirk wanted to keep Angel wondering what he was all about and continued to be generally vague in his responses.

"Persian rugs, I got a good connection and those babies sell for a ton over here."

While Kirk was talking, he flipped off the autopilot mechanism and the loud beep sensor distracted the conversation. The plane's control adjusted to manual and there was a jolt from the yoke.

Kirk told Angel that he had better take over the piloting, to which a nervous Angel gladly agreed. He wanted the distraction to interrupt and change the conversation. Kirk had already planted the seed that would bloom into wild curiosity for Angel and didn't need to push it any further, for the time being.

Angel sat back in his seat, stretched out his hands, and cracked his knuckles, still white from grasping the steering controls so tightly for the last fifteen minutes.

He then asked Kirk,

"So where the hell are we going, man?"

Kirk looked over at Angel and answered,

"Ten more minutes man and I'm landing in New York to meet a friend and then we'll head back"

Angel said,

"That's cool. Ya know I'm on probation. I'm not suppose to leave Massachusetts without contacting my probation officer."

"Relax, man, the sky belongs to no one. You can stay in the plane," Kirk assured him.

After several more minutes, Kirk reached out and grabbed the radio microphone from its control panel holder to announce his approach to the White Plains Airport. Seconds later he was given clearance and runway instructions, which he confirmed his understanding.

He placed the microphone back into the holder and began a series of pre-landing control checks. Angel sat up in his seat and looked forward to seeing if he could make out the landing strip ahead of the plane. The panoramic views were incredible. Angel still could not believe he was flying.

Kirk's plane began making the gradual descent that would eventually lead to a soft touchdown on the runway. As the plane braked down the runway, Angel clapped his hands and gave an exuberant hoot of exhilaration; he reached up toward Kirk with his open right hand in the air to elicit a celebratory "high five" from Kirk.

The plane taxied from the active runway and headed over to a hanger area where he parked the plane and shut down the propellers. Kirk again reached under the seat and pulled out his well documented flight log book and made another entry. Then he reached behind the cockpit seats and grabbed an empty backpack. He told Angel to sit tight and he would be right back.

Kirk walked slowly over to a door in one of the hangers, walked through and closed the door behind him, preventing Angel from seeing him go any further.

Once inside, one of the aviation mechanics asked Kirk,

"Can I help you with something?"

Kirk really had no business in the hanger. He simply wanted Angel to think he was meeting someone there. The plan was to leave the impression that Kirk had followed this routine many times in the past.

"No thanks, I'm just wondering if I can use your bathroom." The mechanic pointed Kirk to the bathrooms and went back to his work on a small Cessna engine.

When Kirk emerged from the hanger, he held his backpack as if it was much heavier then when he left the plane with it. Kirk had stuffed it with toilet paper rolls. Instead of opening the cockpit door, he walked around to Angel's side of the fuselage and unlocked a small baggage compartment and placed the pack inside, making sure that he was in Angel's side mirror and in his full line of vision the entire time. He then came back around the front of the plane and jumped back into the pilot's seat.

"All right let's head back, I got a date tonight, and there is no way I am going to be late for this lady," Kirk told Angel.

He pushed a few buttons and pulled a few levers and within minutes they were once again airborne headed north and back home to New England.

CHAPTER 28

Chief O'Donnell picked up Suzie at her apartment early in the morning to take her to the airport for her flight down to Louisiana. It was so early that it was still dark outside and the only people out were a few early morning joggers and some people walking their dogs. Suzie put her travel bag in the trunk of O'Donnell's car and jumped inside. The Chief had already stopped at the doughnut shop and had purchased a hot cup of coffee for Suzie and a powdered jelly doughnut for himself.

Little Casey had come along for the ride too; she sat in the back seat with her nose out the crack of the window searching for familiar smells.

O'Donnell asked Suzie,

"Are you all set for your meeting with Jesse?"

"Yeah, I'm ready, I can't wait to see him I really miss him. It is so unfair what is happening to him."

O'Donnell reached into his visor in the car and pulled out a small note book and handed it to Suzie,

"I made some notes for you, so you can ask Jesse some questions about the evidence against him."

"Thanks Chief, this is great," as she fingered through a few of the pages.

O'Donnell thought about telling Suzie about the listening device he found under his dining room table the night before, but decided not to worry her about things over which she had no control.

He took a last bite out of his jelly-filled doughnut and saved a little piece for the dog which he offered to Casey over his shoulder. Both of them were hiding their concern over the serious nature of Suzie's trip. Suzie laughed at the Chief and said,

> *"That dog better not be fat when I get back. It's bad enough she won't be jogging with me."*

The airport was about 20 minutes from Meadows and a two and half hour flight to New Orleans. Suzie had booked a flight directly to New Orleans with a return flight from Miami. Miami was where the pawn shop was located that had reported Kirk's gold football ring had been left, the ring that had been in O'Donnell's sock drawer all along.

Both O'Donnell and Suzie felt the pawn shop might provide a break in their investigation. Suzie had not made arrangements for transportation between New Orleans and Miami, but figured she could arrange for a train or shuttle plane once she got down south, depending on how long she could visit with me in jail.

Suzie looked over at O'Donnell and said,

> *"I really appreciate all the work you're doing to help Jesse. He really is a great guy and you will love him when you meet him."*

> *"No problem,"* O'Donnell said, *"I can't sit idly by and watch a guy like Agent Alden get away with framing Jesse, I don't care who it is. Besides, you're like a daughter to me and if it's important to you, it's important to me."*

Suzie leaned over and gave O'Donnell a kiss on his cheek and said, *"Thanks Pop."*
O'Donnell smiled back at her.

> *"Jesse will be fine. I'm sure of it. I'm hearing that the feds are trying to move this case along quickly, and my experience tells me that when they're pushing a case through like they are with Kirk's murder, they're usually worried that their case might fall apart. As soon as you can get back to me with info from Jesse, we'll make sure it falls apart."*

"Make sure you call me after you've spoken to him and then I'll get the info to Mayor Sullivan and he'll get to the senator, and if all the pieces fit...Jesse will be home in no time and Alden will be taking a long vacation in a "federal suite.""

Suzie suddenly realized her task at hand could very well determine her best friend's fate for the rest of his life. Her excitement over seeing her old friend again, was replaced with a nervous and anxious sense of responsibility, and then severe sadness once again, reflecting on Kirk's death. She had not fully accepted Kirk's death, and probably never would. She would never understand why a higher being would allow Kirk to leave this world so tragically and so painfully for everyone behind to endure. It wasn't supposed to end this way. There was so much more to be said, to be done, to be lived.

Keeping busy helped her maneuver through the grief and navigate her life, one day at time. It also meant she had piled up massive emotions which burned deep within her soul. Pulling herself together, she focused her long blinding gaze, which had absorbed far beyond her notebook, and turned the blank pages back into reality and back into the present tense of important notes the Chief had transcribed for her.

She reviewed some of the questions with the Chief during the remaining part of the short ride to the airport. As O'Donnell drove the main entrance of the airport and pulled to the curb by the departing passenger section of the airport, he went over a quick checklist of everything with Suzie,

"O.K. got your license? Got your tickets? Got the notebook? Got your new cell phone? Got plenty of money?"

Suzie peaked into her pocket pouch bag which was strapped around her waist and confirmed that she was all set and ready to go.

O'Donnell wished her a good flight and reminded her to be extremely careful and not to trust anyone.

He also advised her,

"When you get to the jail, you might be video taped and your voice may also be recorded, so just ask the questions to Jesse, don't tell him anything about Alden or anything about our plans, O.K.?"

Suzie nodded to O'Donnell, and responded,

"Don't worry, I'll be all right, I'll see you in a couple of days.

She then bent down to be eye to eye with her four legged friend, and raised her voice to a softer and higher pitch.

Bye, bye Casey. Be a good little girl."

Suzie patted Casey on the head provoking an energetic wagging of her tail, and Suzie got out of the car and walked to the back where O'Donnell opened the trunk and handed the travel bag to her and gave her another comforting hug.

"Good luck, honey."

O'Donnell got back into the car and waited until he could no longer see Suzie inside the terminal. Little Casey jumped over the backrest into the front passenger seat and also looked out the window. The Chief gave Casey an affectionate ear scratch and they drove away, heading back to O'Donnell's house.

The Chief planned on taking a shower and taking Casey for a short walk around the neighborhood and then he would head over to Holyville to see some of his old buddies on the police force.

Holyville was the second largest city in Western Mass and consequently O'Donnell had worked cooperatively on many cases with their police Chief over the years. He was hoping to get some information about Lopez and specifically about the night he was arrested and charged with stealing a car and cocaine possession. The feds might be in charge of the Preston murder investigation, but Holyville's police had jurisdiction over Lopez, and that's where he was being held, pending his trial.

When O'Donnell came home, he parked his car in the garage and walked out to his mailbox on the street, where he retrieved the

Daily Springdale Newspaper and walked inside. He threw the paper on the kitchen counter and took off his hat and coat.

He picked up the dog dish from the floor and filled it with fresh water, placed it back on the floor and then gazed over to the paper. A headline read that the town of Meadows had been awarded national recognition for its recycling efforts and would be receiving an award presented by U.S. Senator Kerrigan.

The article continued by describing an event planned by the Meadows Conservation Commission that would host the award presentation on the town green. The event was to receive national media exposure and would be taking place the very next weekend.

O'Donnell had recalled that Mayor Sullivan was planning on meeting Senator Kerrigan and endorsing him for his upcoming Senate election, during a Western Mass visit. O'Donnell deduced that this must be the event to which he was referring. O'Donnell had hoped he would have more time to prepare and provide information for the Mayor to give to the senator, but was confident he could get the job done. He had always worked well under pressure and looming deadlines.

He decided to skip his shower and dog-walk and head over to Holyville instead. There was no time to waste and he knew that mornings were typically better if you wanted to catch a cop still at the station. He ran back to his bathroom, put a little extra deodorant on, took a swig of mouthwash and spit it out in the sink. He then grabbed his coat, his hat, and headed out to his car and off to Holyville.

CHAPTER 29

Kirk's plan had worked to a tee. Angel Lopez continued to pry into Kirk's personal life on the plane ride back to Massachusetts and was dying to know where he had gotten the pure cocaine that Kirk had given to one of Angel's street soldiers a few weeks earlier. With only about ten minutes remaining in the trip, Angel cut straight to the chase and asked him,

"Hey man. I wanted to ask you something."

"Yeah what?" asked Kirk.

Angel continued,

"The other day one of my guys gave me some blow that you had given to him."

Kirk paused, he was expecting the question ever since they had left the pool hall and he was actually relieved that Angel had finally asked.

Kirk answered in his usual cool demeanor,

"I did? I don't remember that."

Kirk picked up his microphone, ignoring Angel and announced his initial descent to the Westford Airport air traffic control, and then replaced the microphone in the dashboard panel.

Angel pursued his inquiry,

"Come on, man, I'm cool with it. Where'd you get that stuff? I know it wasn't around dis town cuz I ain't see that stuff here."

Again Kirk, paused and fiddled with a few of the pre-landing controls and checked the gauges, rather than answer Angel too quickly.

After a few minutes, Kirk replied back to Angel,

"I'm telling you, I don't do the stuff, but I get it for some friends of mine, on occasion."

"Can you get me some?" asked Angel.

"Nah. I don't really want to get into small street deals, man, I hope you understand, this is dangerous business, ya know," teased Kirk. Kirk looked out over the controls as if not giving Angel the time of day, it was then that he knew he had him right where he wanted him.

Angel was not planning on letting the subject go and wasn't afraid of forcing the issue with Kirk if he had to, once they were on the ground, of course. Angel responded to Kirk's refusal,

"Hey, man I'm not talkin' about small street stuff. I am talkin' about big stuff, where you could make a lot of money," Angel was pushing the point.

"I got everything I need. It's just not worth it to me," said Kirk.

Kirk looked over at Angel's lap and told him to put his seatbelt back on, as he made his final approach to the runway. The plane touched down as smooth as silk and Kirk turned the plane toward his designated tie-down spot and brought the plane to a complete stop, shutting down the props.

"Did you have a good time?" Kirk asked Angel.

"Oh yeah. It was great, man," answered Angel. *"I would love to do dat again sometime."*

Kirk gathered a few of his belongings and made a final entry into his weathered flight log book and then opened the cockpit door and stepped out onto the tarmac. Angel stepped out on his side and walked around to Kirk who was securing the wings with a cable connected to a fastener on the pavement and tying down the propeller blades in a lock position.

Kirk handed Angel a rope and asked him to repeat the procedure on the other side of the plane, which he did. Kirk walked around the back of the plane and opened the compartment where he had stashed his backpack and opened the bag; again he made sure that Angel could see he was opening the same bag that he had filled during the stop in White Plains, N.Y.

Kirk then walked over to Angel and gave him a zip-lock bag with another sample of pure cocaine and said,

"Here you go man, but don't come asking me for more."

Angel was grateful for Kirk's generosity, but wasn't satisfied with the little token, he wanted to score big. Angel knew that he could cut the pure stuff four times over before it hit the street and make ten times more money.

Angel thanked him anyway and said,

"Thanks, man, but I want to talk to you about this some more later, all right?"

Kirk just looked at him and smiled,

"Come on let's go, I got a date and she's a lot better looking than you."

Kirk hopped into the driver's seat of the Corvette and this time he would be doing the driving back to Springdale and to the pool hall where he would drop off Angel. On the ride back, Kirk noticed that his gold chain, which previously sat in his center console, was now missing. He knew that Angel had stolen it, but didn't say anything to him about it. It just reinforced what he already knew, that even though he had befriended him for an entire afternoon, he would never change him. He was just a lowlife scum. Kirk couldn't wait to play the sting on him all the way to the end.

Before being dropped off at the pool hall, Angel asked Kirk if he could have his cell phone number and maybe call him.

Kirk simply responded,

"No, I don't think so, man. I never give it out. I'll be around next week though. I'll try to stop down at the hall."

Angel was determined to not lose a possible new connection for drugs, especially when there was little risk in transporting them to the area. The drugs that Angel has moved through the Northeast corridor in the last year had been cut so many times, it was more like baking soda and little room for much profit, unlike the sampling he had received from Kirk.

Kirk drove into downtown Springdale at about 30 miles per hour over the speed limit and skidded to a stop at a red traffic light, in the center of the city. In the next lane over a Springdale police cruiser pulled next to him at the light and looked over at the vintage Corvette. The cop noticed Kirk and the notorious street thug sitting in the passenger seat next to him. Angel looked over and saw the officer starring at him. Angel whispered at Kirk through the side of his mouth,

"Hey, man, be cool, there's cops right next to you and they're checking us out, you want me to ditch?"

At that moment the officer lowered his window and waved for Kirk to do the same. Kirk looked over at the cop and rolled down his window.

The officer said,

"Good afternoon Mr. Preston is everything all right?"

Kirk responded back,

"Yeah everything is great, thanks."

The officer tipped his hat to Kirk,

"You have a great day, Mr. Preston and by the way, my wife thanks you for helping out at the Boys & Girls Club."

Kirk smiled back and said,

"Hey, it's my pleasure. You guys take care."

The light turned green and the cruiser pulled away from the intersection and Kirk too, continued down Main Street.

Angel couldn't believe what had just happened. He thought for sure that Kirk would have some explaining to do and that the cops might search the car and find Kirk's backpack. He was already taken with Kirk's coolness and whole way of life and this little episode only further strengthened his mystique of Kirk.

"Man, does everybody know you? You like own this town, don't you?" Angel laughed.

Kirk snickered,

"It helps to have a few friends, you never know when you might need one. I take care of my friends and they take care of me. It's all cool."

Kirk pulled over at the next corner and let Angel out in front of the pool hall. As Angel stepped out of the car, he reached back inside to offer a hand shake to Kirk, before he left.

"I'll see you next week, right?" asked Angel.

"Yeah, I'll be around, maybe Friday." Then, Kirk screeched his tires and sped off even before Angel could completely close the door of the car. Angel just stood there and shook his head as if he had just spent the day with a rock star.

CHAPTER 30

Life was getting quite routine in the jail and every day was just like the day before. Nearly every morning I would receive an envelope with an update regarding the extradition procedure back to Massachusetts, with no new information. Most days I wouldn't even open the envelope. I have never received any mail. It wasn't because no one had sent me any, it was because it took two weeks to get to me after going through a screening process and evaluation, and I had only been in the facility for a little more than two.

I did get a few more follow-up letters from the gorgeous strawberry blonde court-appointed attorney, but they were just copies of paperwork. I loved getting correspondence from her. Each letter represented a pack of bubble gum for me. One of my jail mates would trade a pack of gum for every one of her envelopes. He would then lick the gummed portion of the envelope that he believed she personally had sealed. It was a sick place, a different world all together and a different culture where some thrived and others, like me, couldn't believe they were there.

I opened the manila-clasped envelope and on top of the legal documents was a hand written-note, by one of the guards. It read, **You have a visitor today during scheduled hours in the visitors center, please review all procedures herein.** This was great news, a break from my routine. I wasn't sure if it was Cole or maybe Captain Bill who had requested the visitation, but it didn't matter. I was just happy that someone from the outside knew I was here and cared enough to see me.

The next few hours would prove to be the longest since I had entered the jail in anticipation of my contact with the outside world. I read over the visitation procedures a dozen times to pass the time. I did my daily sit-ups and push-ups and wrote a few excerpts in my diary. I found writing to be very therapeutic. I would write about my fondest memories to help cheer me up. Most of them included Kirk and Suzie.

I would read them over and over. In some ways it made my life feel full and more complete. It helped me realize how great life had already treated me. And if I never woke up from this nightmare, then I was at peace with myself. My fate could never be worse than what Kirk had faced, no matter what cards I would be dealt.

At times when I read my diary, I could actually be brought to laughter. I would fondly remember times as when Kirk and I got tattoos in Las Vegas, or how I was parading around the conference room in Indianapolis, thinking I was the center of the world. My ambitions all seemed so petty now, dreams, desires, money. What's it all about? I learned very quickly, in my isolation, that it's about finding peace within yourself and holding on to memories of places, friends and family. No one can take that away, and all the freedoms and all the money in the world can't buy or replace those cherished feelings.

In a strange irony, the worst days of my life were making me more whole as a person and putting my life into a meaningful perspective that I had previously been blind to understand. This tragic circumstance gave me a new appreciation of just how precious life is and to never take good times for granted. But would I ever have any more? Would I be reduced to reliving memories? Maybe my new found peace was just a way of masking a very real fear that I may spend the rest of my life in prison and even worse - be remembered for killing my best friend. But for now, life would be a mystery to be lived, not a problem to be solved.

Whatever it takes, religion, memories, a new purpose, I suppose it doesn't matter - whatever gets you through. If you let it get to you, the bitterness will eat away at your core. Right now, I was O.K. with my "situation." Ten, Twenty years from now? Who knows?

In the outside world you plan for your future . . . weeks, months and years in advance. In jail, it's just one day, one hour at a time and today was going to be a great day . . . I had a visitor.

It was nearly eleven o'clock and almost time to leave for the Communication Center. I had learned how to tell the time by studying the methodical movements of the guards during their daily routines. When the hour arrived, I stood anxious near the cell door. The instruction packet, I had read, indicated that I had only 30 minutes with my guest. I did not want to waste a second of it. Fortunately my escort was prompt.

I turned my back to the food transfer gate in the middle of the iron bars so the guard could secure my handcuffs from the corridor outside my cell, before unlocking and opening the door. After walking through three additional cell blocks, all of them with a separate security detail and procedure, I arrived at the waiting area.

I quickly scanned the plain-clothed people who were lined up outside the room in what looked like an airport security screening area. One at a time, people entered through the metal detector and walked directly to an available phone pod where they would be met with their respective prisoner on the other side of a double-paned and wired glass partition.

One by one, each person was just another stranger to me and I began to wonder if perhaps there had been a mix-up, until I saw Suzie. I had never seen anyone so beautiful in my life. She was truly a vision to behold. Her presence instantly brought tears to my eyes and my new found tower of strength shattered into a weak rubble of emotion. I would have given anything to embrace her, but would have to settle for seeing her face and hearing her voice.

The officer unlocked my handcuffs and pointed to the chair opposite the pod she had chosen, I practically ran to my spot, grabbed the handset from its cradle and with a trembling voice, I greeted her.

"Suzie, my God, thank you for coming. I love you, I love you, how are you? I can't believe you're here for me."

Suzie too, could not hold back the tears and quickly responded,

"Oh Jesse, I have been so worried about you. Are you O.K.?

"I'm fine. It's not so bad. I just want to get the hell out of here."
"That's why I'm here, honey. We have a team at home working on it. We'll get you out. Don't worry."

"I can't believe Kirk is dead," I said to Suzie.

Suzie just shook her head and closed her eyes,

"I try not to think about it, but I can't help it. But that's over now. If Kirk knew you were in jail over this, oh my God . . ."

"Thanks for coming; really, you have no idea how much I have been thinking of you."

Suzie remembered O'Donnell's strict instructions for her to get answers, it was her only chance and she needed to focus on that task.

"Jesse, listen to me, you have to help me. You're being framed and they have a lot damaging evidence on you," she said.

"Why are they framing me?"

"Never mind about that, I'll explain later," she answered.

"Jesse, listen, please. Just answer my questions, please."

"What are they saying?"

Suzie looked down at her notepad and took out a pen. Then she asked,

"Jesse, Why did you go to Indiana and why was there blood on the shirt that you threw away in your hotel room?"

"Suzie, you know my nose, I got so worked up over going to Indianapolis by mistake, I was supposed to be in Minneapolis, I bled all over that damn shirt. Why are you asking about that?"

Suzie tried to stay focused but had to laugh a little.

"Why did you write on a hotel pad, to dispose of the wire?"

Dispose of the wire? I didn't know what the hell she was talking about. I paused and tried to think back.

"Wait. Oh crap....I remember. I was making notes and one of them was about my damn answering machine and the frayed telephone wire. Ya know, I think it was that freakin' machine that screwed me all up in the first place."

"O.K. O.K. never mind that."

Suzie hastily went down the list that O'Donnell had provided, question by question.

"I already know this answer, but I have to ask you. Did you go to Miami and pawn Kirk's football ring?"

I looked at her with a puzzled grin, like she was crazy and said,

"What?"

Suzie said,

"O.K. never mind that too. Why did they find a drop of your blood in Kirk's plane?"

I laughed,

"Hello? Remember my ol' faithful nose? Kirk couldn't get the plane started before I was pinching the bridge of my geyser."

Suzie smiled, shook her head and continued,

"All right, all right . . . here's a serious one. Kirk had a couple of million-dollar life insurance policies. Why were you listed as the sole benefactor on one of them?"

I put my face in my free hand, shaking my head and responded.

"Oh my god, I forgot about that."

Suzie, put her book down and raised her head,

"You mean you knew about that. It wasn't a frame up?"

"No, it's true. Kirk was about to get into some dangerous stuff and thought it would be a good idea to get a policy. He said it had better

odds than a casino blackjack table. But Suzie, this is very difficult for me to tell you."

"What is it?" Suzie asked.

I thought about not telling her, but at this point . . . things couldn't get much worse. I paused for second and swallowed,

"Kirk was planning on finally settling down and getting married and if things worked out all right for him after the scam that he was involved in was over, he was going to switch the benefactor of his policy to his future wife."

She froze and gazed motionlessly into his eyes.

"His future wife? You're kidding? Kirk?" Suzie questioned.

"Suzie, he was going to ask you to marry him."

Suzie dropped her phone and starred down at the shelf of the table in a hypnotic state and sat motionless for several seconds. I called her name, in vane, through the telephone handset, but she could not hear me. After a few more moments, I tapped on the glass and she rapidly blinked her eyes several times and raised her head back to me and lifted the receiver back to her ear.

"I'm sorry Suzie. I'm soooo sorry. I thought you should know how he felt. Kirk loved you. He just wasn't ready before. You know Kirk."

"It's all right," Suzie took a deep breath and exhaled slowly. She then thought for a moment and asked,

"How did you know he was getting into this 'scam thing' anyway?"

"Oh that. That's what probably killed him, you know? Remember how I told you to contact that FBI guy Alden?"

Suzie became more attentive and back on the focus of the case. I continued,

"Kirk didn't trust that guy. They were supposed to meet at the Meadows' High School track and talk about this big sting that Kirk was to secretly conduct. Alden was just using him to get a promotion and he was also planning on scamming some big drug guy out of a lot of cash, which he was going to split with Kirk, on the side."

Suzie leaned forward to absorb every word I was saying.

"Kirk knew this guy was no good, but couldn't resist the temptation of excitement and some quick cash. He asked me to hide in the announcer's booth at the top of the bleacher stands, in listening range, just in case something went wrong, boy was he right, unfortunately dead right. I can't believe what he got himself into this time."

Suzie could not believe what she had just heard and asked,

"Do you think they will believe you?"

"Probably not," I answered. *"That's why I taped all of their conversations."*

Suzie's eyes opened up wide and raised her voice,

"You have all of their conversations on tape?"

"Oh yeah, I have a little recorder machine I used at business meetings and I recorded him and Alden every time they met."

For the first time Suzie felt a huge weight lift from her shoulders. She knew that this was exactly what she needed for O'Donnell to completely blowup the FBI's case.

"Oh my God, this is great, where is the tape?" Suzie asked.

I had to think about it, I usually leave the tape inside the recorder and just fast forward anything I want to save, before recording. I kept it in my business briefcase.

"Hmmmm, let me think, the last time I had the recorder was...Oh damn it."

"What? Where is it?" asked Suzie.

"The last place I used it was in Indiana and I left my briefcase and all my stuff there. After I got fired, I didn't need or want any of it anymore, I had completely forgotten that Kirk's tape was there, shoot." The evidentiary tape had been left in this hotel room.

Suzie tried to stay optimistic and told me not to worry about it. She already had a lot of the information and answers she needed, and she was sure that O'Donnell could work it out somehow.

An announcement came over the public address speaker system in the visitor's center notifying all guests that the visiting time was over. Suzie gathered her notes together and asked me how to get to the train station. I wasn't sure, but I worried, like a big brother, about her traveling alone, especially after getting to know how ugly people can be. I told her to call Cole and I gave her his number. I assured her that he was a good guy that I met down here and he could help her.

My motivation for Suzie meeting Cole was not just for her safety, I had also hoped that she would help restore my friendship with him by telling him that I was being framed for murder. Cole and Bill were really cool guys and befriended me when I needed it most. I felt lousy about betraying their trust and good nature. I knew that Suzie would vouch for me.

I was right in the middle of a goodbye sentence when the phone system line went dead and I was left starring at her beautiful blue eyes. Her smile gave me a new found reason for not accepting this awful and unjust fate. Instead, I felt a new passion to fight for my freedom, and get back out into the beautiful world.

Suzie stood up, threw me a kiss and turned around and walked back to the security entrance from where she had entered. I made sure to absorb her image in my mind in order to help me get through the rest of the day.

Within minutes of stepping outside, Suzie's cell phone rang. She was certain it was O'Donnell checking on her, but it was Detective Murphy.

"Suzie? Can you hear me? It's Murph." Suzie was happy to hear his voice and answered back,

"It's a bad connection, but I can hear you. I just left Jesse and he gave us a legitimate explanation for every single piece of evidence they have on him."

"That's great, the Chief went up to Holyville, so I thought I would check in with you and see what you found out," said Murphy.

The detective continued,

"What about the Miami pawn shop? What did Jesse say about that?"

Before Suzie could respond the cell line dropped off and they were disconnected. Suzie tried to call him back, but could not get a strong enough signal. Instead, she took out her note pad and tried calling Cole, as I had recommended.

Chapter 31

Before O'Donnell left his house to make a visit to some old friends on the Holyville Police force, he decided to set a trap for some unwelcomed guests. The Chief rigged up a hidden camera in his bedroom and set the mode to long play record. Then he walked out to his dining room table where "the bug" was still operational and pretended to call Suzie on his cell phone. He was hoping that his acting job would entice the listeners to appear on his home movie.

"Hi Suzie, how's it going down there? Really? That's great, yup, yup, all right what else did he say? O.K. O.K. Good. I have some good news too. Guess what I have under my bed mattress? Kirk's ring. Yeah I know. It's the same ring all right, yup. This is exactly what we needed. Don't worry, I'm not going anywhere, I'll be out of the house for most of the day, but other than that, it is well protected next to my Smith Wesson. All right, I'll call you tomorrow sometime, O.K.? Have a safe trip back. O.K. bye, bye, you too, bye."

The trap was set. O'Donnell then grabbed his coat and a Red Sox cap and headed out the door. Holyville was a short 15 minute ride from Springdale and the police station was located in the heart of the city. For years Holyville had been known as the breeding ground for gang activity, but in recent years their police Chief had managed to force many of the gangs into nearby Springdale, rather than arrest them, a fact that O'Donnell often complained about to the Chief. He understood their challenges. He couldn't blame them. Their responsibilities were to their own citizens and to their own families. They had to get up and go to work everyday on those streets and some didn't make it home.

When O'Donnell walked through the front public entrance of the station, he might as well have been a Hollywood celeb. Officers and city personnel swarmed around him and vociferously greeted him with open arms. The news of his attempted suicide had been on the minds of all his friends, but most had not had an opportunity to talk to him and offer support. Police officers have always had a brotherly fraternity and Springdale and Holyville was no different. While several people surrounded the Chief in the lobby, a voice from the stairs shouted out,

"I hope you haven't come looking for my job, cuz I ain't fixing to retire quite yet."

O'Donnell looked over his shoulder at his old colleague and shouted back,

"This city couldn't afford me, you don't have anything to worry about."

The two large men embraced each-other and exchanged small talk for several minutes, before being invited to come upstairs and chit chat about things in his office. O'Donnell laughed when he entered Chief Jones's office, because it was just as messy as his and he was humored by the empty doughnut carton on the window shelf.

"Man, it's good to see you. How are you doing, my friend? It ain't right what they did to you over that Preston murder case. It just ain't right."

O'Donnell smiled back and shrugged his shoulders,

"It's all right. You know I was counting the days before I could retire anyway. It just would have been nice to go out with a ceremony at the lodge and receive the gold watch and all, but it's all good. Besides, I've been thinking of doing a little private investigating to supplement my income. I don't know how long I'll be considered off-duty, but I'm sure it won't be for very long. I'm sure they didn't want to risk a contract lawsuit, so laying me off, was probably cheaper."

Jones looked at O'Donnell and said,

"You would make an excellent 'private eye' with your experience; I think that's a great idea. If I can help you in anyway possible, you know I will."

"Thanks," said O'Donnell, *"actually, maybe you can help me. I've been looking into this guy you got in your lockup, Angel Lopez."*

"That scum. What about him?"

O'Donnell took out a pocket notepad and pencil and prepared to write a few things down, when Chief Jones tossed a four-inch file in front of O'Donnell.

"It's funny you should be asking me about him. I just got a call from the feds for a copy of the file too. I told those jokers I would get to it when I had a chance. Who do they think they are? We work 24/7 for evidence and they want to ride in on a horse and take the credit."

"Can I look through this?" asked O'Donnell.

"Sure you can, I don't care," he responded.

O'Donnell scanned each page that related to the most recent arrest of Lopez, the night before Kirk's body was found less than a mile from where Lopez had been caught by police. O'Donnell asked,

"Why did you stop Lopez, was it a traffic thing?"

"No. We received an alert for a stolen car and the likelihood of its location. The cocaine we found inside was a bonus and not what we expected to find when the officers pulled him over. That was his 3rd strike you know."

O'Donnell looked at Jones above his reading glasses and snickered,

"You mean you didn't have to chase him to Springdale?"

O'Donnell continued to take notes from the file, among them was the name of the owner of the car that Lopez had stolen. A French man named Pierre Corriveau was listed on the report as the car's owner, along with his address. O'Donnell asked Chief Jones where the car was impounded and if he could have a quick look at it. Jones agreed to take a ride with O'Donnell, under one condition . . . he pays for a coffee.

After taking all the notes he could use, he thanked the Chief for his help and they both got up and headed to the Chief's 1999 Crown Victoria and drove across town to the municipal motor vehicle impound yard to have a look at the car that Lopez had stolen.

At first glance everything appeared to be normal when they looked at the car. There was the typical broken window, but no hot wire job or anything unusual. O'Donnell asked if he could check the trunk and the Chief directed the yard attendee to open the trunk for O'Donnell to take a look. When the trunk opened, O'Donnell and Jones saw a semi rolled Oriental rug and a USB computer wire and what looked like clumps of human hair. They all appeared to be heavily stained. O'Donnell's intuition was that it was blood, Kirk's blood.

The car was evidence only in a stolen car crime and a drug crime, so it was never combed over for evidence that would implicate a murder. The trunk had been opened before by police, but it took O'Donnell's gut to tell him there was much more to the content of this car than first meets the eye. The items in the trunk told a real-life story and it was the Chief's opinion that the author was dead, and the main characters were in Holyville's jail.

O'Donnell took out a pair of medical-style sterile gloves and put them on his hands. He asked Jones if they had tested the items in the trunk. Jones could not recall seeing any notes on it and didn't think anyone else had. As far as they were concerned, it was a stolen car case and a drug case. There was no need for police to give the car a full forensics check.

O'Donnell scraped a small sample of the dried stain with his Swiss army knife, placed the shavings in an envelope along with a hair sample and then placed the envelope in his shirt pocket. He closed the trunk and asked the Chief,

"Where were the drugs found?"

Jones pointed to the back seat and answered,

"You wouldn't believe it. On the backseat, there was a canvas duffle bag that was labeled dirty laundry. The cocaine was under a few shirts and a couple pairs of blue jeans inside the laundry bag. They found a kilo. The boys tell us it was high grade stuff, nothing like the stuff we normally see from these punks."

O'Donnell walked around the car a couple of times and then took off his gloves and thanked his old colleague for letting him look at the stolen car and for allowing him to take his own sample of evidence. It paid to have friends when doing police work. After a few more minutes they headed out of the yard and drove back to Holyville Headquarters.

They both agreed to make a better effort to stay in touch and maybe even take in a Red Sox game next season. In the meantime, he reminded O'Donnell that if there was anything he could ever do for him, to just give him a call. They parted their ways and O'Donnell got back in his car and headed out of Holyville and back to neighboring Springdale.

While driving back to his house, he pulled his car over into a convenience store mini-mall parking lot where he decided to make a quick phone call to the Frenchman whose car Angel Lopez had stolen. O'Donnell retrieved his note pad and found the phone number and dialed. The gentleman answered the call with a thick, polite French accent,

"Corriveau residence, Pierre speaking."

O'Donnell introduced himself as Springdale's Police Chief and wondered if he could ask a few questions about his car. The Frenchman replied,

"It is about time you called me. I have left many messages with your colleague, Inspector Alden. He told me he would let you know that I called and would like to speak to you." O'Donnell fought back

his anger toward the controlling Alden and simply responded,

"Yes, I am so sorry. I have been very busy and out of the office. Do you have few minutes to speak right now?"

Corriveau agreed to cooperate in any way he could.

"Qui, but may I first ask you a question Chef de police? When will I be getting my auto back?" he cordially inquired.

O'Donnell responded,

"Well, I'm afraid it may be a while, due to the fact that it is being held as evidence in more than just a stolen car charge. So, I can't tell you exactly when."

Corriveau simply replied,

"Oh well, c'est la vie."

O'Donnell asked,

"I was wondering if you could tell me when you first reported your car missing?"

Corriveau paused for a moment and answered,

"Actually, I never reported it missing. I found a note in the airport office that my friend had borrowed it. I did not know it had been stolen until receiving a phone message from my insurance company." O'Donnell interrupted the gentlemen,

"I'm sorry sir; did you say the airport office?"

"Qui, Qui, I am a pilot and I was away on a business trip in my private aircraft. When I returned, my car was not in the parking lot, so I inquired in the office and they informed me that my friend Kirk had borrowed it."

"Kirk Preston?" O'Donnell asked.

"Qui, he is a fellow pilot friend of mine. Our aircrafts were usually next to each others. We have exchanged autos in the past, so I did not think it unusual. He knew where I stored my keys and he left his Corvette keys for me to use while he had my auto."

O'Donnell sat in his car very confused by all this new information and wasn't sure what to make of it. He transcribed everything down on his notepad and would try to decipher it all later.

O'Donnell continued with the Frenchman,

"Why would Mr. Preston need to borrow your car if he had his own there at the same time?"

"Well, you see Chief many times my friend would need my auto because it was larger than his and occasionally he would need to transport items from his aircraft to his residence. I was only more than pleased to help. Kirk was a dear and kind person. I am so saddened by his passing. Did you know him?"

O'Donnell answered,

"Yes, I did know him. He was a fine young man."

O'Donnell's tone changed as he heard the gentlemen talk about Kirk's wonderful qualities. O'Donnell had been so preoccupied with investigating the case he had not thought about Kirk for several days. He still carried a tremendous burden of guilt and sense of responsibility for his death. With Kirk's images in his mind, O'Donnell's attention drifted away from his conversation, while the Frenchman continued to describe Kirk and his genuine qualities.

His mind came back in focus when Corriveau remarked,

"I hope they give his killer a death notice. This Monsieur Thorpe does not deserve to live."

O'Donnell blinked his eyes and rubbed his faced with the palm of his hands, and said,

"Yes, yes, well, thank you very much for your time, Mr. Corriveau. You have been very helpful. I will be in touch if I have any further

questions, and I'll let you know when you can get your car back from the authorities."

O'Donnell flipped his cell phone down and sat idly for a few minutes before continuing home. O'Donnell began to realize that there was much more to this case than anyone knew. All of the police files indicated Angel Lopez had stolen the car. Naturally, the assumption was that he had stolen it from its owner, Pierre Corriveau, who police say called the police to report the theft. But, in fact, it now appeared to O'Donnell that Angel may have stolen it from Kirk. Kirk was the only one who had access to his friend's car within the gated security area of the airport.

If that was the case, why did the records indicate Pierre reported it stolen? Did Kirk report it stolen instead, pretending to be Pierre? If Angel murdered Kirk, was he with him in the plane and did they leave together in Pierre's car? If so, then how or when did Kirk make the phone call to tip the police? And when was Kirk killed? Was Agent Alden involved in some way?

No doubt, there were many questions that still needed to be answered and the labyrinth of clues was too much for the Chief to easily navigate. O'Donnell decided it would be best if he kept this new information to himself. His years of experience would serve him better than involving anyone else this late in the game, and, Angel wasn't going anywhere.

O'Donnell put his note pad away, started his car and pulled out of the parking lot and headed back toward his home. O'Donnell had learned over the years not to jump to conclusions when conducting an investigation, many times the obvious would be the greatest distraction to a successful outcome. He sat back in his car seat with one hand on the lower part of the steering wheel and the other twirling his handlebar moustache, the habit was typical O'Donnell when he was deep in thought, or when he spun his wheels.

As O'Donnell entered his neighborhood he slowed his car down and was flagged to stop by a police officer. The officer was assigned a traffic detail for the local power utility company in order to control traffic while the electric crew repaired a power problem on O'Donnell's street. The officer noticed O'Donnell sitting at the front of the line of cars and walked over to say hello to his old boss.

"Hi Chief, how the hell are ya? We sure do miss you."

O'Donnell smiled at the young officer and answered,

"Hey, Frankie, I'm doing just fine. How are you doing?"

O'Donnell had been on the Springdale force so long that he remembers when the young cop's father served for the department.

"What's going on here?" the Chief asked.

Frankie kneeled down to the Chiefs eye level and replied,

"I don't know, same old crap, I'm just putting in for some O.T. on account of me and the Mrs. are expecting a baby," the cop proudly acknowledged.

"Hey, that's great. Good for you. Congratulations. I hope you're smarter than your dad was," O'Donnell joked.

"I know, don't worry, I've already heard it from my wife. There is no way she'll have more than one cop in the family," Frankie laughed. *Hey, maybe you'll have a daughter and then you'll just have to worry about are all the cops in town."*

The Chief noticed that the one-way traffic from the opposing direction was cleared and hinted to the young cop that he had to get going,

"Well, it was good seeing you. Say hi to the guys for me."

The officer stood up and told the Chief to take care and encouraged him to come back to the station and visit when he had a chance. He took a few steps back and waved him through along with the waiting cars behind.

O'Donnell had been away from his house for about three hours. He was anxious to get inside and check his hidden video camera after setting the bait with his fake phone call near the recently discovered dining room listening device. First, however, he would take little Casey out for a walk and smell in the back yard.

When he came back in the house he reached down and released the leash from the dog's collar and picked up the water dish and began filling it with fresh water. As O'Donnell stood in front of the kitchen sink, he could see a blinking light coming from his microwave oven clock. He wasn't surprised to see that the clock needed to be reset. Whenever the house lost power, O'Donnell would have to go around and reset all the digital clocks and the VCR player.

At that moment, O'Donnell stood motionless, almost in a trance. The water was overflowing the filled doggy dish. O'Donnell just dropped the bowl in the sink and said under his breath, *"those bastards."* He ran to his bedroom and immediately looked for the tiny match he had leaned against the door, to tip him that someone had been in his room. Someone had. He immediately checked the video camera and discovered it had not powered back onto the record mode after the power failure. Just as the feds had planned.

"Damn it," he yelled.

The normally infallible O'Donnell hated to be outsmarted by anyone and was mad at himself for not thinking of using a wireless device to power the hidden camera. He was up against the FBI and he should have known that they think of everything, and have the means to do anything; even if it meant creating a power outage on an entire city block and securing the area from its own residents, until the house was cleared of the uninvited guests.

O'Donnell looked under the mattress where he had set the trap for the FBI. Of course, he did not leave Kirk's ring there, but was surprised to see that the intruder had taken his Smith & Wesson handgun. Even though he had lured the intruders to look for the ring under the bed mattress, he still double checked his sock drawer. He was relieved to find that Kirk's ring was safe in its original hiding place, stuffed inside the black sock in the back of the drawer.

He walked out of his bedroom and over to the dining room table and checked to see if the "bug" was still in place. It had been removed and there was no evidence of it ever having been in that location. O'Donnell figured that the FBI knew that he had tried to trap them in his house and wasn't about to leave anything behind. He was in the middle of a cat n' mouse game and even his own house could no longer be considered a safe playing field.

CHAPTER 32

Kirk Preston and FBI Agent Wayne Alden had met a few more times at the high school track to plan their next move in the operation. Alden would begin each meeting asking Kirk for a detailed summary of what had taken place during his and Angel Lopez's previous encounter. Agent Alden never wanted to risk "wiring up" Kirk, so consequently, he was real a stickler for insisting that Kirk share his every detail with him. The next stage was to tease Angel with the possibility of doing some drug business together. It would be the last step before the big sting.

Agent Alden informed Kirk that the bureau had authorized the use of three kilos of pure Cocaine to use for the bait. He told Kirk that the drugs had previously been confiscated by the Boston division, from a raid on a Brazilian Oil Tanker anchored in the Boston Harbor. From time to time the organization would use stored evidence to elicit more illegal activity and, in turn, make additional arrests.

The plan would be to continue resisting doing business with Angel, further teasing him, and then eventually to sell him a portion of the Cocaine. Alden told Kirk there would be four or five other agents watching the movement of the drugs every step of the way after Angel received the package, but that no arrests would be made. With a high degree of trust and confidence in Kirk among the gang's leaders, the final sting would occur a week or two later and hopefully bring in the next level of gang leaders for the sting.

If all went as planned, it would net a half million dollars of the gang's money and expose the region's kingpins. Kirk told Alden he didn't see any reason why the plan wouldn't play out exactly like he wanted. When Alden brought up the subject of money, Kirk took the opportunity to press Alden for a financial commitment for all of his time and risk. He pressed Alden,

"So, if the FBI is netting half a million, what's going to be my cut?"

Alden expected that Kirk would be asking about the money and was prepared. Alden explained to Kirk,

"You know, it is best to keep a lot of this stuff off the record, I'm sure you understand that the Bureau is taking a risk involving someone from the outside like you to be part of an operation of this magnitude. A lot of guys could get 'the axe' if things were to go wrong."

Kirk looked at the Agent and said,

"Hey some guy getting the axe is the last thing I'm worried about and if something goes wrong, I assume that does not bode well for me." Alden assured Kirk,

"Relax, relax, I didn't imply that anything could go wrong. All right, look, here's what we should do . . . when the time comes to strike a deal with Lopez, let's pad the deal a little for ourselves too, all right? Nobody needs to know."

That was fine with Kirk, but it was the first time that he sensed that Alden was not completely a "company man." He wondered exactly how much the Boston FBI Bureau knew about his involvement, if at all. From the very beginning he thought it was unusual that Alden had been his only contact, but he trusted O'Donnell and the Mayor that everything seemed legit. He had no reason not to trust them.

Alden told Kirk the next time they meet he would bring the Cocaine. In the meantime, he should go ahead and contact Lopez again and work on solidifying more trust in their relationship. Alden left the high school track and arranged to meet with Kirk again in another week and with that, the FBI Agent was gone.

Kirk walked down the bleachers and onto the track where he performed some stretching and warm-up exercises before he began his running routine. Suzie Dillon was also running on the track that afternoon with a couple of her co-workers from the spa. By the time Kirk had made his first pass around the track he had caught up to Suzie. Kirk was happy to see her and jogged alongside her. Suzie intentionally picked up the pace and pulled away from her friends, with Kirk by her side. She and Kirk ran together for the next hour. After their workout, they decided to get together later that night for a bite to eat and catch a movie.

They were a handsome and dynamic pair when they were together. Both of them were fit and both blonde and blue-eyed. Wherever they went, people tended to stare and gravitate toward them. Some wondered if they had spotted a famous Hollywood jet set couple. Everyone in town told them that they were perfect for each other. But, for all the years they had been good friends and had gone on dates, they had never even kissed.

Suzie was actually O.K. with that fact. Although she was very attracted to him, she feared that if their relationship ever turned romantic, their friendship might end, especially if things were not to work out. Suzie was content accepting fate and just enjoyed sharing their time together. Little did she know, at the time, how short her cherished time with Kirk would be.

CHAPTER 33

It was the first time that Suzie had traveled outside of New England and she could not believe how warm the weather was in Louisiana. She loved the fall in the Northeast, but never cared much for the winters. When the temperatures turned cold, she would do her running indoors on her treadmill and would long for the promising days of spring.

Suzie stood outside the jail and called Cole on her phone. When Cole answered the call, Suzie introduced herself as my friend and that I had suggested that she call him. Suzie told Cole she was a life long friend of mine and insisted to Cole that I was completely a victim of circumstance and she was going to prove that I was being framed. It was the reason for her trip to the south.

I know you don't know him very well, but he's a great guy. His best friend in the world was murdered and the police are taking the easy way out by blaming him. He wouldn't harm a fly. He's being railroaded. It's complicated, but he has friends back home, that care and we will not rest until he's free.

She asked if he could recommend the best mode of transportation for her to get to Miami. Suzie's voice was infectious with her natural sweet sincerity and Cole, the typical unselfish southern gentlemen, instantly offered to help. He told her to stay near the jail's entrance gate and he would swing by in ten or fifteen minutes. He was also curious to learn more about his new found friend now charged with murder, especially since he was with Cole when he was so dramatically arrested. Cole asked her to keep an eye opened for a red convertible Jeep, with a Golden Retriever riding next to him in the front seat.

While she waited, she called O'Donnell to check in with him and relay some of the information she had just learned during her visit with me. O'Donnell was in a bit of bad mood. He had just completed searching his entire house for more listening devices and also to see if anything besides his Smith & Wesson handgun was taken.

"Hello, this is O'Donnell," he answered.

"Hi, it's me," Suzie said in her normally cheerful manor.

"Well, hello there, my dear, I've been thinking about you. How is everything?"

Suzie then responded,

"Oh, everything is great. Jesse is fine and asked me to express his gratitude to you for all of your help. He answered every question you gave me in the notebook without hesitation."

"Good, good, I can't wait to nail these guys up here. It's getting personal now," O'Donnell exclaimed in an agitated voice.

"Is everything all right?" Suzie asked.

The Chief lied,

"Yeah, everything's O.K."

O'Donnell didn't see any purpose in telling Suzie about the events that had taken place in his home and at the Holyville police Station. He instead kept the subject of the conversation on her visit.

"So, what's your plan now?" asked O'Donnell.

"Well, I'm waiting for a friend of Jesse's who's coming by to pick me up and help me arrange for my trip to the pawn shop in Miami. Let me ask you something, Chief. Have you ever been down this way before?"

O'Donnell answered,

"No, but I've always had plans to retire somewhere on the Gulf Coast. Isn't it beautiful?"

Suzie responded to O'Donnell,

"Oh, it is sooooo nice. I wish I was here for another reason. I'm almost tempted to stay." O'Donnell reminded her that there was still a lot of work to do to clear me and they could all resume dreaming about their future when their job bringing Kirk's killer to justice was done. Suzie said,

> *"I know, I know, but I just feel like maybe this trip was meant for some reason and that maybe it's time for me to start a new life. What is there at home in Meadows for me? Oh, Oh, I got to go. Here comes Jesse's friend. I'll call you later, love ya...bye."* Suzie grabbed her travel bag and threw it over her shoulder and ran across the street, waving to Cole waiting in his Jeep.

> *"Hi . . . I'm Suzie Dillon."*

Suzie tossed her bag in the rear of the Jeep.

> *"Hey I'm Cole. This is Rudy,"* gesturing to the Golden with the yellow bandana around his neck. Cole directed the dog to jump in the back seat and Suzie hopped in the front and reached around for the seatbelt.

> *"Thanks for picking me up"*

> *"No problem, I'm glad to help."*

Cole never expected to be greeted by such a beautiful girl and couldn't believe she was so friendly to a stranger. It was not what he had envisioned from someone from Massachusetts. People from the Northeast were generally thought of as being snobs and true Southerners were the ones that better fit the description of being genuinely kind.

> *"So, you're down here visiting Jesse?"* Cole asked. *I can't believe he was arrested for murder. I was just getting to know him."*

> *"Yeah, I know. He's one of my oldest and best friends. I am sick over this whole thing. Jesse wouldn't harm a fly and he's being framed for murder, but I know he'll be out of jail soon. I know it. How did you two meet?"* asked Suzie.

"Well, I only knew him for a couple of days. We worked together and we went fishing with a friend of mine on his boat. I can't say I really know him that well though. But I liked him even in the short time we hung out."

"Cole, what's your last name?" Suzie asked.

"Porter, can you believe it? My parents were pretty cruel, don't ya think?"

"No, I think that's a great name," but Suzie couldn't contain snickering as she responded. Cole looked over at her long blonde hair blowing in the wind as he drove and said,

"I can't believe I just shared one of my biggest secrets in life with someone I've only known for a minute."

Suzie laughed again and said,

"I'm sorry.. I didn't mean to chuckle. Don't worry, your secret is safe with me. Really, with me?....Anything Goes."

Oh, you're bad," Cole laughed back.

The two of them had an instant chemistry.

"So where are you heading? And what's your hurry?" asked Cole.

Suzie responded,

"I need to get to Miami for some business, but I don't have to be there until tomorrow. What do you suggest I do? I'm not that familiar with New Orleans?"

Cole paused and thought about it for a minute and suggested that they head down to the docks and see if Bill had any ideas. Cole bypassed the most direct route to the harbor so he could give Suzie a quick drive-through tour of the famed French Quarter. They talked about the hurricane for a while and Cole optimistically described the sense of revival that the area was finally beginning to feel.

"I guess it's true what they say," Suzie remarked, *"No matter what you see on the surface, it's all about the soul. You just can't take- away soul."*

When Cole and Suzie pulled the jeep into the marina parking lot, Cole suggested that Suzie grab her travel bag and bring it along with her to Bill's boat and she could leave it there. He then clapped his hands and gave the dog the signal to jump out of the back and to follow along. Suzie felt excitement from the new surroundings.

She had never seen a pelican in real life and wanted to take a picture with her cell phone of the large pre-historic looking bird perched atop a wooden dock pylon extending out of the clear blue water below. Cole just smiled and shook his head; he didn't want her to know that most of the boaters thought of these birds as nuisances that left unwanted gifts on the docks and on the boat decks.

It was a perfect day, a dry 80 degrees with a gentle breeze coming off the Gulf of Mexico and not a cloud in the sky. Rudy, the dog, led the way down to the end of the dock. It was a familiar path he had made countless times. Cole and Suzie followed to the last slip, where Cole welcomed Suzie aboard his friend, Bill's, yacht. Suzie was speechless and stood on the dock with her mouth dropped open.

"Oh my god, are you serious? This is so cool. I've only seen boats like this in the movies. Are you sure it's O.K. for me to come on board?"

Cole nodded his head in agreement,

"Yeah, it's pretty neat, come on and check it out. Wait'll you see the inside."

Cole walked up to the closed sliding glass-door entry to the main cabin area and tapped on the door. Not hearing any movement, he cupped his hands up against the glass to shield the light so he could see inside.

"Bill must be up at the restaurant. Follow me. I'll show you around. Rudy…you stay here, good boy."

Cole stepped off the boat and onto the dock offering his hand to Suzie to help her from the boat. They proceeded to walk back up the dock and into the closed harbor-side eatery and bar. When they opened the large nautically-designed door with a port hole window, they could see Bill inside, seated at a table with two other gentlemen dressed in business suits.

Bill glanced over at the bright outside light that shone into the dark open room when Cole and Suzie entered and instinctively announced to the couple,

"Sorry folks, we're not open for business."

Cole immediately responded,

"Hey Bill, it's me."

Bill apologized,

"Sorry, buddy, I couldn't see who it was in front of the door. Come on in . . . I'll be with ya in a few minutes."

Cole walked around the empty restaurant with Suzie and gave her a guided tour of the establishment. She gravitated to the inviting view of the harbor through the huge floor-to-ceiling glass windows, freshly installed and still bearing the factory stickers.

Suzie asked Cole,

"So, is this your friend's place?"

He nodded,

"Well . . . , for now it is, although I'm not sure for how long. Bill ran out of money and wasn't able to finish building it. He's trying to work something out with the bank. He didn't have any insurance when the hurricane hit and the half-built building was completely destroyed and he had to start all over again."

The two of them stood silently and gazed at the view of the Gulf and the dozens of sailboat masts rhythmically pitching from side to side. It was hypnotizing to stand and watch the beauty and to hear the repeating sound of clanging grommets against the metal masts and the canvas sails flapping back and forth in the steady gentle breeze. They were momentarily startled by Bill's awakening voice, as he walked up behind them.

"So, aren't you going to introduce me to your friend?"

"Hi Bill, sorry if we interrupted you. This is Suzie. She's a good friend of Jesse's. She's visiting from Massachusetts."

"Hi, Suzie," he extended his hand. *"I'm Billy Turner. It's nice to meet you and it's nice to see someone brighten up this depressing room for a change."*

Suzie politely smiled back and thanked him. Bill then added,

"The last time Cole introduced to me to one of his friends, I ended the day with a swat team pointing their weapons at me."

Suzie replied,

"Oh my god, I'm so sorry. Oh wow, I remember seeing some of that video on the news. That was you guys? I can't believe that happened on your boat. Jesse is such a great guy. He just got caught up in the middle of something. Honestly, you've got to believe me, Jesse is the greatest guy you'll ever know. I'm here trying to help him."

Bill put his hand on Suzie's arm for a moment and said,

"It was pretty unbelievable. The whole thing didn't seem right. I actually really liked his company. I'm sure it will all work out, just keep faith. Come on outside, I'll show you my boat."

Cole told Bill they had already gone down to the boat and they had left Rudy onboard. The three of them walked out the door and Bill turned to lock up. Then they headed down the wooden stairs onto the main dock and toward the boat.

"How long will you be in town?" Bill asked.

"Actually, I have to be in Miami tomorrow, so I'll probably be leaving here tonight or early in the morning," Suzie answered.

"Are you flying?" inquired Bill.

"I don't know, I need to make some arrangements and I was hoping perhaps you could recommend some options for me. I don't travel very much."

Bill jumped on the boat first and offered his hand to assist Suzie. Cole followed behind. As soon as Bill came on the boat he reached into his pocket and pulled out a biscuit and tossed it to Rudy. The dog acted as though he hadn't seen a human in weeks. He wagged his tail with unconditional love and whimpered with glee over his cookie treat and the sight of Bill.

Suzie laughed,

"Now, that's a welcoming committee. Rudy must be your dog, Bill."

"Oh yeah, he's a good ol boy. When I divorced my wife a few years ago, she got the house, she got the car, she got the bank account and she got the pool boy..... I got Rudy...and ya know what? I got the better deal. Anyway, welcome aboard."

Bill unlocked the sliding entrance doors and they entered into the plush main cabin area. Cole offered Suzie a drink and gestured toward the couch for her to take a seat and relax. Suzie would loved to have had a mixed drink, but was still not completely comfortable alone on a boat with two men she didn't know. She asked for a diet soda, instead.

Bill went over to the inside captain's helm and clicked on his onboard computer system.

"All right, let's see," he said. *"You need to get to Miami, hmmm, well, there are no direct flights available at this late stage. Ummm, you could make a connection in Tampa in the morning and take a shuttle flight from there to Miami, but...it's a pretty tight connection. Let's seeeeee, let me try this.... O.K. here's a flight. You could fly out of Gulfport, that's in Biloxi, Mississippi, and get a straight shot to Miami."*

Suzie responded,

"Mississippi? How far is that?"

Bill turned on his radar navigation screen and entered several coordinates and then he spun around in his swivel captain's chair and shouted to Cole,

"Hey, Cole, what are you doing tonight?"

Cole walked over and handed Suzie her drink,

"Nothing, what do you have in mind?"

Bill tore off a freshly printed map with a generated float plan and buoy ETA's and handed it to Cole.

"You want to take a ride to Gulfport?"

Cole raised his opened palm above his head eliciting a "high five" from Bill,

"That's awesome. Let's do it."

Suzie stood up from the couch and asked,

"Are you talking about taking this boat to Gulfport?"

Bill answered,

"Sure, it's only a couple of hours and it's the only way to get you to Miami in time for tomorrow. What do you think?"

He raised his glass to seek a confirmation from Suzie.

She thought she was dreaming. Less than an hour earlier, she was sitting in a dirty jail's visitor center and now she was about to embark on a cruise in a luxury yacht in the Gulf of Mexico. The sudden turn of events was so unexpected and spontaneous, she did not know immediately how to react.

It all reminded her of Kirk. This was exactly the type of adventure that seemed to be around every corner when she was with him. Just that instant thought of Kirk took away the excitement of the moment and replaced it with sadness. She put her emotions in check. Life goes on, she thought. If there was one thing she had learned from Kirk, it was not to waste a minute of it. She composed her emotions, took a deep breath and raised her glass to her new friends and clinked her glass with theirs.

"That would be great," she said. Knowing that I had recommended them as a trusted resource, she felt unusually comfortable with the men, and of course, their furry friend, Rudy, who was already by her side, with his chin in her lap and brown eyes cast upon hers. She had to put her faith in fate. She really had no other choice.

CHAPTER 34

A couple of weeks had passed since Kirk had spent the day with Angel Lopez, befriending him in his plane, and it was time for Kirk to reconnect and move the operation to the next phase. Kirk didn't want to return to the pool hall again, so he left a message with the old bartender for Angel to give him a call the next time he came in. The bartender remarked that he wasn't a secretary for Lopez and the hall wasn't Lopez's office.

Kirk reminded the old man that he was the guy who had been in the hall a couple of weeks earlier and had given him a couple of Patriots Tickets as a tip. The bartender apologized to Kirk, and explained that he didn't realize who he was when he called. He thanked Kirk for the tickets and promised to get the message to Angel the next time he saw him.

Less than thirty minutes had passed, when Kirk's cell phone rang. Kirk might have been a ball player, but he was also a very smart guy. The reason he had been so generous to the bartender when he first met him at the bar, was so he could use his help to contact Lopez. He wanted to make sure that all his cell phone records would show only incoming calls from Lopez and no outgoing calls. If something went wrong, the police would know where to look.

The voice on the other end of the line was a very excited Lopez,

"Hey, my friend, where has you been? I've been waiting for you to come around."

Kirk replied,

"I've been busy, ya know... here, there. I got something you might be interested in."

"I'm listening," said Lopez.

"Yeah, well I ain't talking, but I'll meet you somewhere," responded Kirk.

"You name it, my friend," said Lopez.

Kirk responded by telling him to meet him at the Belmont St. Laundromat in one hour and to come alone. He would be inside doing some laundry in the self service area and would wait for him there.

The instructions Kirk had received from Agent Alden were to try and sell Angel 1 kilo of Cocaine for $50,000 and then wait for Angel to come back looking for more, which he was certain he would do. Then they would make a deal for ten kilos for $450,000 with the money up front, but only deliver the two remaining kilos. Kirk questioned that move with Alden. Kirk explained that if he tried to stiff the "big guys" for that kind of money, they would find him and his days would be over, for sure.

Agent Alden continually reinforced how several agents would be swarming all over Lopez after he received the drugs, to follow the path of distribution. He insisted that Kirk would be protected the entire time. Kirk wasn't buying it, but he kept it to himself. By this time he was certain the FBI would never conduct an operation of this scale with only one guy calling the shots. Kirk decided that he was the one in complete control, not Alden. He could make any deal he wanted and Alden would have no clue.

It was 10:00 p.m. and the only patrons in the brightly-lit Laundromat were three older women reading magazines and a couple of young guys with music headsets, likely from one of the local colleges. They were passively waiting for their clothes to finish a cycle. A television mounted from the ceiling in the back corner was playing an old episode of the "Honeymooners" in black and white. The horizontal hold flickered the screen up from time to time. The sound of the television could barely be heard over the sound of the running washing and drying machines.

Kirk walked in with two laundry bags, one had dirty laundry, the other had some old clothes with a kilo of Cocaine buried at the bottom of the bag. He placed the two bags on one of the work counters in the back of the room. In order to not look out of place, Kirk planned to actually do a load of laundry, even though he had a perfectly good machine at home. He walked over to the coin change machine and made change. He also scanned the entire room for any additional exits and for any camera locations, just in case.

The only attendant in the building was a middle-aged, overweight and unshaven man sitting with his eyes closed, behind a counter wearing a plain and stained white tee shirt. A lit cigarette was dangling from his mouth with an ominously long ash about to fall on his chest. Kirk got his coins and returned to his work area and began to sort and separate his laundry. That's when Angel Lopez came through the door.

Kirk pretended not to see him right away, in spite of Angel's intent to make a big entrance. Angel was wearing a pair of black jeans hanging well below his waist, with a large chain extending from his belt into one of his pockets. He walked with a bouncing, street swagger while chewing a wad of gum. His dreadlock hair hung down in front of his bright red leather jacket, along with several gold chains and medallions.

"Why's a rich guy like you doing his own laundry?" Angel jokingly asked as he approached Kirk.

Without looking up at him, Kirk answered back,

"So I can wear clean clothes. How are you doing, man?"

"I'm smooth, brother, real smooth. I'm glad you called me, bro. What do you got for me?" said Angel.

"Slow down, slow down, why are you so nervous man?" asked Kirk.

"I ain't nervous, friend. I'm excited. You got some candy for me?

"Is that what this is all about?"

Kirk told Angel to sit down and relax. He handed him a men's magazine to look at and suggested he check out the centerfold. Kirk had placed a piece of note paper in the middle of the magazine for Angel to find. It read ***I got stuck with a brick, yours if you want it, $50 g's.*** Angel's eyes widened and he stood up without hesitation and asked,

"When and where can I see you again?" asked Angel.

"What do you mean? I'm here right now. I got two loads to do. I'll be here for about another hour."

Kirk threw him a canvas bag with a tag that said **'dirty laundry'** and said,

"Here, take this laundry bag with you and bring it back," Kirk winked.

Angel dropped the magazine on the chair, grabbed the bag, and practically sprinted out of the Laundromat and into the darkness of the city street.

Kirk picked up Angel's discarded magazine and took out the note that he had written and ripped it up and put it in his pocket. He finished loading his clothes into the washing machine, added detergent and pushed the start button. All he could do now was wait.

He sat down in front of the machine, leaned back and folded his arms. For several minutes he starred through the round window of the washing machine at his sudsy clothes, circling inside, and his mind gradually drifted away to another place.

Kirk remembered how his brother and he used to play space ships on top of the washing machine as small children in their Long Island home. Kirk's childhood was a very private matter to Kirk and a very unhappy time in his life, one that he never spoke about. His parents fought continuously, sometimes even violently, late into the night after drinking. To this day, Kirk would occasionally have a flashback in the middle of the night of his brother, in the bunk bed below, crying from the sound of his parents fighting. Kirk never cried. It was his brother's sadness that made him angry and resentful of his parents.

Kirk had lived most of his life with the guilt of not feeling as sad as some people thought he should have, when he learned of his parent's tragic expressway car accident on New Year's Eve. Sometime later, following numerous family court sessions, Kirk left to live with his newly adopted parents in Meadows and his brother left to live with his grandfather.

It was unusual for siblings to be separated from each other during an adoption process, but therapists at the time argued that the children would stand a better chance of recovering from the trauma, if they were separated and forced to begin a new life, leaving their tragic past behind. Kirk's brother needed years of therapy. After the accident, he became very withdrawn and did not so much as utter a word for years.

There were countless times Kirk wished he could talk to someone about his feelings, but he never felt close enough to anyone in his life to share the burden. By all accounts, Kirk had lived a great life as an adult and was always optimistic about the path in front of him. It was moments like this, however, when he was alone, that he thought of settling down, getting married and having children - children he would spoil with the best childhood any child could ever have.

Inside, Kirk believed that having a family of his own would heal his emotional wounds and finally set him free. He also knew, however, he could never truly separate himself from his life's experiences - no one can. That's what makes us who we are.

Kirk had always been a driven goal setter and most times, an achiever. It was that inner vision that propelled him to excel at everything he did. He understood that he could not commit to a relationship or even think about starting a family until he felt stability in his life. It was one of the reasons he accepted to work with the FBI . . . The prospects of a financial windfall was exactly what Kirk needed. After that, he was ready to move forward to the next phase of his life.

Over the past several years, Kirk's trust fund had slowly begun to dwindle. He was never very attentive to the source of his trust fund money; he just assumed it would always be there - it always had.

His goal was to make some quick cash from the sting operation and sell his car and plane.

Then, maybe he would apply for the coaching position for the Meadows's football team and only then, when he reached those goals, would he propose to Suzie Dillon. For now, however, he needed to focus on the task at hand, one step at a time.

Kirk's first laundry cycle had not even finished, when Angel Lopez stepped in through the front door of the Laundromat, with the "dirty laundry" bag slung over his shoulder. It was obvious he had access to large sums of money fairly close by. His movements were being watched closely by Agent Alden from the outside. By now, Alden likely knew exactly where the local money was being held. But it would take "big money" to fumigate the location of the regional cockroaches.

Angel walked over to where Kirk was sitting,

"I got some dirty laundry for you, my friend," boasted Angel, thinking he was impressing Kirk.

"You want to see it?" he asked.

Kirk looked up at him from his seat and answered,

"No, I believe you. For that amount? I'm not worried about it."

Kirk leaned over to his side and grabbed the second white canvas bag, the one with the drugs, and tossed it to Angel.

"Here, I'll trade you," Kirk said.

Angel grabbed the bag. Normally, he would check to make sure that everything was legit before handing over the money, but Angel felt pressure to stay on Kirk's level of coolness.

"You know, my friend, I have associates that can make that amount a lot higher. You know what I'm saying? We got a ton of dirty laundry, man," Angel remarked.

Kirk stood up and walked over to the washing machine to place four more quarters in the payment slot. He simply said,

"Forget it. I'm not your man, O.K.?, Nothing personal, I just don't need the business."

Angel was accustomed to getting his way and Kirk knew he wasn't going to just drop the subject.

Angel persisted,

"How about just one more time?"

Kirk laughed at him,

"It's always just one more time with you guys, isn't it?"

Angel squinted his eyes. He was embarrassed by Kirk laughing at him and his voice took on an aggressive tone,

"Hey friend, you were the one who called me. What's your problem?"

Kirk initially ignored Angel's attitude and just smiled back at him.

"Hey, if you don't want me to call, I won't. How's that for no problem?"

Kirk then moved in close to Angel's face and stood motionless starring him in the eye, like a prize fighter in the center of boxing ring sizing up and intimidating his opponent. The plan was taking perfect shape. Kirk actually admired Angel's tenacity, but could not allow Angel to think he was not in control at any time.

Kirk lowered his voice to a deep whisper,

"Don't you ever cop an attitude with me, pal, I'll drop you where you stand. I'll call you when I'm damn good and ready. This is my show and that's the way it's gonna stay. Do YOU know what I AM saying?"

Kirk starred him down for a few more seconds and then turned away. Angel avoided any further confrontation and silently walked away without his customary swagger, holding Kirk's laundry bag in his hand.

CHAPTER 35

Chief O'Donnell had less than a week to compile all the evidence they had discovered and present it to Mayor Sullivan for his meeting with U.S. Senator Kerrigan. O'Donnell felt it wasn't enough to just point the finger at Agent Alden. He needed to lay out a theory of exactly how Kirk Preston was killed and what role the FBI played in his death. Suzie wasn't scheduled to be back home for another couple of days from her trip down south, so at Detective Murphy's request, he agreed to meet with Murphy to go over the loose ends of the case.

O'Donnell decided to ask Murphy to bring the stains he had found in the Frenchman's car to a crime lab for testing. The car Lopez had stolen was still a bit of a mystery to O'Donnell and a piece of the puzzle that he needed to fit. O'Donnell didn't want Murphy to know about the break-in at his house and the stolen Smith & Wesson revolver. He was concerned that Murphy would lose confidence in the Chief's leadership and might quit the team in fear of losing his job and jeopardizing his career. O'Donnell completely understood the risk Murphy was taking to work on this case, a case that was moved under the vast FBI umbrella. He admired Murphy for his trust and confidence in this highly sensitive matter.

With the break-in and compromised sanctity of his home still fresh in his mind, O'Donnell suggested they meet in Forest Park to discuss the developments of the case. It was an unseasonably warm 60-degree day, with a bright blue sky. Most nights, this time of year, the temperature would drop to below freezing and then warm up during the day. O'Donnell asked Murphy to meet at the lower duck pond. He would be waiting for him at one of the waterside rustic picnic tables.

Early morning would typically welcome a very thin layer of ice on the ponds in the park which would quickly melt when the sun reached above the thickly wooded tree lined bank surrounding the water. Even in the height of the winter cold, there would always be a flock of ducks that called the Forest Park Pond their home. When the main part of the pond froze, the ducks would migrate to a section of the pond that emptied into a babbling brook. It was a favorite spot for families and retirees to spend some outdoor time feeding crusty stale bread to the resident birds.

O'Donnell intentionally arrived at the picnic area thirty minutes earlier with Casey, to feed the ducks. The Chief brought along a bag of bread containing end pieces that he had been saving for some time. He also brought a thermos of coffee that he made at home for Murphy and himself to have while meeting.

Casey wasn't sure what to make of the ducks. Never before had she seen so many in one area. When a duck emerged from the water to come up on the shore, Casey would bark and corral the duck back into the water where it belonged. A group of school children nearby was more amused by Casey's playful actions than the novelty of feeding the ducks.

Detective Murphy arrived in his personal car and parked near the picnic area. He walked over to O'Donnell and placed some papers and envelopes on the table, along with a box of doughnuts. Then, he walked down to the water's edge and greeted the Chief. O'Donnell tied Casey to the base of an old Oak tree and walked up the small embankment area to the table and poured two cups of coffee. They both sat down on opposite sides of the table and talked for a few minutes about happenings at the police department and about Suzie.

Murphy expressed his feelings for Suzie to the Chief,

"I really miss her. I spoke to her for just a minute, but we lost the cell connection. It must have been tough for her to see Jesse like that."

The Chief agreed,

"Yeah, but it sounds like it was a very productive meeting. She got all the answers that we need."

"Really? That's . . . great," said Murphy.

O'Donnell sensed that Murphy's response wasn't exactly lined with sincerity. He wondered if Murphy didn't feel a bit of jealously over Suzie's attention to her old friend. O'Donnell considered that Murphy may not have been aware of their long plutonic relationship.
O'Donnell added,

"Yeah, I can't wait to hear more from her. Ya know, Jesse and Suzie grew up together. They're like second cousins or something."

"Oh really, I didn't know that. No wonder she's so passionate about getting him out," Murphy responded with a different tone.

At that very moment Murphy's phone rang. He looked down at the display and could see that Suzie was calling him.

"Speak of the devil. Here she is now. Hello... hey... I'm here with the Chief. We were just talking about you. Good, good, how about you? Excellent. What? ....Oh, that's O.K. I know... I couldn't hear you either. Sure, hold on," Murphy passed the phone over to the Chief.

"She wants to talk to you."

O'Donnell placed the phone to his ear and answered,

"Hello, my dear, it's about time you called back."

Suzie was standing on the back of the boat, which was still at the dock. She wanted to make sure he was aware of her new travel plans.

"Hi Chief, I'm sorry I didn't call you back. Everything went perfectly with Jesse. I'll be heading toward Miami in about an hour, so I wanted to let you know. We just need to get some supplies for the boat ride. What's that?.... Oh, I said a boat ride. Yeah, these two guys are taking me to a harbor near the airport in Biloxi on a beautiful yacht and from there I'm flying straight to Miami."

The Chief jumped in,

"Whoa, whoa, slow down a second. Who are these guys?"

Suzie answered,

"It's OK. Don't worry they're really nice. They're friends of Jesse's and I trust them."

Suzie stood on the listening end of a fatherly lecture from O'Donnell about strangers for several minutes and then handed the phone over to Bill at his request. Bill answered the phone and also just listened to the Chief for a minute or so before handing the phone back to Suzie again. After she said her goodbyes and put her phone away, Bill said,

"That must have been your dad."

Suzie rolled her eyes and smiled at Bill,

"Well . . . sort of."

O'Donnell handed the phone back to Murphy. Murphy quickly put the phone back to his ear and said,

"Hello . . . hello? hello? Huh. Oh well. We must have gotten disconnected again."

It was clearly evident to O'Donnell that Suzie did not share the same feelings about Murphy that he felt toward her. He put his phone away and told the Chief how great it was to hear her voice and how he wished that he could have gone with her. The Chief agreed, but reminded the young detective that there would be plenty of time for that later, but for now... Suzie was counting on the two of them to do the necessary police work.

O'Donnell reached into his pocket and took out a small sample of what he believed was a blood stain from the stolen car and gave it to Murphy. He asked him to bring it to his friends at the lab and see if he can get a match with other evidence in the case. Murphy asked him where he got the sample.

O'Donnell said it was another sample he found in the plane and wanted to make sure he wasn't missing anything. O'Donnell was the only one who had discovered the stains in the car and his years of intuition thought it best if he kept his theory to himself, for the time being, even from Murphy.

O'Donnell asked,

"O.K.... so... what do you believe are still the biggest hurdles facing Jesse?"

Murphy thought about it.

"Well, certainly the ring and the photograph of Jesse in the pawn shop. But, I would have to say that the new life insurance policy is pretty damning. It points to a clear motive, and that's every killer's Achilles for sure."

As Murphy was talking, O'Donnell was thinking to himself that Murphy was right. O'Donnell was confident he could disprove the pawn shop evidence, after all he had the ring, but explaining a million-dollar life insurance policy would be a daunting task, especially since the beneficiary was not a family member and was also the accused, a prosecutor's clear motive argument.

O'Donnell asked Murphy if he had heard any other scuttlebutt around the department about the case. Murphy told O'Donnell that things had been very quiet. It was as if the case was solved and most of the attention had moved to other affairs of the city, including the process of hiring a new Chief. O'Donnell was a little surprised that they had initiated a national police Chief search. O'Donnell's official status was that he was on temporary leave. The Chief had always assumed that he wouldn't be going back to the department, but this was the first time it was publicly being made clear.

O'Donnell wanted to learn more about what the "rank and file" guys on the force were saying. Murphy responded that as far as he had heard from others, the directive to hire a replacement Chief was coming from the Mayor's office. More specifically Mayor Sullivan himself. This surprised and even angered O'Donnell a bit and he couldn't accept that it was true, especially because it was the Mayor who was secretly helping to solve this case by hand delivering the evidence against Alden to the senator. Evidence that could exonerate me.

While on the subject of the Mayor, Murphy asked,

"When are you meeting with the Mayor about the Preston case?"
"In a couple of days. That's why I'm anxious to get everything in order," answered O'Donnell.

The Chief seemed to be a bit distant and Murphy sensed that he had touched a nerve about O'Donnell's lifetime friend pressuring for his replacement. Murphy downed the last sip of coffee in his cup and stood up from the picnic bench.

"Well...maybe I should be going then. I'll get this sample to the lab and let you know as soon as I hear anything."

O'Donnell lifted his head up and came back to focus, after a long stare at the water.

"Oh....O.K..... yeah, great, that would be good. Hey, thanks for everything." Murphy grabbed his belongings, said good-bye and headed back to his car.

The Chief walked back down the small hill and released Casey from the tree and took her for a short walk around the park, before heading back to his house.

CHAPTER 36

It was about four o'clock in the afternoon, when the boat finally pulled out of the docks to begin the 4-hour cruise to Gulfport. Bill and Cole had procured supplies and food for the trip and Bill had submitted copies of his float plan to the harbor-master and sent another one to the marina in Biloxi before heading out.

The sun was just beginning to set and their boat was the only one in sight that was heading out to sea. In the first 30 minutes of the trip they passed nearly two dozen shrimp boats returning from their daily harvest. Each vessel chugged along with a flock of seagulls following behind in hopes of a free meal of shrimp from one of the deck hands. It was a beautiful sight.

Boat after boat appeared in the distance with their huge double winches extending from both sides of the boat to support the hefty hanging nets. Nearly everyone signaled their horn and waved to Bill at the captain's helm as they passed nearby. Suzie was impressed with the friendly nature of every boater out on the water. Cole explained to her that boaters belong to one huge family, and everyone looks out for each other.

No one was respected more than the local fisherman. They worked long hours and wore their fingers to the bone. Most captains were 3rd generation fishermen, as kids they dreamed bigger dreams, as adults they trolled a destined legacy, with little hope to catch a different future. Like their fathers before them, they had families back on land that depended on them. Their weather beaten faces showed the strain of years at the sea. Most young men, joined their aging dads to lend a hand, and then never left when father time called.

Suzie, too, could not help but get into the custom and found herself waving at every opportunity. Soon the yacht would make its turn at a large green buoy marker and begin to head due East, leaving the picturesque sunset behind the boat and in perfect view from the stern's seats.

Bill and Cole joined Suzie on the back of the boat and brought a plate of fresh fruit, along with some cheese and crackers and placed them on a table next to Suzie's chair. Suzie looked up at both of them,

"Hey, who's driving the boat?"

Bill and Cole laughed and answered,

"We like to call him Ray." Suzie took off her sunglasses and peered over her shoulder and into the empty main cabin,

"Ray?" she asked.
Cole then explained,

"Ray is short for Raytheon. The boat is on a GPS radar control. The computer is driving the boat. For the next three hours, we can just relax. What can I get for you?"

Suzie asked for a glass of water with lemon. She put her sunglasses back on and leaned back in her chair,

"I could get very used to this lifestyle I'll have you know." "Isn't it great?" said Bill. He added, *"I'm glad you agreed to the trip to Gulfport. I'm afraid this may be one of my last voyages. Those guys you saw me meeting with in the restaurant were from the bank. I don't think I have any choice, but to sell the boat to cover the completion of the building. So....let's enjoy her while we still can."*

Suzie was in a very comfortable teak chair with soft built-in hunter green cushions. When the custom chair reclined, it automatically opened a leg rest, for sunbathing or simply lounging. Cole and Bill sat on each side of her in two professional fighting chairs equipped for deep sea game fishing. Rudy was in his customary corner of the stern above the warm and soothing sound of the engine compartment, sound asleep.

For the next three hours they would relax together and talk about everything from politics to potato chips, but most of time they were just silent. It was a wonderfully relaxing time. Bill and Cole were perfect hosts. Time and again, one of them would walk into the galley and return with a gourmet treat for Suzie to sample and of course, Rudy was always sampling a small nibble, too, down by her feet.

The glistening sun was setting on the distant horizon and the water shimmered from its reflecting radiance. Two large wakes created from the two powerful propellers converged together to create a natural cresting effect. The continually changing motion of the water was mesmerizing and akin to watching the dancing flames of a roaring fire. Occasionally during the cruise, a pair of frolicking Dolphins could be seen jumping just beyond the wake following behind the boat's path.

Suzie's mind was far away from the anxiety of thinking about her best friend in jail or about the murder of her beloved Kirk, at least for now.

CHAPTER 37

Agent Alden and Kirk met for the last time in the stands of the high school track before the final phase of their sting operation was to take place. There was a light misty rain falling, but not enough to discourage several joggers from taking their faithful laps around the track, Kirk included. When Alden arrived, he and Kirk went to the top of the stands in front of the announcer's booth to discuss the next and final steps of the drug bust. Kirk took his towel and whipped down a spot for them to sit on the aluminum bench.

Kirk gave Agent Alden an envelope containing the $50,000 he had received from Lopez in the laundromat and Alden quickly placed it in the inside pocket of his jacket. Alden congratulated Kirk on the operation so far and assured him that the remaining phase would be equally as smooth and successful. Alden questioned Kirk,

"How do you plan to meet with Angel again?"

Kirk responded,

"Well, I left it kinda open and told him that I would contact him. I also told him, however, that I did my laundry every week at the same time and same place. So, my guess is I won't need to call him."

"I bet you're right," Alden agreed. *"O.K... Here's what I suggest..."*

Alden continued to lay out the plan, step by step, just as he had done from the very beginning. Alden described what Kirk should expect from the kingpins above Lopez. Lopez was a high ranking "lieutenant" in the gang, but wasn't a "shot caller" in the organization. Alden was certain that if the stakes were raised, which was the plan, Lopez would not continue to be the contact and all the relationship building he had made with Lopez would have served its purpose and no longer of value to the sting.

Alden felt it was important to keep the gang believing the drug supply was coming from outside the area and using Kirk's plane again would help sell that idea. He instructed Kirk to be prepared for his new contact to give him only half of the money up front and insist on completing the transaction when they see the entire product.

Since Alden and Kirk had never intended on delivering the promised amount anyway, they would have to be content with the up-front money and arrange for a drop-off location for the two kilos they had for the operation. Kirk was unclear about the instructions and asked Alden to repeat his plan.

"All right, listen carefully. Try to make a deal for 12 kilos. That should cost the gang half a million. If they only give you half of the money up-front, then at least we have 250 thousand."

Kirk interrupted,

"Yeah, I get that part, but what happens when I only deliver two kilos instead of 12?"

Alden explained,

"That's going to be my problem. You won't be anywhere near. When you get back, you will contact them with a secured pick- up site where they think they're exchanging the remaining order for the rest of the money. They'll pick up only the two kilos instead. My guys will be all around and following them everywhere they go and once we learn locations and whom they answer to, we'll step in and make the arrests. But we'll keep a portion of the money for ourselves, to, you know, finance our part of the operation."

Kirk nodded and wasn't worried about his part, but was concerned that he may not be getting his fair share of the money, especially since the take could be half of what Alden had originally proposed.

Alden looked at Kirk and said,

"All the bureau is expecting is $100 thousand of the gang's money. If all goes well... you and I will split the other $150 thousand."

The rain began to fall a bit harder and Alden thought that the sight of two people sitting in the bleachers may look strangely out of place. So, they stood up and walked down the metal stands and onto the track. Before Alden left, he wanted to make sure that Kirk was perfectly comfortable with his responsibilities and again, assured him that his team would be there the entire way if anything went wrong.

"The only time we can't follow you is when you're in your plane."

Alden reached into his pocket and pulled out a small GPS tracking device.

"When you get the money from the gang, turn this switch on, and place the tracker in the bag and keep it with you in the plane and with you at all times. That way we can know exactly where you are. All right then. We should avoid talking or meeting again until the deal goes down."

Alden handed him the device with his left hand, grabbed Kirk's other hand tightly with his right hand and stopped for a moment until he had Kirk's undivided attention, looked him directly in the eyes and said,

"Good luck, we'll meet when you get back. This is it."

Alden stared for another moment then turned away and ran through the rain to his car and drove away.

CHAPTER 38

O'Donnell still felt uneasy about being in his own house. His safety and personal space had been irreparably violated. The house that was once a home of love had been replaced with a house of deceit. Aside from his sleeping hours, O'Donnell preferred to be out of the house as much as possible and today was no different. With Casey by his side, O'Donnell took a car ride out to the countryside, west of the river and out to the municipal airport in Westford.

Although it was a cold late fall day, Casey wouldn't be happy unless her head was out the passenger's window and her ears were flopping in the wind. Of course, O'Donnell was more than happy to accommodate his little girl. So, with the window down and the heater on full, Casey and O'Donnell drove west; through the winding hill town roads, while listening to light jazz.

O'Donnell's best thinking always took place when he was driving and he thought a ride to the apparent crime scene, might help him imagine what took place on the night Kirk Preston was brutally murdered. Since O'Donnell was driving in his own personal car, he did not have the access to the airport grounds, beyond the automated gate that his patrol car normally allowed him. So he pulled his car over to the side of the road, near the gate and put the car in park. For the next twenty minutes, he sat and watched cars coming and going through the gate.

Each car had a transponder on its window that would activate the gate to open and allow for entry. Without the transponder, a security officer would need to be contacted to override the system. It had not previously occurred to O'Donnell that if the murder had taken place in Kirk's plane, as the blood evidence found in the plane indicated, then the assailant would either have had access or be with someone who had access to the gated entrance.

O'Donnell was putting his thoughts down on a note pad, when his cell phone rang. O'Donnell looked down at the display and recognized the incoming call as Detective Murphy.

"O'Donnell here," he answered.

"Hi Chief, its Murphy how are you?"

Before answering, O'Donnell took the phone away from his ear and pressed a feature button and watched the display.

"Hey I'm doing all right. Where are you?" O'Donnell asked.

"I'm in Springdale, I just left the lab," Murphy answered.

O'Donnell flipped over his notebook to a fresh page and said,

"Oh good, well....was the sample I gave you blood?"

"Oh yeah, it was blood all right. I won't be able to get a DNA analysis on it for a while, but I thought I would let you know that it was blood type B Negative."

Chief sat silently for several seconds.

"Chief, Chief are you there?"

"Yeah, I'm here. Sorry about that I got distracted for a minute..... O.K., thanks for taking care of that, let me know when you have the final report. What's that? Oh...Suzie will be home tomorrow.... right, right, O.K., good enough I'll catch you later.... bye."

O'Donnell flipped his phone closed and put his phone back on his belt. He was stunned by Murphy's call. The blood stains he had found on the computer cable in the stolen car were definitely Kirk's - B negative - but there was another type as well, AB Negative, not Kirk's, not Lopez's.....O'Donnell tapped his pencil several times on his note pad and then hastily wrote the name of the only suspect in the case that matched that type of blood...... Jesse Thorpe.

He pressed so hard on the paper when he underlined the name that it broke the tip of the pencil right off. He was frustrated by the news. He couldn't know for certain, but AB negative blood type was among the rarest types and clearly pointed the finger, once again, directly at the man O'Donnell was working so hard to free.

It didn't make any sense, O'Donnell thought. Could the test have been wrong? Could the killer coincidently also share the same rare blood type as Jesse?.. Perhaps a member of Lopez's gang? That's it, he thought, he'll go with that theory for now. That's got to be it.

Whatever the answer was, O'Donnell decided to keep the information to himself and stay on the course he had already chartered. O'Donnell's years of homicide investigating provided an instinct that told him there was still much more to the case than anyone knew and he was beginning to see the signs of a disturbing pattern, a pattern he needed to trace much more clearly.

CHAPTER 39

The boat cruise was the most fun Suzie had experienced in a long time and certainly since the recent sad events in her life. She arrived in Gulfport exactly as Captain Bill had planned, and promised to get together with the two of them very soon and reciprocate the kindness they had showed to her. She called for a taxi at the Biloxi Marina and soon was on her way to the airport and onto her short flight to Miami. When Suzie arrived in Miami she went directly to the hotel located at the airport and checked into a room to freshen up and to change her clothes. It was still early morning and she had a few hours to unwind before reviewing her plan for her pawn shop visit.

Suzie took off her shoes, propped up a couple of pillows and laid down on the comfortable feather bed. She called for room service to bring her an order of Eggs Benedict, a glass of orange juice and a carafe of black coffee. Then she decided to call her apartment and check to see if she had any phone messages. The first two messages were from the Spa and the next couple of messages were from the rental office at the apartment complex.

The messages from the complex said it was in reference to Jesse and asked that she call them when she had a chance. Suzie assumed it had to do with the late monthly rental payment. The complex was a popular location in the city for single professionals and there had always been a waiting list for vacancies. Suzie did not return their call. She had enough on her plate and did need to do more dishes.

Within a few minutes, room service delivered her breakfast and wheeled a cart into the room and set it in front of the large window that overlooked the airport and surrounding city. Suzie tipped the bellhop for delivering the meal and sat down with her notes at the small table and ate her food, while pondering her next mission.

O'Donnell was meticulous about details and had provided a list of things to inquire about when Suzie was at the pawn shop. He had written down a reminder to Suzie that the photograph of Jesse had been e-mailed by the owner's daughter. He recommended that Suzie approach the owner as a local news reporter and not as an investigator. Since, the whole ring thing had to be a fraud; O'Donnell didn't want the owner to get suspicious of Suzie's line of questioning.

When Suzie finished her breakfast, she stepped into the shower and then laid out the clothes she was planning to wear. Since Nicky Cardoni was not expecting a reporter to come by his shop, she decided she would use every weapon God had given her to get his attention and a few minutes of his time.

She had brought a pair of snug fitting blue jeans and a low cut thin white cashmere sweater for her introduction to Cardoni. Her long natural blonde hair hung over her shoulders and her tan made her blue eyes and gorgeous smile light up the room. She added a touch of intoxicating Chanel perfume and a few sparkles to her plunging neckline.

She stood in the bathroom looking in the mirror and repeatedly rehearsed her entrance to the pawn shop, until she felt confident of conveying a noticeable first impression. Then she took a big breath, grabbed her room key and notebook and headed to the lobby of the hotel where she hailed a cab.

The pawn shop was located in the heart of a mostly Cuban part of the city. The streets were bustling, peppered with a symphony of color, a sensory explosion of sights, sounds, and smells. There were street vendors every few feet that had set up stands selling hats, cigars, watches and fresh fruit. Along both sides of the streets were groups of people sitting on tenement steps listening to their calypso music fill the hot sultry air. It felt like you had stepped out of the cab and into another country, vibrantly alive with energy and flavor.

The pawn shop was actually a bit of an eyesore in the otherwise diverse and uniquely beautiful neighborhood. It starkly clashed with the colorful Latin culture. The store front windows were dirty and guarded by thick security fencing. Large, half functioning, neon signs flickered an advertisement for the shop's "check cashing" service. Suzie entered the heavy front door to the sound of a loud security buzzer activated by a light beam positioned just inside the door. She was welcomed by a blanketing and malodorous smell of cheap musk cologne.

The interior of the store was cluttered with a plethora of unwanted gifts from wall to wall and from floor to ceiling. Items were stacked atop each other 3 feet high. There were guitars, cameras, VCR players, instruments, power tools and fur coats. There was an old six-foot jewelry display case with a cracked glass top held together with a yellowed tape. It was filled with old coins, antique estate jewelry, guns and knives. Behind the case was a desk with an inattentive middle-aged, lascivious-looking man sitting behind counting and sorting stacks of cash.

On the wall behind him was an outdated swimsuit pin-up calendar next to a hanging fly-strip encrusted with years of dead flies which turned like a wind chime from hell. The man clearly thought he was a gift to all women, but looked more like a perverted porn star wanna-be. Cardoni was the kind of lowlife guy who, when he drove his car, would aim for dead road kill, just for kicks.

Without looking up, he blurted out in a raspy voice,

"I'll be right with you."

After his mutter, he coughed until he hacked and then cleared his throat. He curled his sealed lips inward to hold back a belch and then convulsed his stomach and exhaled a spewing blast of garlic tear gas.

Suzie responded in her gentle and sweet feminine demeanor,

"No problem, take your time."

The sound of her innocent voice immediately got his attention.

"Uh, uh, sorry about that, young lady. I wasn't expecting to see such a...a..."

Suzie stepped forward, took a deep breath to avoid breathing too closely to him and extended her hand,

"Liz Clayton. Are you Mr. Cardoni?"

"Call me Nick, please."

He wiped his hand on his pants and reached for hers and greeted her. He was a short man with a muscular build. He was baldheaded, with an obviously colored black mustache. His right arm had a large military tattoo on his forearm and each hand donned a large gold nugget ring. He wore a gold watch on one wrist and a thick gold chain on the other.

"Hi, Nick, I'm a reporter from the Herald, I was hoping to ask you a few questions."

"Ask me a few questions? Pardon my French little lady, but what the hell do you want to talk to me for?"

"Well....I'm doing a weekly series for the paper and highlighting small business owners who run unusual types of businesses. I thought a pawn shop would be interesting for our readers, and by the way.....it's very good advertising........for free," she added.

Cardoni nodded his head and begrudgingly agreed,

"A couple of minutes can't hurt," he added.

"Great," Suzie exclaimed.

"How long have you owned this business?" she asked. *"Oh...I'd say about 10 - 12 years now. After I got out of the Army, I worked for a while, but decided I wanted to work for myself, instead of for the man. Ya know what a mean?"*

"Sure, sure absolutely that's the American dream."

Suzie was repulsed by his every word and could feel his eyes exploring her body when he looked at her. He really thought he was something special. She played along and wrote down everything he said. She wasn't sure if anything that he said was actually important, but thought she should leave that judgment to O'Donnell and Murphy.

Suzie continued,

"So, do you work alone? Is this a family business?"

Cardoni snickered and smiled,

"No, I don't have any kids and I'm not... shall we say...... currently married."

Suzie knew that she had just gathered important information, since it was Cardoni's daughter who had supposedly sent the e-mail and photo to O'Donnell.

"Aren't you afraid of crime, with all this valuable inventory, Nick?"

"I've never had any problems, and if I did, I would take care of it, if ya know what I mean?"

Suzie looked around the room and said,

"You probably have a sophisticated security system anyway."

Cardoni leaned in and whispered to her in a smug manner,
"Promise me you won't print this?" He said to her, bragging over his masculinity,

"I'm the only security system I need in this joint. I don't want no camera watching me teaching anybody a lesson, ya know what I mean?"

Suzie continued to ask questions that were more specific to the business, to keep him from suspecting her real purpose. But she couldn't leave until she had least brought up the subject of Kirk Preston's football ring.

"Now...I remember that you were recently in the news about some murder connection...or something...what was that all about?"

The question instantly touched a nerve with Cardoni and he quickly ended the interview and said that he really needed to get back to work and couldn't comment. Suzie had a sense that she may have pushed her luck too far and felt her heartbeat begin to race.

"So...... what's the most unusual item that you ever pawned?" Suzie tried to get back on track.

"Look lady, I gave you enough time, now would you please excuse me?"

Suzie was tempted to say something. She had never disliked someone so soon after meeting them. It was hard to hold back. She couldn't wait to get outside and take a deep breath of fresh air, absent the odor and filth of the classless vulgarian's store. So, without hesitation, she said,

"Thank you for your time, Mr. Cardoni. We plan to run the business profile in a couple of weeks." She turned away and walked out the door.

CHAPTER 40

A week had passed and if Kirk's theory was correct, tonight would be the night that Angel Lopez would arrive, unannounced, to the Laundromat. When Kirk walked in with his laundry bag he felt like he had stepped into a time warp. The same people were sitting in the same chairs. The black & white television was playing another episode of the Honeymooners and the same old man was snoozing behind the counter.

Although Kirk had only been to the Laundromat once, he too found himself in a routine. He walked over to the same sorting shelf, in front of the same washing machine and proceeded to make change in the vending machine, just as he had done the previous week.

But that was where the similarities ended. As predicted, Angel Lopez made his usual entrance, but this time he was not alone. He walked through the door and stood still, turning his head from left to right he scanned the room to see if Kirk was indeed there. When he spotted Kirk sorting through his dirty laundry, he turned, walked back outside and within seconds re-entered with another man by his side.

Kirk could see every move from a reflection in a large mirror on the back wall of the room. For the first time since the operation had begun, Kirk felt an unfamiliar and nervous anxiety come over him. He tried to remain calm by focusing on his laundry sorting. But the sudden mood change in the room was unavoidable. Angel's accomplice had a different presence about him. He was not your typical street thug. He walked with a certain aura and authority that was difficult to describe.

In any other surrounding or circumstance one would assume he was a successful professional. He wore wool dress slacks, a turtleneck sweater with a scarf under a full - length brown trench coat tied at the waste by a matching belt and freshly polished leather shoes.

Angel walked in front of the man toward Kirk and called out Kirk's name.

"Hello, my friend. I thought I might find you here," Angel announced.

Kirk looked up at Angel and then glanced at the man standing next to him.

"Kirk, I want you to say hello to Vincent. Vincent is a friend of mine visiting from out of town for a few days."

The man took off his right leather glove and stepped forward within reach of Kirk.

Kirk shook his hand and said,

"Boys doing laundry tonight?"

Kirk turned away in a somewhat disrespectful manor and went back to the task of sorting his clothes. The man put his glove back on his hand and stepped backward and responded,

"Actually, we might be doing a lot of laundry. I could fill a lot of dirty laundry bags. I just wanted to check out the facility first.... To tell you the truth, though...., I'm not very impressed."

As quickly as the man had walked into the Laundromat, he had turned and walked out. Angel followed him out of the building and then walked back in a matter of minutes and came back over to Kirk.

"Hey man, sorry about the surprise like that. Vincent can be a moody guy. He doesn't like Springdale."

Kirk looked up at Angel,

"I don't like surprises, why did you bring somebody here like that? This is why I didn't want to get caught up like this with you, understand?"

"Sorry man. I know, man. It's just that I got to survive out there man, just like everybody else. I don't call the shots...it's kinda complicated, ya knows what I'm saying man?" Angel tried to explain.

He continued to talk in a low voice.

"Ever since I met you, friend, opportunities have come my way for the first time. Ya gotta help me."

Kirk put his last bundle of clothes in the washing machine and entered the cycle time and walked back to his chair.

"Look Angel, I like you, I don't know why, but I do. Maybe it's because we both had tough childhoods or something I don't know, but I can't help you. I'm sorry if I led you to believe I could. I didn't mean to."

Kirk felt he could push Angel a little because he appeared so desperate.

Angel backed down and slumped his head down to his chin,

"I'm sorry man. You're right. I guess... I just get used to getting my way on the streets. You see...I gave the laundry bag to my big guy and he gave it directly to Vincent. That was my mistake, man."

Kirk saw his opportunity begin to slip away, and changed his strategy. *"Why do you need these guys anyway? They don't care about you. How are you ever going to get anywhere if you're not calling your own shots?"*

Angel just sat silently listening to Kirk and said nothing. Kirk continued to encourage him to stand up for himself and take control of his life. Kirk began to listen to himself talking and couldn't believe he was actually trying to mentor to a street punk like Angel, but he was.

Angel said that he was in too deep now to get out and pleaded with Kirk to do one more deal and that was it, just to get Vincent off his back. After that he would tell his boss that Kirk's connection got canned and any more deals were impossible. Of course it was exactly what Kirk was hoping to hear all along and it was the plan that Agent Alden had laid out in detail.

"Angel, listen to me carefully. I said that the last time was the last and I meant it. If I do this now, I can't ever see you again, do you understand? Even at the pool hall or anywhere, understand? Say 'yes'."

Angel agreed. Kirk was prepared to offer twelve kilos to Angel for $500,000 dollars even though he only had two at his disposal.

"All right, how do you want to do this?" asked Kirk.

Angel tore a scrap advertising insert out of a magazine sitting on the counter and wrote the number 50/2m on the paper and handed it to Kirk. Kirk looked down at the number and tried his best to keep his composure. He deduced that Vincent had given him the authority to buy 50 kilos of pure cocaine for two million dollars.

Kirk calmly took the scrap paper and crumpled it up and threw it in a trash basket filled with empty detergent bottles and used softener sheets. He walked back over to Angel and said,

"I'll need the dirty laundry bag filled first."

Angel shook his head from side to side,

"I wish I could friend. I can do half."

Kirk responded,

"Give me whatever you want. If you give me half, I'll bring you half. I never use my own money. Tell your guys whatever you want."
Angel agreed,

"O.K. O.K. I'll worry about my guys, you take care of yours."

Kirk handed Angel an extra set of his Corvette keys, with the alarm button attached. He instructed him to put the money in the dirty laundry bag and place it behind the driver's seat. The car would be waiting for him next week, same day, same time, outside the Laundromat.

Kirk told Angel that a couple of days after he gets the dirty laundry bag with the money he would contact him and tell him where he could pick up the laundry bag with the drugs.

Angel warned Kirk that he was likely going to be followed by Vincent's soldiers every step of the way and they won't be taking their eyes off of the bag of money for a minute after it's dropped off in the Corvette. He also told him that these new guys don't carry small stuff. They're all fully automatic, referring to their weapons of choice.

"I can't see you again, all right?" Kirk said to Angel.

Kirk gave Angel a pretend slow motion right hook punch to the jaw, and said,

"Now, get out ta' here and start taking care of yourself. What are ya gonna stay a punk your whole life? Come on, take control will ya?

Angel stood up and thanked Kirk for saving his life and warned him again about Vincent's men. With that, Angel walked out of the Laundromat and out of Kirk's life.

For a brief moment Kirk actually felt sorry for Angel and a bit guilty for setting him up. He knew that when the pick up of the drugs revealed the sting that Angel would probably face a death sentence by his own gang. But that feeling faded quickly when Kirk remembered, how Angel had used the system when he was younger and had gotten away with murdering an innocent man and then spent his second chance in life ruining lives on the street with drugs and violence. Kirk believed in destiny and that we had very little control over life's circumstances. Angel made his bed long ago.

CHAPTER 41

O'Donnell had only one more day before a scheduled meeting with Mayor Sullivan about the evidence he had uncovered and there were still gapping holes in his theory. Suzie's flight was due to return that night from Miami and O'Donnell was counting on her to fill some of those holes. Murphy agreed to pick her up at the airport, while O'Donnell plugged away in his home office.

The Chief sat at his computer and worked for hours researching all the casts of characters where he had been focusing his efforts. His search engines revealed mostly old newspaper references to stories that contained the subject's name somewhere and didn't help much. O'Donnell was persistent though. He was very accustomed to endless and tireless investigating, often without reward. But occasionally, it would all pay off with the stroke of a button.

O'Donnell had entered an Internet search for Wayne Alden without much success and then, by error, it happened. He had entered Nicholas Cardoni in the same search window prior to deleting Alden's name first. Consequently, the search started for both names together. Before O'Donnell could stop the search process, a screen appeared with several hits.

O'Donnell clicked on each result and one after another made reference to a specialized Army combat division in Vietnam, where Alden and Cardoni served side by side. One site displayed an old photograph taken of a platoon garbed in their heavy combat gear posing for a picture. Alden and Cardoni were standing together arm in arm.

"You son of a bitch," O'Donnell whispered toward the screen.

O'Donnell clinched his hand into a fist and pumped it in vindication of his discovery. The computer screen had become an illuminating epiphany, the veritable "aha" moment that would ignite the bombshell, blowing apart the government's case. This was a corner piece in a puzzle that would instantly allow all the missing pieces to fit.

Not only did the revelation dismiss the pawn shop evidence, but it also placed Alden in the director's chair of his own maniacal scheme to line his pockets with filthy greed, the method to his twisted madness. O'Donnell deduced that Alden had his parasitical cohort plant the initial call to O'Donnell early on in the case, and steer the indisputable evidence toward me. And then he had O'Donnell dismissed from the case to avoid the Chief offering any conspiracy theories.

O'Donnell printed the article with the picture and filed it in his expandable folder. He pondered at the thought of just how many previous cases he could have solved over the years if the Internet had only existed.

He logged out and shut his computer off, before taking a brisk walk with Casey around the block. After walking out the door, he flipped open his cell phone and checked the display. The phone indicated it was 5:00 p.m. O'Donnell was expecting a call from Suzie anytime and didn't want to miss it. He made an entry on the mini keyboard and checked the display, then flipped it closed and put the phone in his coat pocket.

O'Donnell had spoken to Suzie earlier in the day and had planned to meet at her apartment when she arrived to talk about her trip. O'Donnell told her that she would probably be very tired and it would be easier for her if they met at her place. The real reason, however, that he suggested the location, was due to the whole break-in and bugging ordeal, which he had chosen not to share with Suzie or Murphy.

When Suzie came back to her complex, she found an envelope taped to her door, with her name written in ink on the outside. She took the envelope off and put it between her lips as she juggled with her apartment keys. Murphy was a few steps behind, carrying her travel bag for her. She opened the door and turned the light switch on and held the door open with her foot for Murphy to come in.

Suzie grabbed the envelope walked over to adjust the thermostat temperature, which she had lowered before she left.

Murphy asked,

"What's that notice all about?"

She answered,

"Oh I don't know, it's the rental office again, they've been trying to get a hold of me for Jesse's apartment, I just know it. Do you think I should pay for a month of his rent? It's probably cheaper than having all of his stuff put in storage somewhere."

Murphy thought about it,

"Gee I'm not sure. He might not be back here for a long time," Murphy said.

"Don't be so negative, we're gonna get him out. Hey, could you please call the Chief and let him know we're here?" she asked.

Suzie walked into the kitchen and put on a pot of coffee and cleared some books and boxes from her kitchen table in preparation for their meeting. She opened her travel bag and retrieved the notebook that contained all of the notations she had made both from the jail and from the pawn shop. She placed the book on the table along with a few extra sheets of blank lined paper.

"I called the Chief. He's already on his way over here. He must have checked your flight arrival," said Murphy.

Before he could finish his breath, the buzzer sounded indicating that he was waiting to be let in outside the ground-level entrance door. Suzie ran over to the intercom system and activated the remote door lock release and then unlocked and left her door slightly ajar.

Within a minute, Casey came sprinting through the door to greet her long lost friend. Suzie got down on her knees to hug the excited bundle of happiness. Casey jumped up on her chest and licked Suzie under her chin and wagged her tail out of control with excitement.

"And here I was thinking she had fallen in love with me and would never leave," O'Donnell said as he walked through the door and saw Casey's excitement.

"Oh . . . come over here you, and give me a hug," Suzie said to O'Donnell. She looked over at Murphy, too, and said,

"I can't believe I missed you guys so much and I was only away for two days. Come here, Casey, I got a treat for you...." Suzie walked into the kitchen and Murphy and O'Donnell followed.

"Who wants coffee?" she asked. *"Sit down guys, relax, I'll get some cups."*

She tossed a milk bone cracker to Casey and the dog ran under the table to protect her treasured prize.

"We missed you too, honey, and we worried about you," said O'Donnell.

Murphy jumped in,

"Next time you go anywhere, I'm going with ya, and that's that." *"Sounds good to me," Suzie said. "I'd love to show you around New Orleans. It's really coming back strongly. It's taking a while, but it's coming back. I met some great people and it was sooo warm."*

"I hate to change the subject, but I got a meeting with Sullivan tomorrow morning and we got work to do," O'Donnell reminded his team.

"First of all, how's Jesse doing?" Murphy asked.

"He's hanging in there, it's been tough, I could tell. But overall? Under the circumstances? I think he's doing remarkably well. He is incredibly grateful for everything you guys are doing. I told him all about you guys."

Suzie moved her notebook in front of her and opened the cover and flipped over the first few pages.

"I don't know who killed Kirk and neither does Jesse, but I'll tell you someone who does, and that's that FBI Agent Alden."

Suzie went on to describe about every encounter that Kirk had with Alden at the high school track and everything they had talked about.

"Ya know, Jesse was in the announcer's booth taping every conversation for Kirk?"

Murphy had not heard this news and his eyes widened with interest.

"He taped the conversations?" he asked.

O'Donnell interjected,

"Well....it's strictly hearsay though. We can't use that without the tape."

"Who's got the tape?" inquired Murphy.

"Probably the FBI. Jesse left it in his hotel room in a briefcase out in Indiana. The Feds were all over that room." O'Donnell explained.

"Yeah, but Jesse wouldn't lie," Suzie insisted.

"I know, honey, but no jury in the world is going to believe the accused, just on his word," O'Donnell responded.

Suzie continued to run down every piece of evidence and repeated the answers that she had been given. With every explanation, O'Donnell felt more confident that he could, at the very least, present reasonable doubt in the case. For the next hour, Murphy and the Chief transcribed Suzie's answers, which dispelled every accusation that had been made by the FBI and by the media.

"And then I got to the pawn shop. Oh, my God, what a creep that guy was."

"You went to the pawn shop?" asked Murphy surprisingly.

"Yeah, you didn't know I was going to the pawn shop?"

They both Looked at O'Donnell and he just shrugged his shoulders.

"I thought we talked about that, huh," said O'Donnell.

Suzie described the shop and Cardoni,

"That guy gives me shivers just thinking about him. Yuck. Not only didn't he have a daughter, he didn't even have a security camera. I mean come on. They're calling him a witness? What a joke."

The Chief already knew that the Miami connection was "in the bag," but didn't want to tell Murphy or Suzie. If he had only investigated the guy earlier on the computer, he could have saved her a trip she didn't need to make, but her description of Cardoni simply added credence to his discovery.

O'Donnell then said,

"Never mind about Cardoni. Tell me a little more about what Jesse heard from the announcer's booth when Alden and Kirk talked."

"Well....we didn't have a lot of time to go into detail, and he couldn't remember everything, but he did say he heard Alden's plans to make a big drug deal and only deliver enough to make an arrest. Jesse said it sounded like he was trying to scam the gang out of money for personal gain."

O'Donnell's wheels were turning at laser speed and he was writing down his every thought with his right hand and twirling his moustache with his left.

"When are you meeting with the Mayor?" asked Murphy. O'Donnell answered,

"Tomorrow morning. In his office."

"Do you want me to come along?" Murphy asked.

"No, I can handle it. I'm pretty sure I got this one pegged. There are still a few problems, but I can deal with those later."

Suzie asked Murphy if he had learned anything more about the case. Murphy thought about it for a minute.

"No, not really, the prosecutors are keeping tight lipped about it. They're pretty confident. I did hear that two of the Fed guys had just left for Louisiana, though. That usually means the extradition process must be close and they'll likely be escorting him back here soon for the initial hearing."

"Really? That's interesting. I wonder if Jesse has been assigned an attorney yet," said O'Donnell. *"See if you can find out, cuz we got a lot of information that would help. Man...I was hoping we could break this thing open before the proceedings started, but I'm not sure now,"* added O'Donnell.

"Well...you must be a very tired young lady, so I think we should wrap it up. I can finish my work at home," said O'Donnell. *"There's just one very serious question remaining, however,"* added O'Donnell.

"What? What is it? ...."

O'Donnell looked at Suzie and asked,

"Is Casey coming with me or staying with you?" Both Murphy and Suzie laughed at O'Donnell's humor.

Suzie said,

"Well....let's ask her."

Suzie told the Chief to get his coat and walk toward the door, but not to say anything to the dog. He did as she suggested and Casey's head popped up off the floor and her tail began to vigorously wag. When the Chief opened the door and didn't say anything, Casey stopped in motion and froze like a statue, except for tilting her head to the side in an inquisitive manor. Suzie stood up and said,

"Awwwwww... will you look at that. Casey, do you want to go?"
And like a gate had opened at a horse track, Casey ran

past the Chief and out the open door. The Chief just smiled and quickly said...

"Bye........got to go."

Suzie asked Murphy if he wanted to stay for a second cup of coffee, but he too thought that she was probably tired from her trip. Instead, they agreed to a rain check and to talk to each other the next day. Murphy suggested maybe dinner or a movie or something. Suzie thought that would be great.

CHAPTER 42

It was a Monday morning and an official holiday, Veteran's Day.

Government offices were all generally closed, but Mayor Sullivan was working in his Springdale City Hall office. His itinerary for the day included a meeting with Chief O'Donnell, a parade, and an event in Meadows where US Senator Kerrigan would speak and lay a wreath at the town's war memorial. It was another beautiful sunny day and the Chief decided to take his vintage Indian Motorcycle out for one last time before winterizing the fluids and disconnecting the battery for the season. Before leaving his garage, he placed his files in one of the side leather saddle bags on the motorcycle.

O'Donnell put on his fur-lined pale yellow leather jacket with the Indian logo on the back and a pair of thick gloves and a hood underneath his helmet. He wheeled the bike out of the garage before kick starting the loud roaring engine. O'Donnell adjusted his goggles and his side mirrors and then cruised out of his driveway and down to city hall.

Because the main offices at city hall were closed for the holiday, O'Donnell was able to pull his motorcycle right into a vacant parking spot in front of the hall's front entrance stairs. He turned the motor off and removed his gloves so he could gather his files. He headed up the stairs and into the large granite-pillared rotunda which led to the Mayor's executive office suite.

While O'Donnell was entering the building, he thought about all the daily visits that he made over the years to visit the long running Mayor. He also thought about what Murphy had shared with him just a few days earlier about the Mayor's efforts to find a permanent police Chief replacement.

The Mayor's receptionist was not working, so O'Donnell bypassed his normal routine of checking with her before knocking on his inner office door. The Mayor was dressed up in a suit and tie with a carnation pinned to his lapel and sitting at his paper stacked mahogany desk making notes. He heard the knock on the door.

"Chief? Is that you? Come on in, come on in," he announced.

The Mayor stood up from behind his desk and walked around to greet his old friend.

"Don't tell me you took out the Indian? You crazy old man."

"Of course I did. It's probably my last chance."

The Mayor took the Chief's jacket and hung it up on an antique coat rack in the corner of his office.

"I thought we would sit in the conference room. The desk is a little bigger. How about a coffee?"

The two men walked into the large boardroom, sat down opposite each other and exchanged pleasantries for a few minutes before O'Donnell untied the string that held his expandable folder secure and removed several sheets of paper.

"All right,...... it's going to be quite awkward talking to the senator about this you know? Especially after an outdoor ceremony," the Mayor noted.

"I know, I know, but what alternative do we have? This is not a local problem. This involves the Federal Government," O'Donnell explained.

"I know, I'm just saying...it's going to be difficult accusing a Federal Agent of intentionally framing an innocent man."

"Hang on for a second, let me show you what I got first."

The Chief spread out his papers and began presenting his case like a seasoned attorney.

"First of all, let me begin by reminding you of the first day I met FBI Agent Wayne Alden in this very office. The purpose of his visit was to seek our recommendation for a civilian that could assist his office with a drug investigation. My recommendation, as you know, was Kirk Preston."

"Over the course of several weeks Preston and Alden met to discuss a strategy that would entrap high-level gang members to expose their operation. This was, of course, a highly top-secret project, and one I believe that only Alden had knowledge of, since the FBI would never approve of a civilian participating.

The operation was an extremely dangerous one and it is safe to assume that Preston's only interest would be one with a large financial incentive. Without the Bureau's involvement, it is also safe to assume that Alden would not have the resources to compensate Preston for his high risk. I believe that Alden formulated a plan to procure a large sum of money from the gang, without the ability to deliver the expected drugs. Are you with me so far?" O'Donnell asked.

"I'm listening," said the Mayor.

"O.K..... Kirk Preston used his airplane to transport the drugs from some other location. I believe that he was strangled with a cord and killed in a deal gone bad by a member of the gang. His body was then placed in the trunk of a nearby car. The car was stolen and driven thru the gate and dumped at the base of Mt. Tom. A stolen car was pulled over on that same night with drugs inside, less than a mile from where Kirk's body was found."

"The stolen car? It was stolen from the airport where Kirk's blood was found, and there was blood found in the trunk of the car, too."
The Mayor took off his glasses and interrupted,

"Was it Kirk Preston's blood?"

O'Donnell responded,

"No. I believe the blood belonged to the killer."

The Mayor put his glasses back on and asked,

"Was there any of Preston's blood present?"

"Well......no, but there is more."

The Mayor had been impressed up to this point, but had trouble connecting the dots in a convincing formation.

"Let me continue.... when Kirk's strangled body was discovered. Alden had a serious problem. He was directly responsible for Preston's death. When a possible suspect emerged, he took the opportunity to pile-on incriminating evidence to avoid being the focus of an internal federal investigation."

"His only threat to exposing his involvement was me. That is why he removed me from the case, stating federal jurisdiction. He claimed jurisdiction because the crime scene took place on the property of an Air National Guard Field. That's how he was able to control the investigation."

The Mayor sat back in his chair and rubbed his face,

"Well...a lot of coincidence, I'll give you that. But, what about that Jesse Thorpe guy? How could he be set up in so many different ways? I am not sure if you have enough. A steady stool needs four legs you know, and you're teetering on only two."

"Hang on Sully," O'Donnell continued.

"I can explain every shred of evidence. Remember the pawn shop guy who had received Preston's diamond football ring?"

O'Donnell reached into his shirt pocket and placed the ring on the table and spun it like a coin.

"I've had this ring since Preston's funeral."

The Mayor grabbed the ring and put it in his palm and said,

"That just means that the guy was a nut, probably just wanted to be on TV."

Then O'Donnell slid over the military picture and said,

"Oh I agree. He's definitely a nut. Here he is with another nut named Wayne Alden in Vietnam."

The Mayor picked up the photo and removed his glasses again and held the picture close to his eyes.

"That son of a......" he put the picture down on the desk, looked up at O'Donnell.

"I'll talk to the senator right after the Veteran's ceremony. I think it would be a good idea if you were there, too, in case I need you to answer any questions. I can't promise anything, but the senator is a good man and I'm sure he will at least listen. I'm giving him a nice endorsement so I expect he'll be willing to do at least that."

CHAPTER 43

For an entire week, Kirk found himself thinking a lot about his life and about friends and the journey that had taken him to where he currently was in his life. Kirk was admired by so many people for everything he had done, yet when he thought about his life, only a few monumental events ever came to mind. He remembered his sad brother the night their grandfather came into their room to tell them the news of their parent's deadly car accident.

He remembered being carried off the football field by his teammates the day they won the championship and the day he first flew solo in his plane. Perhaps it was the pending danger he was facing, dealing with the gang that fueled his inner thoughts of mortality and purpose. He thought about Suzie, how sweet she was and how selfish he was to lead her on for so long.

Kirk had it all, yet he marked his storied life by only a few short titled chapters.

Before he drove to the Laundromat for the last time, he made a list of people to call to just say hello. He was feeling melancholy and alone and wanted to hear the voices of those who brought him comfort. He sat down in his living room and thumbed through a photo album that Suzie had made and given to him at a surprise birthday party she had thrown for him some years earlier.

Suzie was the first person he called.

"Hello Suzie? Hey it's Kirk. What's going on?....Really ? Me? Not much, just sitting around, I got a few things I got to do. Listen, ummm, there's something I ummm... want to tell you...I.., I was thinking that we should, maybe, if you want, maybe we could go somewhere, away, like some place different, together, maybe. I don't

know...I've been kinda bored with this town lately. You know what I mean? Let's think about it O.K.? Hey, I'll call you later and we'll talk more. Suzie....ummm, bye."

He had planned on calling a few more friends, but didn't. He put his hand on the telephone handset and then he took it off again. Then he picked it up and dialed a number in Virginia. The phone rang about ten times before a soft voice answered on the other end.

"Hello."

Kirk could barely hear the person on the other end.

"Derek?" Kirk asked.

"This is Derek," the soft voice answered.

"Derek, It's Kirk calling."

The line went silent and Kirk wasn't sure anyone was still there.

"Derek?"

"Hi Kirk, I'm here," said the man in a somber tone.

"Derek, I just wanted to see how you're doing. It's been way too long."

There was another long silent pause.

"I know why you're calling, it's because of the money," Derek said. Kirk answered,

"I don't know what you're talking about Derek, I just wanted to say hi and hear your voice. Are you having trouble with money?"

"It's gone, it's all gone," Derek's voice trembled.

"Derek? Are you O.K.?" again a long silence.

"I lost the entire fund in the market, all of it," followed by more silence.

"Derek? Derek? Listen to me. I don't care about money. It's not important. Derek, I just wanted to talk to my brother, that's all. I just wanted to hear your voice. Derek?"

The voice became even fainter and then Kirk's brother said,

"I'm sorry Kirk, I'm so, so, sorry," and he hung up the phone. *"Derek?"*

Kirk hung up his phone and sat for a while thinking about his brother. Kirk knew that the family trust fund had run dry, but always thought it was his own endless squandering exploits that were the cause. He never thought for moment that his brother had somehow lost it.

Kirk and Derek were very different and yet, very much the same. When they were separated, after their parents died, Derek withdrew from everyone close to him. In some ways Kirk did as well. While Kirk turned to athletics as a means of escape, Derek turned to computers. For most of his life he had become somewhat of a recluse and lived in his own cyber world, rarely leaving his one bedroom apartment. He didn't have any close friends or any significant relationships.

Kirk fought for most of his life not to be his father's son, but Derek was not as fortunate. Derek's struggle with the demons of alcohol he had inherited from his parents would ultimately close the door on his world and shut out all who cared and wanted to help. His computer screen would be his only window and his keyboard his only touch.

Following the adoption, all records had been sealed tight. It was not until Kirk turned 21 that he could petition the courts for access to the documents that would allow him to know where his brother lived. Derek went to live with his grandfather for ten years in Virginia prior to the grandfather's death and Kirk lived with his adopted parents in Meadows, until they left for Europe when he was 18, also leaving him alone.

Kirk picked up the phone again to call his brother and tell him he wanted to see him, but when he dialed the number, all he heard was a busy signal on the other end. Kirk got up out of his chair and grabbed a jacket and a laundry bag and walked into his living room to turn off the television, before leaving for the Laundromat for the final phase of the sting. The television had been set to a regional cable news station and they were recapping the top stories of the day.

Kirk was just about to turn the set off, when he saw a picture of the man he last saw in the Laundromat with Angel Lopez. He grabbed the television remote and increased the volume to catch the tail end of the news story. The news anchor reported,

> *"55 year old Vincent Armando a reputed organized crime boss from Providence has been found dead of an apparent knife wound in Springdale. There are no suspects at this time, but authorities believe it was an inside job, among warring turf factions. Police are asking for anyone with information to call....."*

Kirk grabbed his remote and turned the set off and sat back down on his sofa to think about what he had just heard. Vincent Armando was the accomplice and Angel's boss. He was also the stranger who Angel had escorted to the Laundromat the previous week to meet Kirk.

Kirk sat idly, wondering if Angel had heeded his advice and taken control of his life. His mentoring to the thug was not intended to inspire murder in-order to get ahead. Could Angel have been so misguided? Kirk wondered.

Kirk wasn't sure how these events would affect the operation and in spite of his reckless abandon thus far, he contemplated not driving to the Laundromat as he had planned for Angel to drop off the money. But after a few minutes, he decided he was in it too deep and it would be equally as dangerous to cross Angel at this point. The dice were in Kirk's hand and all the players were waiting for his high stakes next toss. He decided to continue as if he had no knowledge of the news.

He sensed an uneasiness looming over him by how smoothly things had progressed with the sting operation. Although he was in control, the new players in the game had changed the stakes and he was untested in the new league and unprotected. As he entered the city in his Corvette, Kirk was very aware of his surroundings and felt vulnerably exposed.

Nights in the inner city had become the heartbeat for a nocturnal culture of criminal indigents on every level, from drug gangs and their turf wars to gutter rats pursued by street strayed alley cats. Tonight, however, there was a different feeling on the cold concrete grounds, a feeling of deadly and imminent peril. The tension in the air was so intense; it was palpable with the taste of doom. The ever present pockets of gang cockroaches had all scurried and scampered into their holes and hideouts.

Kirk's naturally confident demeanor was replaced by an insecure paranoia of every car and movement around him. He sensed, in his rearview mirror, a feeling that someone was following and watching him. There seemed to be patrol cars everywhere and very few people on the streets. A spotlight beam from a state police helicopter passed over Kirk's car and randomly searched side streets and rooftops like a giant exterminator's flashlight in a darkened basement.

Kirk came to an open intersection and felt target trapped, exposed as he waited for the changing signal of a red traffic light and considered making a U-turn and heading out of the city and back to Meadows. He sat starring in his mirror as a lurking dark car, with tinted windows, loomed uncomfortably close behind him. Inside the car, from his rearview mirror, he could see three figures oddly crammed into the front seat, a driver and two passengers shoulder to shoulder. Kirk kept his head forward and kept his eyes in a watchful focus of their every move.

The light from a cigarette lighter flamed and illuminated a shadowy black face, as the man lit a cigarette in his mouth. The passengers' window opened and plume of smoke rose out of the black sedan. Kirk heard a voice from the car yelling something at Kirk. Their car raced the engine like a dragster on the starting line of a race. The driver of the car laid on his horn and flashed his high beam headlights at Kirk and raced the engine again to an even higher confronting pitch.

Kirk's entire body entered a physiological fight or flight debate. His jowls felt a welling drench and his lips turned sand dry. Kirk didn't know how to react or what to do. For the first time, he had lost control. Without moving the visible part of his body frame, he slowly removed his seatbelt and reached under his seat for his 9 mm hand gun and placed it on his lap, all the while, never taking his eyes off the mirror or moving his head.

So this is it, he thought to himself. This is how it ends. What a pathetic waste I have been. A selfish, arrogant show-off who thought he was invincible. How fitting it is that the lowest of the low should control my destiny and pen my final chapter. I am what I have become and it is what it is. Kirk put the shifter in park and unlocked his door. He cocked his gun, closed his eyes and took a deep breath.

The horn from the car behind sounded again along with another horn and still another. When he turned his attention forward, he noticed that traffic light had turned yellow and he had missed the entire green light signal sequence. He exhaled in relief, realizing that the car behind him had simply tried to get him to move on the green light.

When the light finally turned green again, Kirk immediately left the stop line and pulled to the side to gather his composure. The car passed by and the passenger gestured his finger of discontent with a vociferate punctuation. Kirk continued down Main Street and onto Belmont where the Laundromat was located.

He parked, locked his car and proceeded inside. The room was completely empty, the television was off and there was no attendant in sight. Kirk first walked over to the spot where he had previously met with Angel, but decided to switch to an area that was not in direct view or bullet path of the street-front windows.

Kirk had been so preoccupied by the news story that he had forgotten to bring any dirty laundry with him to use as his decoy. He tried sitting down for a few minutes and reading a magazine, but felt completely out of place. How would he explain what he was doing there if anyone saw him and asked, he thought. He threw the magazine down and decided to abort the operation and ran out of the store and jumped into his car.

He left the city on the most direct route and headed across the river toward Westford. Kirk instantly felt safer after leaving the city. It was unusual for Kirk to feel scared. He was always so confident and secure in everything he did. Whether it was intuition or gut instinct, Kirk wasn't comfortable and he wanted no part of the operation any longer. He decided to keep driving. Next to flying, nothing calmed Kirk's nerves better than driving in his car.

He readjusted his mirrors and popped a CD into his player and lowered his window just a crack. Kirk reached into his glove compartment and took out a cigar, clipped the end off and lit it up.

He reached down in front of his seat and lifted the seat release lock and pushed his bucket seat back to stretch and relax his tense body. When he pushed the seat back, it would only move one position. He lifted the lever again and pushed back with added force by pushing his foot against the floor panel, but again, could not move the seat back.

Kirk reached behind his seat and blindly felt for something that might be hindering its movement. He instantly recognized the feel of the canvas dirty laundry bag on the floor, behind the seat. In the short time he had been inside the Laundromat, Angel must have been waiting in the darkness, waiting for the Corvette to appear. He stashed the bag of money in the car and quickly vanished.

Kirk pulled over to a mini-mart convenience store parking lot, loosened his seat belt and got out of the car. He tilted the driver's seat forward and retrieved the bag. He threw the bag onto the passenger side floor and got back into the car and continued to drive. He pushed the interior dome light on and glanced down at the laundry bag. Attached to the drawstring on the top was a scribbled note that read,

I took your advice. I'm calling the shots now...50k/2M Co-pilot.

Kirk's feeling of ease and relief was replaced with one of fear and anxiety. How did he find himself so close to the region's inner gang operations and be caught in the middle of a major drug deal? Did his advice to Angel, to be a man and take control of his life, actually cause that gang leaders death?

Every phase of the operation had gone exactly as planned, until now. Kirk had four times more money than he expected. He had two million dollars of dirty money, and a completely different plan from what Alden and he had discussed.

CHAPTER 44

Chief O'Donnell left Springdale's City Hall on his Indian Motorcycle with plans to enjoy the unseasonable good weather and take a short ride and visit some friends before attending the midday ceremonies in Meadows as the Mayor had requested. By the time he cruised into Meadows and approached the town green, there were already approximately 250 to 300 people waiting for the festivities to begin and for the senator to arrive.

Town volunteers had arranged dozens of chairs facing a temporary stage with a podium where the dignitaries would speak to the crowd. The stage was adorned with red, white & blue swaging and American and state flags. To the side of the stage, stood the Meadows marching band, awaiting a direction to play the National Anthem. To the opposite side, stood a seven-person Civil War company, complete with authentic period uniforms, muskets and swords.

It was always a tradition in Meadows to have the company fire a twenty-one-gun salute during Veteran's and Memorial Day ceremonies and particularly when there were visiting dignitaries in attendance. There were several war veterans dressed in their military attire, including one elderly townsman - a Normandy raider in World War II. There were also a couple of Boy Scout troops present to lead the crowd in the pledge of allegiance. United States Senator Kerrigan had arrived with his entourage of assistants and interns and was working the crowd, speaking to potential supporters.

All three of the area's television affiliates were set to cover the senator's speech and were set up in different vantage points on the green. The senator's visit to Meadows was two fold. He was delivering a national recognition award for the town's recycling efforts and delivering a speech in support of our troops overseas.

The senator had hoped his appearance in the Western part of the state would be seen as a declaration of his dedication to environmental concerns and to the politically-charged subject of our military actions.

It was no secret that Senator Kerrigan had aspirations of running for the Presidency. His staff was responsible for the multiple press releases announcing his important speech, hoping, of course, for wide coverage. Before the event began, the senator granted interviews to all of the media present, which delayed the beginning of the program. Mayor Sullivan had planned to speak with the senator immediately following the ceremonies in a private area set up for their brief meeting, concerning the Preston case and the apparent improprieties of the FBI.

O'Donnell sat on his motorcycle and watched from the back of the gathering on the green, munching from a bag of kettle pop corn and waving to friends and children as they walked by. A member of the town's historical society walked up the stairs of the makeshift stage and tested the microphone located at the podium. Within minutes the stage was filled with prominent speakers and participants of the program.

Seated behind the podium, were Senator Kerrigan, Mayor Sullivan, the honorary WW II veteran and a representative from the town's conservation commission. A member of the select board welcomed the crowd to the Meadows town green and thanked everyone for attending. The host asked all to rise for the playing of the National Anthem.

O'Donnell stood up from his motorcycle and placed his right hand on his heart. Following the music, the crowd applauded the high school band's rendition of the anthem and the host asked the crowd to remain standing for the pledge of allegiance, by a member of Meadows' Boy Scout Troop #14.

The senator was asked to walk down from the stage and join members of the local VFW in laying an ornamental wreath at the war memorial monument next to the stage. The senator stood facing the monument as a boy scout played an emotional stanza of taps on his bugle. The senator stepped forward and bent down to place the wreath and then stood up, took a step backwards and gave a salute to the memorial.

Breaking the silence of the solemn moment was the commander of the ceremonial Civil War Company shouting his commands to the officers to ready their arms for the twenty-one gun salute. The standing crowd could be seen covering their ears in anticipation of the firing. It was a ceremony they had all experienced before. The muskets were raised in formation and the commander raised his sword and lowered it swiftly signaling the first of three rounds to be fired. The sound from the rifles reverberated from the green throughout the village, a flock of crows took flight from the trees on the green and smoke from the muskets rose slowly into the cool autumn air.

The focus of the crowd was naturally on the firing muskets and no one, with the exception of those on the stage, had noticed that Mayor Sullivan had collapsed and fallen face down on the platform. The moment had seemed to stop in time and move in slow motion. O'Donnell's vision of the stage zoomed in like a long distance camera. His senses had temporarily blocked out all of the sounds and exterior sights surrounding the stage and his tunnel vision watched as people scrambled about the stage in a chaotic reaction to the fallen Mayor.

Most instincts would lead people to believe that the Mayor had suffered a heart attack, but O'Donnell feared something far graver. His fears were confirmed when he could see someone roll over the Mayor and discover a pool of blood underneath him and an unmistakable bullet wound to the forehead. People suddenly began to scream, then yell, and scramble in all directions for protection.

The few seconds of pandemonium felt like several minutes. In spite of the angst of the moment, O'Donnell's years of experience and training immediately brought the surreal moment into a clear focus. Tuning out the screams of horror, he began to absorb every movement. His instinctive attention turned to the sound of an off-road motorcycle speeding away from the green. O'Donnell quickly reached for his cell phone, opened it, and then closed it. There was no time to waste. He put on his helmet; kick-started his motorcycle and took chase after the other bike, leaving the town green and the chaos behind.

He raced down the center road of town at double the posted speed limit, keeping the smaller motorcycle in his line of vision at all times. He recklessly passed cars on the right and then weaved back to pass on the left, on the one lane road. In hot pursuit, he turned into Forest Park in an all out chase. O'Donnell had ridden motorcycles his entire life and knew from the sound of the bike he was pursuing, that it was a two-stroke model designed for off-road racing. If the bike reached a wooded dirt path then O'Donnell's Indian street model would lose its powerful street advantage. O'Donnell continued to race down the paved park road and as he had feared, lost the dirt bike at the entrance of the woods.

He stopped at the side of the road and shut his motor off to hear the direction of the off-road motorcycle's motor. Again, he took out his cell phone and looked at the screen. The sound of the motorcycle took on a lower gear and raced to higher rpm pitch. O'Donnell understood the driver's action to mean he was climbing a steep hill. The Chief had grown up and spent his entire life in Springdale and countless hours in the park. He knew every trail and path in the 100-acre forest. If his assumptions were correct, there were only two paths out of the woods that the racing motorcycle could take from the top of the steep hill.

O'Donnell kick-started his motorcycle and sped down the road to the other side of the park and to the path that he guessed the rider had taken. O'Donnell slowly drove up the trail and slowed his bike down until he could hear the sound of the oncoming dirt bike. The Chief decided not to sit and wait, but rather, he spun his wheels and headed directly toward the approaching sound. In a straight section of the trail he could see and hear the other speeding motorcycle coming directly toward him.

Like a scene out of a medieval gladiator movie, the two motorcycles faced each other like armored horsemen and throttled in a deadly game of chicken directly at the face of their challenger.

O'Donnell did not flinch and showed no intention of veering off the center of the path. It seemed as if the stand off lasted forever, both bikes barreling down the path, challenging each other head-on with their lives. At the last possible second, he flinched, the dirt bike turned and darted off the beaten trail and impacted a large Oak tree on the side of the path, throwing the rider through the air and into another tree.

O'Donnell's momentum carried him past the impact site. He turned his head over his shoulder and slid his bike to a stop; spinning and whipping the back end around 180 degrees. Without setting his kick stand down, he dropped the vintage Indian on its side and ran to the motionless rider. As the Chief ran, he threw off his gloves and unstrapped his helmet, dropping them both in the wake of his leafy path.

The man's body was a medium build and he was wearing a black leather jacket, and black leather racing pants with knee-high motocross boots. His helmet was jet black with a full-length tinted visor. The Chief grabbed his shoulder and turned the lifeless body onto its back. O'Donnell's experience over the years of responding to accidents, served him well in responding properly, but when he felt the riders pulse on the side of his neck, he instantly knew that the man had suffered a fatal hit. There was no pulse. Tremendously shaken over what had just happened, O'Donnell reached for a nitro pill, swallowed it without water and sat down next to the body to catch his breath.

O'Donnell then reached down and unhooked the chin strap of the man's helmet. He stopped momentarily, fearing what he was about to discover. Then, he slowly lifted the man's visor and uncovered the hidden face behind the dark-tinted helmet shield. It was the face of detective Brian Murphy.

It was chilling. A moment unlike any the Chief had ever experienced. He stood up and felt nauseous at the sight of his discovery. He walked away from the body and took a seat on an old tree stump. He placed his face into his hands and sat silently for several minutes.

It all began to make sense, but O'Donnell couldn't immediately process the meaning or motive behind Murphy's unconscionable actions. O'Donnell had suspected that the young detective was not entirely on their team for a while, but couldn't be sure. One of the reasons he had issued new cell phones to Suzie and Murphy as part of their investigating the Preston case, was to watch their every move.

O'Donnell had purchased phones that had an integrated GPS function that allowed the Chief to follow their movements. It was the reason that O'Donnell continually checked his phone device. Over the course of the last couple of weeks on several occasions, Murphy was monitored visiting the federal building and FBI Agent Alden's temporary residence.

His fearful suspicions of Murphy suddenly become abundantly clear. Murphy was Agent Alden's henchman. He had infiltrated the Chief's trust and co-piloted Alden's flight to destroy the all knowing Mayor and Chief with one stone. Murphy was just an unwilling pawn, dispensable if necessary, to keep Alden's hands unsullied. The deadly crash became the final curtain call of his tragic play.

O'Donnell needed more time to think, but now wasn't the time. The Chief could hear the faint sounds of sirens in the distance and nearby only the peaceful sounds of the wind cutting through the trees. He called the Springdale Police number and asked that they dispatch a cruiser and an EMS vehicle to the park.

Then, he walked over to his motorcycle and lifted it up onto its wheels and lowered the kick stand. He picked up his gloves and his helmet and with his head hung low, walked down the trail to the clearing that led to the paved road and waited for the response team to arrive.

CHAPTER 45

In spite of what television and the big screen portray, police work is intrinsically about doing paperwork. No one knew this better than Chief O'Donnell. Following the events in Meadows and the chase and crash in the park, O'Donnell expected to be at his old police headquarters for several hours into the night, answering questions, completing reports, and providing information. It was a peculiar position that he found himself in, sitting across from investigators that he had once trained on the techniques of gathering, recording, and reporting testimony.

For several hours detectives repeatedly went over the Chief's minute by minute account of what had taken place. They sat in an open area of the station that looked more like a newspaper office. Desk after desk and officer after officer, each divided by 5 foot indescript partitions, with little privacy, were busy taking phone calls and interviewing witnesses. The detective interviewing O'Donnell was nearly ready to let the Chief go, when he received a phone call at his desk.

The seasoned cop answered the phone and listened to the caller speak for over a minute before replying. He agreed to something and then hung up the phone and looked over at O'Donnell and relayed the message he had just heard.

"Chief, we're not quite done. If you could just follow me, we have just a few more questions."

The two gentlemen walked across the open headquarters and into a private room next to the Chief's old office. They entered the room to find three other men, from the force, sitting around a conference table.

"Chief, come on in, have a seat. We have just a few more questions for you," said a man from the District Attorney's office.

The Chief looked around the room and nodded his head to the other two plain clothes men that O'Donnell knew as administrators from the police commission.

"Chief, we've all had a pretty tough day around here and we need to clarify a few things, if you don't mind."

O'Donnell looked around the table.

"Yes, it' been a horrible day."

"Don't worry, I know the routine better than any of you guys, with all due respect," he said.

"Good, well...you're a straight, no-nonsense guy O'Donnell, so I am not going to beat around the bush. Before we go any further, I need to be on the record as having read you your rights," the man announced.

O'Donnell took off his glasses and demanded an explanation.

"What the hell are you talking about?" he yelled.

The men around the table were very uncomfortable with the sudden change in mood and one of the men stood up from the table and walked over in front of the closed door and stood guard.

"Thomas O'Donnell, you are being charged with the 1ˢᵗ degree murder of Mayor Patrick Sullivan. You have the right to........"

O'Donnell was in complete shock and couldn't even hear the remaining instructions given by the prosecutor until he heard his name repeated as if he was asleep in bed and someone was trying to wake him.....

"Chief,..... Chief, do you understand what I have just read? Chief...You need to answer me, Chief!"

O'Donnell looked up and replied,

"Yes, ...yes I understand."

The prosecutor then continued,

"O.K. good, now would you like to continue?"

O'Donnell knew they had nothing, so he agreed to answer more questions and be recorded doing so, but first asked why he was subject to the arrest. The prosecutor referred to his notes and read a synopsis of evidence and preliminary testimony that they had gathered.

"Well Chief, among the key points we found is the murder weapon found at the scene was a handgun belonging to you."

The Chief jumped in,

"That gun was stolen from my house."

"Well, we have several eye witnesses who watched you flee the scene at a dangerously high rate of speed. We also know that you met with the Mayor earlier in the day at his office and we have evidence that supports that you were very upset over his firing of you and his search for a replacement. We also know that you have not been yourself lately, well...with the suicide attempt and everything. And there is still the matter of the young detective and his untimely death. We believe detective Murphy was, in fact, in pursuit of your arrest when you fled the scene after the shooting. I'm sorry Chief, but I'm afraid that you're going to have to spend the night here in a cell, unless you want to say something?......

O'Donnell knew that nothing he could say at this point would change his present circumstance. He was being charged for shooting the Mayor and possibly for Murphy's death, too. He shook his head and said,

"You're wrong. I know you're just doing your job, but you're wrong. I will reserve my statement pending council."

With that acknowledgment, one of the men stood up and removed a pair of handcuffs from the back of his belt and placed them on O'Donnell. He was escorted, as a courtesy, by his former colleagues. Out of respect, they brought him down a back staircase, out of sight from his former staff, and processed him in private before being locked in a holding cell for the night.

Before the attendant left O'Donnell in the cell, O'Donnell asked him for a piece of paper and a pencil.

"Chief, you know the rules. I can't give you any contraband while you're in a cell. I'm sorry Chief."

O'Donnell apologized for asking the young cop.

"I'm sorry. I'm not thinking straight. I think I just need to write some things down on paper, so I can work this out. I wasn't trying to get you to break the rules."

The uniformed guard responded back to the Chief,

"Hey, it's O.K., it's been a long day."

The guard walked away from the holding area and returned a minute later with a pad and a pen clipped to the cover.

"I'm the only one on duty for this shift. I can't give it to you, but I'll be damned if I didn't drop it right outside your cell and forgot to pick it up."

O'Donnell thanked the officer and promised to be very discreet when he used it. The first thing he began to write was all of the evidence that Murphy had provided during their meetings. Everything that Murphy had said and done now had to be re-evaluated. This included the blood samples he claimed that he had tested. Everything was fitting into place. O'Donnell figured that Murphy must have worked for the FBI and was in cahoots with Alden all along. He was likely the culprit in bugging the dining room table and probably breaking in O'Donnell's house to look for the ring and for stealing the handgun.

He also surmised that Murphy had manipulated the Chief's relationship with the Mayor, by fabricating the story about the Mayor's desire to replace the Chief right away.

"God, how could this happen," O'Donnell heard himself say out loud in his cell.

O'Donnell always thought it was unusual that someone like Murphy would leave a successful law career in Boston and come to Western Massachusetts to start all over again as a police detective. Murphy was placed by the FBI, inside the force, to find and expose corruption in the city's law enforcement community.

Over the course of time, he had been coerced by his superior, Agent Alden, to help in the secretive drug sting operation. When things fell apart and Kirk was killed, Alden threatened Murphy with his authority to frame the detective for masterminding the operation. Murphy knew first-hand that Alden was corrupt enough to do it and had the power to follow through with his threat. He had already seen him do it. Alden would not go down alone and Murphy knew it. It is nearly impossible to conquer a superior who has abandoned civility.

The only way Murphy could keep tabs on O'Donnell and Suzie, was to get close enough to them and get inside their operation. When it became known that the Mayor was about to share facts in the case with the senator, there was no other alternative but for Murphy to take out the Mayor. Stealing O'Donnell's gun and using it to kill Mayor Sullivan would take the Chief out of the picture as well. It was a perfect plan and so far...it was working to a tee, at least for Alden.

O'Donnell's mind was spinning in so many directions he didn't stop to consider he was sitting in a jail cell, charged with murder. It was a strange twist of irony. His tireless efforts to free someone, who had been framed and imprisoned for killing his best friend, put him in the identical predicament. It was a bizarre anomaly, to the say the least.

A guard for the holding area appeared from around the corner, with a video camera. He proceeded to mount it on an adjustable four-foot tripod, directly outside of and pointing to O'Donnell's cell. The guard stood behind the camera and focused the lens to encapsulate the entire interior of the Chief's cell. He then pushed the record/monitor button and started to walk away. The Chief called out to him,

"Hey, what the hell is this? Don't I have some sort of privacy rights? What if I have to use the can?"

The guard walked back over to the Chief and said,

"Chief, I'm sorry about this. I'm just following orders. If it were up to......"

The Chief interrupted the nervous young guard,

"Who gives an order for someone to be videotaped? It's humiliating enough as it is."

The guard stepped forward and said,

"Chief, you've been put on a suicide watch, I'm sorry, really, I'm sorry for this, but it's for your own protection."

O'Donnell sat back down and the reality of his situation began to unfold in his mind. Again he struggled with the question, how could this have happened? His life had taken on so many unpredictable contrasts. Only weeks earlier, he had been reading retirement brochures in his office. Since then, he had been relieved of his life-long career, nearly died and was admitted to the hospital, had his house broken into and caused the accidental death of a fellow cop. To top it all off, he was sitting in a jail cell under a suicide watch and facing a 1st degree murder charge for killing his oldest and trusted friend. His life as he knew it, had just ended, again.

O'Donnell's throat felt like there was a lump stuck halfway down, the physical manifestation of an overwhelming sense of guilt. His conscience was heavy with his indirect involvement in all three deaths, Kirk's, Sullivan's and Murphy's. His emotions of guilt fueled a raging hatred for Alden and his selfish unscrupulous exploits. It was the unfinished work of revenge that kept O'Donnell from completely self-destructing under the pressure. Quitting was never in the Chief's lexicon.

The Chief was physically and emotionally exhausted, but sleeping was out of the question. When he closed his eyes, visions of the Veteran's Day ceremony played repeatedly in his head and the sound of the gun echoed in a surreal hollow. The scene would then alternate with a replay of Murphy's motorcycle racing toward him, with no room to pass.

The process of incarceration was as familiar to O'Donnell as riding his Indian. Over the 40 years of law enforcement that O'Donnell had logged, he had locked up literally thousands of bad guys in the same holding area where he presently sat. But never had he imagined that all of the occupants would be presumed undignified, until proven guilty.

He was fully aware of every procedure. First thing in the morning, he would receive a visit from either an attorney or bondsman. By nine o'clock he would be transported to the court house for a preliminary arraignment and then would likely be denied bail and immediately be transported to the county jail outside of Springdale for a lengthy stay, awaiting trial.

He also knew that keeping quiet, as difficult as it would be, was essential to a successful process and positive outcome. O'Donnell believed that his destiny would not be shaped by the choice of his words, particularly since there was no one, outside of Suzie, that he felt he could trust. O'Donnell also felt he should no longer confide in or involve Suzie in the case. It was too dangerous. He planned to advise her to leave the area, as soon as he could get a message to her.

The long agonizing night was compounded by the sounds of other detainees in the adjacent cells. Everyone, with the exception of O'Donnell, was under the influence of some sort of substance. Yelling, screaming and moaning fell upon deaf ears in the holding cell. The Chief thought about the immeasurable damage to everyone in society that illegal drugs had caused. Whether it was the junkie on the street, the prostitute on the corner, or the corrupt FBI Agent in his office, the cost was devastating.

CHAPTER 46

The discovery of two million dollars in a laundry bag behind his seat made Kirk reconsider Alden's carefully laid out plans. Only he and Angel knew how much money was stashed in the bag and only he and Alden knew what he was going to do with it. Alden recommended that when Kirk received the drug money he take a plane trip to throw off the gang. It made sense, since Angel was likely keeping a close eye on the money and a flight would end their surveillance ability.

With his brother's phone conversation still fresh in mind, he decided that a flight to Richmond, Virginia would be the perfect opportunity to visit him. And with his new found wealth, he could perhaps help out his brother with his money concerns. There was plenty to go around.

Kirk figured that Angel's boss from Providence likely didn't give Angel his blessing to make the deal. He didn't become a kingpin by making stupid or risky decisions. His refusal to deal with Kirk must have angered Angel into taking action into his own hands. If it was true, then Angel was in big trouble. In any business, killing your boss seldom leads to a promotion.

Before leaving on his flight, Kirk placed a package into a shipping receptacle, located at the airport. He addressed the box to a fictitious location with Agent Alden's name and Federal Building office as the return address. In the package, he had placed the tracking device that Alden had provided to him and designated it for "air mail" delivery status. Kirk didn't trust Alden any more than he trusted Angel and if Alden was going to watch Kirk's movement, than Kirk was going to throw him off, too.

When the courier would be unable to deliver the package, it would automatically be rerouted back to Alden's office. If Alden was monitoring the device, Kirk would have more freedom to move around on his own terms and time-frame. Kirk was a brilliant thinker and, sadly, the world would never realize his true potential. He climbed into his plane and followed his normal pre-flight ritual, which included an entry into the flight data book of his four-hour trip to Richmond. It would be his final entry.

CHAPTER 47

Chief O'Donnell must have dosed off after all, in spite of the all night ruckus chorus. He was awakened by the sound of his door being unlocked by the morning shift guard. He had developed a cramp in his back and a migraine in his head from lying on the thinly cushioned single bunk. When he opened his eyes, it took a few seconds for him to focus and remember where he was. The man who was standing in front of him was wearing a black pin-stripped suit and a grey overcoat.

"Good morning Mr. O'Donnell," greeted the stranger.

O'Donnell rolled over to his side and managed to reach the floor with one of his feet and then pushed against the wall to sit all the way up and sarcastically replied back,

"Yes, thank you. Isn't a wonderful morning?"

"Mr. O'Donnell, I'm Attorney Gustafson and...."

O'Donnell stood up on his feet,

"Yeah, yeah, I know you're a court-appointed lawyer, blah, blah. How about you let me use this beautiful commode and I'll be right with you unless of course, you would enjoy watching me."

O'Donnell was not in good spirits, for obvious reasons.

"Mr. O'Donnell. I'll be happy to wait for you outside. But, perhaps you would like to use a private bathroom in the office outside the holding area instead. Oh and by the way, you're partially correct. I am an attorney. I am a US Attorney."

He stepped out of the way and offered the open cell door to O'Donnell to walk through. O'Donnell apologized for his rudeness and asked for the man's understanding. He walked into the washroom alone and used the facility, washed his hands and his face and walked back out.

"Mr. O'Donnell, I was wondering if I could have a few minutes with you?" the attorney asked.

O'Donnell was still not himself. Even on a good day, it took him a while to wake up. He was not a morning person.

"Gee....I don't know. I'll have to check my schedule. Did you have an appointment?"

The man was growing a little impatient with O'Donnell's dry sense of humor and said,

"Mr. O'Donnell, I am here to help you. It concerns Agent Alden. But, if you would prefer that I wait thirty or forty years?"

Again, O'Donnell apologized and responded to the man and willingly agreed to speak to him. Gustafson had procured an office in the record's department on the 2nd floor for the two of them to discuss the events of the previous day. O'Donnell followed the man upstairs without handcuffs or even a uniformed officer's escort. Even O'Donnell thought that this was highly unusual considering the charge against him. The two men entered the empty room and Gustafson closed the door and invited O'Donnell to sit down. He also offered him a cup of coffee, which the Chief gladly accepted.

"Mr. O'Donnell, let me explain why I am here and hopefully you can enlighten me to a few questions I have, all right? Good. As I mentioned I am a United States Attorney here in the Commonwealth and I need to clarify a few things, if you don't mind?"

O'Donnell took a sip of his coffee and placed the cup back down on the conference table.

"Excuse me, sir....with all due respect. I appreciate your apparent 'pull' around here, but I have not spoken to council yet and until I do so..."

"Mr. O'Donnell, perhaps we have gotten off to a bad start. Let me back up a bit and try again. I happen to know that you did not shoot Mayor Sullivan, O.K.? So, since you are correct and I do have 'pull' around here, I highly recommend that we have a friendly discussion. And then I use my 'pull' to let you sleep in your own bed tonight. How's that? Can we try again? Or should I head back to Boston? Yes or no?"

O'Donnell's judgment over the last few weeks hadn't exactly helped him out very much, so he parted from his conventional wisdom and offered to take a chance in the hopes of receiving some sort of impunity and answer whatever questions the man asked. But first O'Donnell had to ask,

"How do you know I didn't shoot Sullivan?"

The attorney responded,

"O.K. listen. Here's how it works...I'll ask the questions and you will answer. All right?"

The Chief sat back and sipped his coffee.

"Some very disturbing documents were given to me that were found on Mayor Sullivan's body that make some very serious accusations about a federal agent. Are you aware of any such information?"

O'Donnell didn't quite know where the man was going with his line of questioning, but felt secure enough to allow the conversation to continue.

*"Yes, I am aware of some **indisputable facts** that were articulated on paper."*

The attorney said,

"Look, just answer the question yes or no and I will make the judgment as to the factual validity of evidence, O.K.? O.K. Did you

supply the Mayor with these documents with the intent of forwarding them to Senator Kerrigan? Yes or No."

O'Donnell now felt like the conversation was more of a deposition and was reluctant in being overly cooperative. O'Donnell's instincts began to fill him with incredulous feelings toward the man's real motive in speaking with him.

"Now you listen to me, Mr. Attorney, if you would like to talk about the events of yesterday, I will do so. If you want to muscle me into giving you leverage on some future case, forget it."

"All right. Look...... this is very difficult for me," explained Gustafson.

"Let me speak off the record for a moment, to be fair. I assigned Agent Alden to Springdale a couple of years ago. I also assigned Brian Murphy to work under you, here at the department. Both the Mayor's office and your office were the subject of a federal corruption probe, which as you know, yielded no results, yet."

"It has come to our attention that Agent Alden has not been, shall we say, 'forthright' with the bureau. For the last few weeks he has been under internal review for reasons I am not at liberty to say. What I can say, is that I personally need to know, before the courts and the media know, what allegations are being raised against my subordinates."

O'Donnell understood exactly what it was all about. The attorney only cared about saving his own butt and had little or no concern for anyone else's welfare. O'Donnell felt more in the driver's seat and offered a proposal to the federal attorney.

"I will share everything I know with you, tomorrow morning, after I have slept in my own bed."

O'Donnell reached out his hand for Gustafson to shake. The attorney ignored O'Donnell's outstretched arm and looked at the wise old Chief. He knew he met his match, but decided to call his bluff.

"Thank you very much for your time, Mr. O'Donnell. I will have someone escort you back to your cell."

O'Donnell stood up and threw his empty coffee cup in the basket and winked at the man for playing his little game so well.

"Yes...well if you 'need me' you know where I can be found." O'Donnell said with a smile. Gustafson opened the locked door, stepped out of the office and signaled for an officer to approach.

"Officer, would you please handcuff and bring the suspect back to his cell. And please take the main stairwell down to the basement level passed his comrades. I think ankle cuffs are appropriate, too, for this murderer. He is very uncooperative. Thank you for your help. I appreciate it."

The officer walked behind his former boss and whispered in his ear,

"I'm sorry about this Chief. You do understand, don't you?"

O'Donnell kept his eyes forward and answered,

"Don't worry about it. You're just doing your job. I'm the one that should be sorry."

O'Donnell put his hands behind his back to help the officer. As the officer and O'Donnell walked out of the office and through the record's office, O'Donnell noticed a Springdale Newspaper sitting on one of the desks.

The above the fold headline read:

Police Chief is Suspect in Rampage, Kills 2

The Chief stopped for a moment and looked at the paper and then lowered his face and walked down the familiar corridors and passed his former co-workers shaking his head in a stunned disbelief. When he arrived back to the basement holding area, there was another attorney waiting for him.

"Excuse me, officer, where has this man been?" asked the man.

"It's O.K. I had a meeting with someone," answered O'Donnell on behalf of the young officer.

"And who might you be? The court appointed suit, I assume."

O'Donnell had little confidence in young inexperienced public defenders. They were generally well meaning professionals, but O'Donnell felt this case was far too complex for a recent law school graduate to handle.

The young attorney introduced himself to O'Donnell as a partner in the area's most prestigious law firm. He went on to say that the entire firm had been retained by an anonymous client to represent him. O'Donnell could not believe his ears and asked the man to repeat his introduction to him, to make sure he heard right. The young defense lawyer asked the officer to uncuff O'Donnell and to immediately open a client conference room for an attorney/client briefing.

The two men entered the room and the lawyer took immediate control of the situation.

"O.K. now listen carefully, I don't know where you've been for the last thirty minutes, but we have a private hearing with a judge in less than one hour. Here, put this on and keep listening."

He handed O'Donnell a garment bag which was already hanging in the room. It contained a suit, shirt and tie already tailored perfectly to O'Donnell's measurements.

"We have already spoken to the prosecutor's office and they are allowing us to meet in private chambers, with a judge. Do not speak, unless spoken to by the judge. I can't go into details right now, but we have supplied the District Attorney's office with a copy of a television tape taken in Meadows clearly showing the shooter in the act. We intend to ask for a wave of bail hearing and agree to house arrest, pending further investigation. The firm believes a house arrest at this time will protect you. Do you have any questions Mr. O'Donnell?"

Before O'Donnell could answer, the young attorney continued...

"Good, put this suit on. Take this shaver and comb. Make yourself presentable. I need to sign some papers, so let's get going. I have never kept a judge waiting and I don't plan on starting today."

The longest night of O'Donnell's life had led into the fastest morning he could remember. In minutes, he was escorted out a rarely used back entrance of the building reserved for cafeteria deliveries and placed in an undercover, window-tinted vehicle by a plain clothes officer with the young attorney by his side, every step the way.

The Chief sat in the back seat between an officer and his new high profile council. He leaned over to the attorney and asked,

"Whom did you say hired you guys to help me?"

The attorney looked back at him and said,

"Shhhhhhhh, here..... you need a mint," and didn't say another word.

The next two hours were a blur to O'Donnell. He had no participation or input in the process and only spoke two words during the entire morning....

"Not guilty."

By noon, O'Donnell was sitting in front of his own television, in his own living room watching the national cable network reporters return to the small Western Massachusetts community for another sensationalistic news story. The reporters took their scripts directly from the Springdale Newspaper headline and weren't even aware that O'Donnell was at home and that the initial charges against him had been dropped.

Because the investigation was still open in Murphy's death, O'Donnell was required to remain in his house and wear an ankle bracelet. The law firm had hired a full-time 24 hour security officer, complete with canine support, to sit outside on O'Donnell's street in front of his house. Visitors to O'Donnell would require clearance from the officer and the law firm, before entering onto the property.

The Chief couldn't bear to watch any more of the pathetic news coverage. He shut the TV set off and called Suzie to let her know what was going on. Suzie had picked up Casey the night before, when O'Donnell had called her. She had not heard from the Chief since and was anxious to see him.

"My god, how are you?" Suzie asked. *"It is so good to hear your voice. I want to see you. When can I come down to the jail?"*

O'Donnell answered,

"Suzie, I'm at home, everything is all right. I want to see you too.

I'm so sorry about Murphy. We really need to talk." Suzie was surprised and happy to hear that O'Donnell was at home. She had no idea he had been released.

"I'm coming over right now," she told him.

"Suzie, actually I can't have any visitors until 5:00 tonight and you have to call this number...."

O'Donnell gave Suzie the contact at the law firm.

"Wow. You hired those guys?" Suzie asked.

O'Donnell answered,

"Well....no, I was thinking maybe ....you did."

Suzie snickered,

"Did you forget I work at a spa?... I will see you at five."

CHAPTER 48

I had mixed feelings about this day. I knew it was coming. In some ways I was looking forward to being extradited home and in other ways, I felt like the Gulf Coast was my new home. I had been notified by the warden's office that an escort was scheduled to arrive sometime in the mid-morning hours to bring me home to Springdale to face my fate choir.

There is something about New Orleans that is absorbed into your being. I don't know what it is. Maybe I lived here in a previous life and maybe my ancestry was calling me home. Whatever it was, I had a feeling I would return. The music, the food, the water, and the history of the people... it definitely called on my soul. It was warm, inviting comfort.

The guards at the jail I've come to know were actually a really nice group of guys. I sure don't envy their daily tasks. They delivered a fresh set of clothes and an extra bar of soap for me to feel better and look better during my trip home. My normal five minute cold shower was replaced by a ten minute steaming hot one, courtesy of the warden for my exemplary behavior. When I took my final procession passed my fellow jail mates, I received a strangely heartwarming applause. They knew I wasn't free, but somehow just leaving the building was an event for most of them, and they all wished me well.

The processing room was the same one I had entered through when I first was arrested, but the process was reversed. I received my personal bag, which contained the belongings I had with me when I first arrived. I was instructed to check off each inventoried item and sign the form. The clerk stamped several documents with large inked stamps and then stapled the bundle and handed it to the assigned officer.

I walked out of my temporary home and never looked back. I was placed in the back of a rented sedan and driven to the airport by two plain clothes, but armed, officers from Springdale. They were both quiet and very professional. They made it very clear that they were both carrying weapons and had authorization to use them, if necessary.

We were the last passengers to board the three-hour commercial flight back to New England. Prisoners are customarily held in a secured waiting area in the concourse and then notified by the airline when the other passengers are seated. I was seated between the two officers in the front row of the airplane.

As the plane lifted off, I thought of Kirk, like I so often did. The plane banked sharply to the right and I could see the beautiful aerial view of the coastline below. The speckled white dots of boats in the water trailed long white wakes behind. I could see a couple of large oil tankers being guided by tug boats through the narrow channels.

I wondered if Cole and Bill were among the vessels. I also wondered if I would ever see another sight as beautiful as that again. I wanted to make sure the moment left a warm imprint in my memory for the lonely and dark days possibly ahead of me, within prison's cold concrete walls.

CHAPTER 49

The Chief was pleased to be home, but still felt imprisoned. He couldn't leave his house, didn't want to watch television and had already burned the newspaper in his wood stove. Instead, he sat in his worn recliner, with a hand knitted blanket on his lap and played a word search game in a crossword puzzle book. At his side, were his telephone and a wooden spatula he used to itch his leg behind his ankle bracelet.

The monotony was broken by the sound of the doorbell and the opening of the door. It was the abrupt arrival of a team from the law firm. Four representatives entered the house, each with one briefcase and one laptop. Three eager members of the team walked in to greet O'Donnell before he could get out of his chair and the third member paraded through every room with a portable electronic detection apparatus that resembled a small satellite dish, with audio headphones attached.

When the technician came into the living room, he gave the remaining team members a "thumbs up" signal that one would assume meant that they were cleared to speak confidentially.

"Good afternoon, Mr. O'Donnell, I hope the anklet is not too uncomfortable for you. We have people working on having it removed, so… please be patient a little while longer."

The gentlemen introduced the other two men and one woman to O'Donnell. He qualified them as O'Donnell's exclusive team of "all stars" and requested that the Chief be completely open with them, while they asked him to disclose all the information he knew.

They were the best in the business and often beckoned to defend the most indefensible.

The leader of the team explained that their client's request was a bit unusual. The client asked that we start from the beginning with the Preston case and work forward.

Ordinarily a defense team's objective is to prove the accused innocent of the charges against him. In this case, their goal was to prove innocence by exposing guilt. The plan was to present a portfolio of evidence to the District Attorney's office. In essence, they were being asked to prepare a case for the prosecution from the perspective of a defense team that would know every possible loop hole.

O'Donnell walked into his bedroom and retrieved a cardboard storage box full of the voluminous materials he had uncovered. He carried it back to the living room and placed it on the floor. The team was impressed by O'Donnell's extensive work and was anxious to get started. Each team member grabbed a hand full of papers and went their separate ways to different rooms in the house. The Chief was amazed at the efficient clockwork the team exhibited.

O'Donnell remained in his recliner and one by one, the investigators would enter the living room and ask a quick and direct question and then return to their respective work areas. This went on for nearly two hours, before the leader summoned the team back into the living room for a preliminary summation.

Each team member sat on the floor with their legs crossed and their laptops in front of them on the floor.

"*O.K. Darren, you go first, what jumps out at you?*" the man pointed to the first investigator.

"*Thanks, well, among the papers I took, I found a printed picture of Agent Alden and Nicholas Cardoni together very intriguing,*" he picked up the photograph and passed it around the circle.

He asked O'Donnell to share with the others exactly who Cardoni was and what role he played in the evidence.

"O.K. Well, I made a few phone calls and discovered something else even more intriguing than their military association. Cardoni had worked for the FBI for a while, following his time in the service."

O'Donnell jumped in,

"Really? Oh....this is good. I wonder why he left."

The young man continued,

"He didn't leave. He was dismissed after his participation in a drug importing case he was working on. Apparently some of the confiscated evidence suddenly disappeared. It was never found. There doesn't appear to have been any charges against him, but my source tells me he was dismissed anyway. The FBI doesn't screw around."

O'Donnell was at the edge of his seat,

"I knew that guy was as crooked as my Adirondack walking stick. Did your source tell you what he allegedly stole?"

"Oh yeah...he sure did...three kilos of pure cocaine."

O'Donnell slapped his leg and pumped his fist.

"Oh my god, that no good bum. That's it! He was the link. I knew it. So it's true then, Alden and Cardoni were accomplices and only in it for the money and the agency had no clue."

Alden lied about the cocaine bait evidence. It never came from a tanker confiscation, as he had implied. It had come from his old Army buddy, Nicky Cardoni. They were planning on exploiting Kirk as the pawn in their own criminal enterprise and splitting the untraceable mob money, and if Kirk got killed in the process? Well..... it would leave more money for them.

"Good job, Darre. Stay on that for a while and see what else comes up. Cindy, go ahead..."

"O.K. thanks. I found some hand written notes by the Chief, regarding some blood stains found in a stolen car. The Chief tells me that Brian Murphy had the sample tested. Well, so did I, I had a

field forensics' guy get permission from our judge to make a field test at the impound yard. He just sent me a text message. The sample he tested, was O positive... could be anyone's.. Probably Kirk Preston's. He's on his way with an imprint from the computer cable to match to the coroner's casting of Kirk's fatal neck wound. We should know within the hour."

Nice job, Cindy, please follow up with the others tonight and cc me as well. Pete, go ahead."

Just as he was about to present, there was a knock at the door. One of the men signaled for the other to answer the door. It was the security officer with Suzie standing behind him. O'Donnell stood up from his chair and shouted for Suzie to come in. Suzie pushed herself passed the uniformed escort and rushed to O'Donnell's open arms where they tightly embraced. She kissed him on the cheek and said to him,

"I'm so sorry for what has happened. I'm sick about Murphy, I thought I knew him. I feel so violated, how can anyone be so evil, and the Mayor, oh Chief, the Mayor. I am just glad you're okay."

One of the team members asked her if she had been cleared and she responded that she had. He then asked her if she would wait outside. O'Donnell stopped the man and insisted that she be allowed to stay.

"This is Suzie Dillon, she compiled a great deal of this evidence, and she's like a daughter to me. I assure you she's O.K. I want her here with me to hear this. She can be trusted."

They returned to the living room and Suzie apologized for her interruption and introduced herself to each of them, but not until she gave O'Donnell a big hug and a kiss on the cheek. The team leader continued,

"All right, where were we?... Oh yes... Pete, go ahead"

"Thanks. Well I grabbed the folder that pointed to motive. It looks like Agent Alden had the most to gain and the accused Mr. Jesse

Thorpe he also had a policy motive, so I'll need to look at him a little closer. There was, however the matter of a trust fund life insurance policy for three million which has already been distributed."

Suzie interrupted,

"Excuse me, I don't mean to stop you, but I don't understand why Kirk would have a life insurance policy for his own trust fund?"

The young attorney answered,

"Well, there are several reasons why one might direct their trust fund as a beneficiary. Many trust funds continue to operate as a charitable trust. Some funds are automatically passed on to dependents. In this case, however, the beneficiary was clearly Kirk's brother."

O'Donnell and Suzie looked at each other as if they didn't clearly hear what he had said.

"Wait a minute.... Kirk's what?" asked Suzie.

"Kirk's brother," said the man as he looked down on his notes. *"Let me see...here it is...Preston...Derek Preston. It's a sealed file, but I was able to get a little information. He lives in Richmond, Virginia.*

Once I can eliminate Jesse Thorpe and Derek Preston from the motive list then I can better shine the spotlight on Alden."

Suzie looked at the Chief and exclaimed,

"I can't believe Kirk had a brother. But wait, remember when one of those television reporters ask you why Kirk had flown his plane to Richmond the night before the murder? Do you think Kirk went to see his brother? If he did, maybe he knows something. Do you think?"

The lead attorney responded,

"Anything is possible, we'll try contacting him.

Well, that's enough for today. We all have our work to do. We can follow up tomorrow. Thanks, Pete. Excellent job, all of you, excellent work. All right everyone, please complete a full footnoted narrative for me tonight and a prospective agenda for tomorrow. Any questions? All right good. We will see you back here again tomorrow at noon. Mr. O'Donnell, Ms. Dillon, It was a pleasure meeting you both. We will show ourselves out. Have a pleasant evening."

The team walked out of the house together and then left in separate vehicles. They took with them the cardboard box of files. After O'Donnell closed the door and locked the lock, he turned to Suzie and took a deep breath,

"Wow!...those guys are unbelievable. I need to sit down. Holy cow...wow, it's no wonder the rich always get off, when they can afford guys like that, yikes," O'Donnell remarked.

Suzie just sat still. O'Donnell asked her,

"Are you all right?"

"I'm fine," Suzie answered. *"You think you know someone really well and then a stranger that you never met comes along and blows it all apart."*

"You mean Murphy?" asked O'Donnell.

"Well of course, Murphy, but I'm talking about Kirk

I never knew Kirk had a brother. Why wouldn't he tell me that? It's just weird. I thought we were close and now, it's like, I don't know who he was."

O'Donnell put his arm around Suzie and consoled her,

"Hey, hey, I'm sure Kirk had his reasons. He was very private about his past. You know that."

Suzie wiped a tear from her cheek,

"I know. I don't know why that upsets me so much. I guess, I guess I just thought that we shared so much and now,...well..I don't know."

O'Donnell handed Suzie a tissue,

"Don't think about it, dear. Kirk was a great guy. Hey you know what? Let's get some delivery, what do you think? I'm starving and I can't go anywhere. What do you want pizza or Chinese? Or, do you need to get back for Casey?"

Suzie shouted,

"Casey? Oh my god! I forgot her outside in the car, poor little thing. I'll be right back."

Suzie ran outside and opened the door to her car and Casey jumped out and bolted for the front door. Suzie opened the door and the dog ran full speed to O'Donnell and jumped up onto his lap on the recliner and started licking his face.

"Hey little girl, I missed you too," O'Donnell laughed.

O'Donnell, Suzie and Casey spent the rest of the evening together and shared a large order of Chinese food and just spent quality time together, without television, without news. Even though they both still had the weight of the world on their shoulders, somehow the burden felt lighter, with the law firm's team doing all the work. O'Donnell was more confident than ever that there would soon be closure to all of the recent events.

Suzie continued to feel depressed. They talked about Murphy. Suzie felt much betrayed by his pretend friendship and was glad she had not grown closer to him, in spite of his advances. Suzie was a beautiful woman. Having advances made toward her, was something she was quite accustomed to. She liked Murphy, but never felt a real connection, as the one she held so deeply for Kirk. His death, nonetheless, was disturbing, but his dishonesty was unforgivable.

The subject of the Mayor and Murphy came and went throughout the evening, but Suzie's thoughts could not leave the news she had learned of Kirk's brother. Suzie said to O'Donnell,

"I'm very tempted to contact Kirk's brother. I know they say that these kinds of conversations seldom go very well, but there is a part of

me that feels empty, and if I can speak to him, maybe I'll feel closer to Kirk. What do you think?"

Chief answered,

"I don't know, I don't really see how it could help, and if it goes bad, it might even hurt worse. Maybe you should be thinking more about Jesse? You know if this law team can pull this case together, as it looks like they will...Jesse will be free and back home in a matter of weeks. Now that's something good to think about."

Suzie agreed and complimented O'Donnell for his wisdom. But, in the back of her mind, she still couldn't stop thinking about Kirk or his brother.

CHAPTER 50

O'Donnell slept like a log in his own bed and Casey's whimpering to go outside woke him around 10:00 in the morning. He hadn't overslept like that in weeks. He felt completely refreshed. After walking the dog in the back yard, he waved to the security guard sitting in his patrol car and grabbed the newspaper from the mailbox.

The Chief walked into his bathroom and turned the shower handle on and let the water run until the temperature was nice and warm. While he was waiting in his bath robe, he flipped over the newspaper and saw a very different headline from the previous day. The font was only half the size, but O'Donnell was pleased that the paper at least reported that the Chief was no longer a prime suspect in the Mayor's killing. As a follow up to the lead story, the newspaper also reported, *Jesse Thorpe Returns to Face Charges.*

O'Donnell had heard that the extradition was taking place, and hoped that the law team could make some quick progress and maybe delay the start of the hearing. The Chief reached into the shower to test the water temperature. Then he ripped the end of a plastic bread bag and wrapped it over his foot to protect his ankle bracelet from getting wet and then stepped into the soothing hot shower.

O'Donnell came out of the shower, towel-dried his hair and put on a pair of slacks and a sweatshirt. He grabbed his reading glasses and the newspaper, walked into the living room and sat down with a fresh brewed cup of black coffee. As he reached for his cup he noticed his answering machine's light was blinking and he had missed a phone call while he was in the shower. O'Donnell reached over to the machine and pressed the play button.

"Hi, it's me...maybe you're still asleep," it was Suzie leaving a message.

"I wanted to call you and let you know, that....well, I couldn't sleep at all last night. There's just too much on my mind. Anyway..... please don't be mad, but..well, I'm on my way to Virginia. I know what you're probably thinking, but I just have to meet him. I love you, and I'll call you,.... bye"

O'Donnell wasn't surprised. He knew she wouldn't let it go. He just prayed that she wouldn't get hurt. She was way too sensitive for her own good. O'Donnell's fatherly instincts understood that she needed to do this, whatever the outcome, good or bad.

Suzie had booked a flight to Richmond right at the airport counter and boarded immediately. She didn't check any bags. She just brought along a backpack with a change of clothes and few small toiletries. Before the plane took off, she called the spa to let them know she was not coming in again. The owner was not pleased and informed her that the spa really needed to hire someone and if that new person worked out, then Suzie might not be needed anymore.

She completely understood her bosses' dilemma and apologized if her absences had created any problems for the shop. The only problem, the spa manager told her was her apartment supervisor that kept calling, looking for her. Suzie asked for the man's number and promised to call him right away, which she did.

"Hello. This is Suzie Dillon in 617. I had a message to call the office," Suzie said.

"Yes, thanks for calling," the voice responded.

"We have been trying to get a hold of you for quite some time, regarding your friend, Jesse Thorpe?"

"Oh, I'm sorry, I've been traveling a lot and I....."

"It's O.K. Ms. Dillon; we have a package that was shipped to Mr. Thorpe and we signed for it. We really can't keep it here any longer. Could you?...."

Just then, the flight attendant asked everyone to turn off the electronic devices in preparation for takeoff.

Suzie quickly asked the apartment supervisor to send the package over to O'Donnell's house. She gave them the address and then apologized for having to hang up so quickly. Suzie stashed her phone away in her bag and sat back for her short one hour flight to Richmond.

She practiced in her mind, over and over...Hi Derek? You don't know me, but I was a close friend of your brothers... She tried to imagine what he looked like, did he have a family? wife? kids? When did he see his brother last? She had played every scenario imaginable in her head, except for the one she was about to live.

When her plane landed, she went directly to the car rental counter and asked for the smallest and cheapest car available. As usual, a man behind the counter was smitten with her radiance and offered her a free upgrade to a full-size model complete with a GPS features for no additional cost. Suzie accepted, and winked at the rental agent and walked away with a little extra hip action, much to the man's delight. No one ever liked to see Suzie go, but they always loved to watch her leave.

Suzie was actually quite happy she had accepted the larger upgrade. There was a torrential downpour as she exited the airport and the GPS would prove to be very helpful in guiding her onto a busy highway in the blinding rain. Sheets of rain blanketed the road and had ponded reservoirs of water which her rental car plowed through like a boat. After several minutes of verbal prompts, the navigation system led her off the interstate and onto a busy, secondary road. She stayed on this road for about twenty minutes, before the audio prompt instructed her to turn right on another path.

She came to a stop at the programmed location in front of an efficiency complex. Suzie wasn't convinced that she was at the right place, in spite of the electronic guidance. The attached single floor apartments looked like they had been renovated and converted from a motel at one time. The parking lot was directly in front of the building and each spot lined up with its respective exterior door. She was able to pull directly up to the unit where she was told Derek Preston lived.

Suzie lowered her visor and opened a lighted mirror to look at herself. She applied some fresh lipstick and a drop of perfume just below her right ear. There were flocks of butterflies in her stomach, none flying in formation, but there was no turning back. She could never live with herself if she did not follow through with speaking to Kirk's brother.

She had to meet him, hoping it would put closure to Kirk's death.

She opened the car door and ran, without an umbrella, through the rain to his numbered door. She took a deep breath and knocked. She stood and waited, but there was no response. She knocked again and then listened for any sound of movement inside, but she heard nothing. To avoid becoming completely drenched, Suzie ran back to her car and jumped inside and sat for a few minutes, considering her options.

Her heart began to sink at the thought of coming this far and not at the very least meeting him. She sat silently, starring through the blurring sheets of rain cascading down and covering her windshield. The windshield wipers were set on the intermittent mode and every sequence conjured another vision for Suzie as she contemplated her situation. She saw Kirk's casket, then me sitting behind the jail's glass window, the Chief in the hospital and later in an ankle bracelet and then Kirk again. At that very moment, something from deep inside triggered an uncontrollable emotion and she began to cry. Most of her life, her sweet tears had come from laughter and now they rolled from a bitter sadness.

Her tears bled from a heartfelt wound that would not heal. It may have been that she had never truly mourned Kirk's death. Preoccupied with proving my innocence and her denial of her loneliness, never allowed her the process of reflection and closure. And now, it seemed that any hope of finding some peace by being near Kirk's brother was setting behind a dark, bleak cloud.

Just as her tears had begun to run dry, the rain, too, began to let up and she decided to approach the door one more time and knock a little harder. Again, she waited. This time, she heard a faint voice from inside the door, *"it's open,"* the voice said. Suzie turned the doorknob and pushed the door open. The room was dark and musty and she didn't immediately see anyone inside.

She slowly and cautiously stepped in and purposefully left the door slightly open behind her, if for some reason she needed to exit quickly. It was a large open single room efficiency with a kitchen off to the side and an unmade double Murphy bed which collapsed into a wall. The room was full of book shelves with hundreds and hundreds of books. The far corner of the room looked like a NASA Command Center; there were four or five flat computer screens all lit up with actively rolling and streaming stock market graphs and charts. In the other corner was a single treadmill machine facing a shaded window, the only one in the room.

Suzie timidly and slowly walked forward,

"Hello? Hello, are you there? Hello, Derek?"

A man walked out from the bathroom door and walked toward Suzie with the aid of a metal crutch that was fitted around his lower right arm. He limped toward her in the dimly lit room,

"Hi I'm sorry, but I was unable to get to the door. Can I help you? I don't often get visitors," he said in a strangely slow and soft voice. Suzie couldn't see his face from where he was standing. She walked closer to him, to introduce herself, but he turned his face away.

"Hi Derek, my name is Suzie. I knew your brother Kirk. We were very close and I just wanted to talk to you and extend my sympathies to you."

The man turned away further from Suzie as she extended her hand to him and he responded in a soft fragile tone,

"Yes, well... I never knew my brother very well. But thank you. Did you come all the way from Massachusetts just to see me?"

"Yes, yes I did."

His back was still turned away from Suzie. He was clearly uncomfortable with her being there. Suzie also felt strange. She never knew that Kirk had a brother and just being near him felt weird. It was as if she was near a part of Kirk that had been taken away from her. The frame of his body and his movements were amazingly similar to Kirk's except for an apparent handicap and a shaved head. There was no mistaking though, he was definitely a Preston.

There was an awkward silence for several seconds or so. Suzie could hear the man sniffling and struggling. He could no longer fight the emotion. He raised his free hand to cover his eyes and began to cry.

"I never knew my brother," he cried.

Suzie approached him and put her hand on his shoulder to comfort him. She felt a chill.

"I never knew my own brother," he repeated.

Suzie hugged him from behind and tried to console Derek, even if it meant lying to him,

"It's .....O.K.. Your brother loved you very much. He was a great man and he loved you."

Suzie did her best to control her own emotions, but to no avail. They stood, as strangers, yet as one soul together in the middle of the room and wept. It was important for both of them to finally release their sadness and it was wonderful that they could be there for each other.

He dropped his crutch on the ground and turned his body to face Suzie and fell toward her, quickly hugging her tightly.

"Thank you for coming, thank you," he whispered to her. *"You are an angel. You are truly an angel."*

He kissed her on her neck and squeezed her even tighter. He cried on her shoulder and she cried on his. This odd closeness didn't bother Suzie. It's as if they both had been waiting to begin their healing, and now, by fate, they were here for each other.

"I should have been a better brother," he sobbed.

"It's O.K.. It's not your fault. Really it's O.K." she assured him.

He kissed her again on the neck, just behind the ear, this time longer and now with passion. He exhaled his warm breath onto her soft supple skin. Suzie began to instantly feel uncomfortable. The supportive hug had turned awkwardly affectionate. Suzie dropped her arms to the side and tried to lean away, hoping he would release, but he continued his embrace of her. Suzie's breasts were pressed firmly against his chest. She felt her heart pounding as she struggled for every full breath. She fought to channel her fisted hands up to her chest between their two wedged bodies and tried to push him away.

"Don't fight it. I need to feel you, my angel," he insisted.

"No," she whispered back to him with more urgency, *"I can't do this, please, let go, please stop."*

He released his clutching grasp and leaned away from Suzie.

For the first time, in the darkened room, their eyes made direct contact. Suzie's eyes instantly widened then became absorbed deep into his, melting away, her eyes slowly closed.

She felt her body go limp and her knees buckle. A chilling rush climbed the back of her neck. She stood speechless and motionless and felt a conscious disconnect with her being. The world had stopped. Suzie's world had stopped. He pulled her fainting body tight to his body again, kissing her and whispering softly into her ear,

"Suzie....it's all right... it's me, Kirk."

CHAPTER 51

The "all star" legal team arrived at O'Donnell's house promptly at 12:00 noon, with an entire afternoon of case study to conduct. Pete, one of the investigators from the previous day was absent. The team entered the house led by an officer of the court. The officer, immediately upon entering, approached the Chief and asked him to take a seat. He knelt down in front of him and removed the house arrest ankle device.

While leaning over and rubbing his ankle, O'Donnell thanked the team for their quick work on having the court-ordered bracelet removed. Just as the previous day, the legal team sat down in a circle on the floor in the living room. This time, however, they had four large cardboard boxes, instead of O'Donnell's one box. Evidently, the team had been working around the clock, gathering pieces of the intricate jig saw. The puzzle was taking form and the image of Agent Wayne Alden was predominately the central figure. The team would focus on Alden all afternoon.

Before the team separated into their work areas, they conducted an informal discussion about Alden and yearned to know more about him from the Chief's experiences. O'Donnell talked about their first meeting in the Mayor's office and his best recollection of what took place.

"I should have suspected that he was up to something. I never liked the guy, but he did have plenty of authority. Springdale was in a losing battle on the streets against these drug gangs. I suppose I overlooked his motives because of my love for this city. This used to be such a great place."

The Chief went on for several minutes describing what the city was like when he was their age. In an effort to bring O'Donnell back to the subject of Alden, one of the investigators asked,

"When was the last time you saw Agent Alden?"

O'Donnell paused,

"Well...let me think. I'm not sure I saw him again or least if I did, I didn't speak to him. All of his meetings were with Kirk at the Meadows High School track."

One of the team asked,

"Were those the meetings that Jesse Thorpe heard from the announcer's booth?"

O'Donnell nodded in agreement,

"Yes, did I already tell you about that?"

The investigator replied,

"No, that was information that we gathered from Jesse himself."

O'Donnell seemed surprised,

"You've spoken to Jesse?"

In a matter of fact legal tone the attorney answered,

"Yes, we are representing him and we spoke to him this morning, as a matter of fact, Pete, one of the lawyers you met yesterday, is with him right now."

"Wow. You will be representing him?" O'Donnell asked.

The team leader jumped in,

"Well, technically, no, but our client has requested that we turn this case upside down. I am confident that when we do, Jesse will land on a soft cushion, and be completely exonerated of his charges too. We are only in the early stages, but we have a second team, back at the firm, already preparing a civil trial against the Federal Government.

So that should tell you something about our confidence," informed the Attorney.

O'Donnell said with a grateful emotion,

"I don't know who hired you, but boy am I glad you guys came around. I think Alden's fall from his pedestal has already begun. At least that's what the US Attorney, back at the jail told me..."

"Whoa, whoa, wait a minute...you spoke to a US Attorney? When? Yesterday?"

The silence was deafening. Everyone stopped what they were doing a looked up at the Chief. The team leader snapped his fingers and pointed to Cindy.

"Cindy, this one's yours."

Cindy flipped open and turned on her laptop and said,

"O.K. Chief, tell me exactly what he said, word for word, as best as you can."

The Chief went on to describe their conversation and his arrogant demeanor. O'Donnell was a pro at remembering details. His photographic memory exposed Gustafson's mood at the time and developed a theory for his changing tone, during their meeting.

The team found it interesting that O'Donnell sensed a moment of vulnerability and weakness from the federal official when he spoke about "his people."

O'Donnell continued,

"The guy even said that there was some sort of 'internal review' happening with Alden. He said it was off the record."

The team laughed in unison.

"A US Attorney off the record and about his own negligence? Yeah, right. He needed something from you and he was just trying to be chummy."

After hearing these new revelations, Cindy excused herself,

"I need to make a few calls, so if you don't mind...I am going to head to the other room and get to work."

The others continued to talk about Alden, Murphy, Kirk and everyone else involved in the case. During the course of their discussions and questions, the security guard watching the house from the outside came inside the front door.

"Mr. O'Donnell...there's a package here for you. Where would you like me to put it?"

O'Donnell looked over at the officer and asked him to just place it in the hallway and then thanked him for bringing it inside.

Cindy walked back into the living room and interrupted the session.

"Hey guys, are ya ready for this?...You're gonna love this one...the internal FBI investigation on Alden? Well, my source tells me that Alden was sitting at his desk watching his computer do a live tracking of a package and the package came right to the federal building door.

Apparently, he ran down to the security desk and tried to intercept the box before security could run it through the screening machine, but he was too late. Guess what was inside the box that was addressed to him?... an FBI GPS tracker and a kilo of Cocaine."

"What?" yelled one of the team members.

"It gets better....there was a note inside that said, I can't go through with your sting."

O'Donnell stood up with excitement,

"Who sent him the package?"

Cindy answered,

"They couldn't tell me. I'm working on that, I'm sure that they're trying to cover that up. I did find out though, that the package had originated from pick up location number #119. I ran a data base of

the courier's locations and #119 is located at the *Westford Municipal Airport,"* she added.

O'Donnell sat back down with a smirk on his face.

"That's Kirk for you. He was very special, one unique guy. Ha! He covered all the bases. He wasn't going to go down alone. Not Kirk.....ha... I love it. He knew all along that Alden was gonna screw him for the money, unbelievable. I wish I could have seen Alden's face.

The Chief looked up to the heavens and said,

"That's classic Kirk, simply classic."

Cindy responded,

"Well, it's fun information, but knowing the feds, it's going to be difficult to get anything out of them. Hey, at least we know that Alden is no longer in a position to sabotage our case."

"Great, excellent work, Cindy. With Murphy and Alden out of our way, it'll be a lot easier. We still need to pin the tail on Alden's operation with Kirk, if we're to spring Jesse. Keep going everyone. Pete should be here shortly. He'll fill us in on Jesse's information."

The team split up and worked for the remainder of the afternoon, with an occasional question for O'Donnell, to keep them on track.

CHAPTER 52

Kirk brought Suzie a tall glass of ice water and a couple of aspirin and handed them to her. She was sitting on a small love seat couch and still in a mild state of shock. Kirk pulled a computer office chair up in front of her and sat down. He picked up her feet and gave her a foot massage, to calm her nerves. Kirk would always give Suzie a foot massage after she ran in her marathons, it always helped her to relax.

"Please don't say a word. Let me explain everything from the beginning and please remember," he paused..... *"I love you very, very much. I never meant for this to happen like this."*

Kirk looked at Suzie sitting on the couch, with a tissue box on her lap, completely confused.

"When I was eleven years old, I lived with my parents and my twin brother Derek on Long Island......"

For the first time in his life, Kirk was sharing his deepest thoughts and memories of his tragic childhood, while Suzie sat and gazed into a deadman's eyes brought back to life and into his childhood.....

"After the fatal accident, Derek went to live with our grandfather and I was adopted and moved to Meadows. The social workers and the courts believed that we would have a better chance of living a 'normal life' if we started over without each other together to relive our memories of the past."

"My brother, Derek, was not as fortunate as me. My grandfather was a wealthy man and did his part to provide for us through a trust

fund, but he did nothing to help parent Derek during some difficult and impressionable years. When our grandfather died, Derek and I were only eighteen years old."

"I wasn't even allowed to contact him and it took years for me to even find out where he lived. It wasn't until just a few years ago that I spoke to him for the first time. Derek had not lived well. Even when we grew up together he was always sad. He never wanted to play ball or do anything. Looking back, I suppose he suffered from depression even then and battled with it his whole life. When we turned twenty-one, I finally was able to unseal the records of his adoption and I contacted Derek." "He had lived most of life as a recluse, never leaving this very room. He was a genius when it came to computers. I learned lately that he had hacked into some system and began controlling our trust fund,... from his own computer. From what I can gather, he traded in tech stocks and in commodities. I never even knew."

"When the market crashed, he lost everything, millions. I knew something was wrong. All of my accounts had run dry. He came clean just a few weeks ago when I called him on a whim. He was sick over it. I didn't really care. I never worried about money. In fact, when the funds ran dry, I just assumed I had blown it all away."

"Well, the next part is kind of complicated...I came into some money, a lot of money. And I was worried about Derek. So, I decided to fly down here and see him."

Kirk stopped for moment and borrowed one of the tissues from Suzie's box. He turned his eyes away from her and lowered them to the floor. He wiped his eyes and blew his nose.

"This part is very difficult," he said to Suzie.

Suzie put her feet on the floor and leaned forward and took Kirk's hands in hers. She had never seen him like this before. Kirk was always a tower of strength and rarely showed any sensitive emotions.

"It's O.K. Honey, you don't have to...."

"No, I can do this, it's all right" Kirk said, *"When I came to the door of this apartment he didn't answer my knock. I listened and I could hear the sound of the telephone receiver, off the hook. I tried the door handle and the door opened,"* Kirk paused and took a breath.

"When I came inside, I saw Derek hanging from the light fixture. He wasn't moving or breathing. His limp body was just slowly turning. It is an image I will never be able to erase, ever. I ran over and cut the cord down with a knife from the kitchen, but it was too late."

Suzie dropped to her knees in front of Kirk and hugged him around his legs, as he cried.

"There was blood all over him and on the rug beneath him. He had hung himself with a computer cable. The wire had severed its plastic coating and cut into his throat. There was nothing I could do." "I sat on the floor and held him in my arms for an hour. His pain had finally come to an end, after so many years. A part of me had just died too. He was my identical twin and he was gone. I couldn't leave him there and I didn't want anyone to know what he had done, he was too proud and the family name had already endured too much. I couldn't bear to explain to anyone about his life, about my life. I wrapped him up in the rug and put him in the car and drove back to the airport. I carried the wrapped up rug with his body inside and placed it in my plane."

"I flew his body back to Massachusetts..... He deserved so much more. Flying the plane was one of the most difficult things I had ever done. It was a very cloudy day, a deep thick layer of clouds. I am not instrument trained, so I rarely fly above the clouds where I can't see land. But on this day I did. Something just drew me higher and higher. I broke through the cover and it was like another dimension. A clear sky, peaceful, alone, separated from the world. Suzie, you know I was never a very religious kind of guy, but when I was alone

with Derek and flying near the heavens, I felt as though I was in God's presence. I talked with God and with my brother. I prayed for him. I was at peace and I felt that he was already in a better place. Derek had always feared living more than he feared dying."

"All that remained now was a soulless body. When I got back home to Westford Airport, I placed his body in the trunk of a borrowed friend's car and drove him to a place that was special to both of us, Mt. Tom. The mountain was a place where Derek and I once played together as kids, during a family trip to Massachusetts. It was one of the few happier memories that we held on to. When I moved to New England, it became my most favorite place to rock climb."

"I put my wallet in his pocket with all my I.D.s, and clipped my phone to his belt. Then I gently laid him down at the base of the mountain. I put my climbing boots on his feet and left the climbing jacket that I always used with carabineers attached, next to his body. I was originally planning on climbing with Jesse on that day, so they were the only extra clothes I had with me."

"I even trimmed his hair to my length. I knew that when he was discovered, they would assume it was me and he would have a proper burial. Please Suzie....I never meant to hurt you or anyone. I just needed some time to myself. Please try to understand. The old Kirk died and was left on that mountain too."

"So, I have been living in Derek's apartment, as Derek. I was nearly ready to find a way to contact you. I really was. I haven't watched television or read any news. I had no idea, of all the problems that I had caused back home. Please, please understand me. I needed time and now I feel reborn. I love you so much and I promise you, I will make this up to you and all of my friends. I can't change the past. I know that."

"When everyone thought I had died, a life insurance policy replaced all of the family money that Derek had lost. I didn't feel guilty accepting the money; there was a death, even though it was suicide. I

know he is smiling down for the first time and I know he's free. No one can ever know what happened, no one. It's too late now. I will always be Kirk to you, but always Derek to the rest of the world."

Kirk stood up and held Suzie in his arms.

"Help me start a new life. I will love you and I will consider each and every day a gift. I want it all, you, a family, everything."

Suzie squeezed Kirk in her arms and cried a river for him and for her, a river of flowing sadness carrying them together to an oasis of peace.

What Kirk had not shared with Suzie was the whole drug sting operation. They would later talk in detail about what had happened. Suzie explained how much she knew from working with O'Donnell and from her trip to New Orleans. Kirk described how he borrowed his friend Pierre's car at the airport. Pierre's car also had a gate transponder and could leave the gated area without security's knowledge.

He then drove to Holyville where he had left Derek's body in a crevice on Mt. Tom, and how afterwards he planted the bloodied rug and the computer cable back into the trunk of his friend, Pierre Corriveau's car to be discovered later as evidence. He also left the third kilo of cocaine on the backseat, in the dirty laundry bag as the cheese for the rat's trap.

Then he called the rat pack leader, Angel Lopez, and told him his Corvette had been followed and he would need to change the pick up location for the drugs to a different car. He informed Lopez he parked the car in a parking lot near Mt. Tom, in Holyville. He described exactly where the car was located and where to find the keys. Then he called the Holyville Police. He impersonated Pierre Corriveau, and reported the car stolen and tipped them off to where he suspected the thieves might be.

The keys were no where to be found, and just as Kirk had planned, Lopez smashed the window to get the drugs and, minutes later, he was out of the picture, no longer a threat. Arrested for possession of a controlled substance and grand theft auto. But thanks to the diligent work of Chief O'Donnell, finding Kirk's planted evidence in the impounded car trunk, Lopez was subsequently booked on 1st degree murder charges for strangling football star Kirk Preston over a drug deal gone bad and initiated by FBI Agent Wayne Alden.

Lopez was also charged with the murder of his gang boss, Vincent Armando. By the time Lopez was being locked up, Kirk was already asleep on a bus, heading back to Richmond. It was a brilliant twist; Kirk had framed Angel Lopez for his own murder, finally putting him away, along with Alden for his dastardly deeds that ultimately and unfortunately killed the good Mayor and the impressionable young detective. They both did themselves in, driven by selfish greed. The tainted money would now help rebuild Kirk's life and the insurance policy proceeds would take care of and redeem his closest friends.

Suzie sat there, taking it all in, in disbelief, yet the reality provided her with a miracle. Her Kirk was alive and she was in his arms.

CHAPTER 53

The legal team was finishing their session at O'Donnell's house and informed him, the remaining work would likely be taking place at their office. They all thanked him for his help and for his generous hospitality. They reminded him that, although the bracelet had been removed, he was technically not supposed to leave his residence.

O'Donnell asked them what the next step would be and if he would hear from them. They could not give him a definite answer to the time frame, other than to say... the legal process moves slowly. They promised to do everything they could to move it along. But unless some new "breaking evidence" was to come along, it would likely be several weeks, if not months.

O'Donnell was hoping it would all end sooner and before any trials started. He saw them to the door and wished them well, offering his help to them, at any time. O'Donnell closed the door, turned and stumbled over the package on the floor that had been delivered earlier in the day. He finally picked it up and placed it on his dining room table. O'Donnell walked back into the living room for his glasses and for a pocket knife to open the box.

He put his glasses on and read the return address on the package. It read: Holiday Inn Indianapolis, Indiana. O'Donnell didn't bother with the pocket knife. He quickly ripped the box opened and read a note on the top which said, *"Dear Mr. Thorpe, we found a few items, which you must have left behind, during your last stay with us. We hope you will visit the Hoosier State again real soon. Have a nice day."*

O'Donnell scrambled through the Styrofoam pellet packaging and picked up, from the bottom of the box, the mini recording machine with tape. With his heart beating and his hands trembling, he nervously pressed the rewind button. When the tape stopped, he pressed the play button and turned up the volume. The next sixty minutes played as clearly as a bell, every minute of every meeting between Kirk and Agent Alden that I had secretly recorded at the high school track while hiding in the announcer's booth. O'Donnell kissed the recorder and sang out loud,

"I love.....the folks from Indiana."

This was it - the "blue dress" evidence that would indisputably blow the case wide open. It was only a matter of days before the law firm had authenticated and copied hundreds of tapes and announced there would be a "bombshell" news conference on the steps of Springdale City Hall at 5:00 pm Friday evening and another at 9:00 pm later that same night.

The firm knew exactly how to use the press to its full advantage and would maximize the live coverage, nationwide. The media, which had been so cruel and judgmental to all in the early stages of the case, would now be their most effective ally. The courts of our government move slowly, but the courts of public opinion move with satellite swiftness. The firm distributed tapes to every news director, producer, editor and writer in the Northeast market.

For the next several nights, members of the legal council team appeared on every cable news program from New York to Los Angeles. The incredible story of how a local hometown hero got caught up in some high stakes game of drugs, murder, and an FBI cover up was too tantalizing to resist for a rating hungry media. Excerpts from the tapes I had recorded played continuously, with subtitled text streaming below a still photograph of Kirk in an old high school football uniform.

The clear evidence was devastating to the FBI. The official statement from the Bureau was that they were conducting their own independent investigation and would allow due process to unfold. They were obviously planning on hanging Alden out to dry and not accepting any responsibility for his unethical actions.

The legal team would not go into detail, but alluded to additional evidence that would expose Brian Murphy's involvement in the cover up and the killing of Mayor Sullivan, brainwashed in a Manchurian way to unwillingly act out Alden's superior commands. It was a slam dunk that shattered the backboard glass and would be only a matter of days and some routine paperwork before I would actually be free.

CHAPTER 54

Suzie spent the night with Kirk in Derek's Richmond apartment. They never went to sleep. Instead, they sat snuggled together on the couch and talked. Kirk lit a candle on the coffee table in front of them and shut all the remaining lights off. The glow from the single flame flickered light upon the walls and ceiling and warmly glowed upon their faces. They sat there embraced, all night.

Both Suzie and Kirk felt a need to begin their relationship and most other aspects of their lives over again. They knew they could never go back to Meadows and needed to leave Virginia as well. Kirk agreed that a move was in order and that he could afford to take her anywhere in the world to start their lives together.

Suzie shared and described the feeling she had when she was in New Orleans and how being on the water was spiritual to her. She suggested the Gulf Coast might be a good place to start. In many ways, Suzie's intuition came from an inner feeling of hope and renewal. It may have been from a subconscious sense. Just like their own lives, New Orleans, too, was recovering from a tragedy and rebuilding from its inner soul outward.

In the morning, Suzie called O'Donnell to check on him. She couldn't tell him about Kirk. Possibly, when the time was right in everyone's lives, the truth would be divulged among their closest confidants. Until then, it was a secret that could not be shared with anyone, even with her dearest of friends.

O'Donnell was excited to receive Suzie's call. He was so ecstatic to tell her the news of the newly-found tape, and the press coverage, that he never even asked about her visit in Virginia. He expressed his elation for the reward of their hard work and for the soon-to-be justice against those responsible for ruining so many lives.

"I can't believe it's almost over," O'Donnell said. *"The law firm tells me that they even think Jesse could be out as early as next week. Can you believe it? And that's not all ..."* O'Donnell hardly took a breath between sentences...

"They called from the police station. The commissioner asked me if I wanted to come back as their full time Chief, on an interim basis, until they decide what direction they're going. He wants me to help chart a course for them. I haven't decided yet. Everything is happening too fast."

"That's wonderful. I am so happy for you and for Jesse. This is awesome," said Suzie.

The Chief continued,

"Where are you? Can you come over later? I thought we could open some Champagne and celebrate. I still have to stick around my house."

"That sounds excellent. I would love to. But, actually Chief,... I'm still in Virginia. I'm not sure when I'll be home. I've really learned a lot about Derek and gotten to know more about him, and....well, I feel as though, I'm sort of needed here right now, so.... I think I'm going to stay a bit longer. But, keep that Champagne on ice and we'll have it with Jesse. I'll call you later, OK? ... Oh Chief...one more thing... you were right...everything worked out just fine. I'll call you later, thanks...I love you, bye.."

Suzie hung up the phone and told Kirk the good news about the case and that Alden had one foot inside the jail door already. Kirk was thrilled that things had moved so quickly and with great results.

He hugged and kissed Suzie again and said,

"You made this all turn out right you know. You are amazing. You really are."

Suzie smiled up at Kirk,

"Thanks. It wasn't all me, though. The Chief worked really hard on this case, ya know. It also didn't hurt that we had the best law firm in the Northeast on the case,"

Suzie squinted her eyes at Kirk as if he had something to do with it.

Kirk then said,

"Really? You had a law firm help?" he smiled back at her and winked his eye.

CHAPTER 55

It seemed like it all happened in a past life, when I look back at it now. When I really think about it, I wouldn't have changed a thing. I try to picture what my life would have been, if I was still selling sneakers for a living. What little I knew back then and how little I appreciated things and friends. It sounds kind of corny, but it's true - there really is a rainbow behind every rain cloud.

I'll never forget when the Chief and I pulled into the marina parking lot in New Orleans with a 40-foot truck full of our life's possessions. It all seems like a distant dream now. At the end of the lot, against the backdrop of sailboat masts and an endless blue horizon was the restaurant, the restaurant with a huge sign on the roof written in illuminated cursive lettering;

Jesse's.

When I think back to Suzie and who I thought was Derek standing outside and giving me the keys to my restaurant, I can hear their voices as if they were standing in front of me right now,

"Hi Jesse!! Hi Chief!! Welcome to Jesse's," and then tossing me the keys.

It still gives me a chill, just thinking about it. When I walked up to the outside door, my feet did not touch the ground - it was like a dream that floated my being ahead of my body. I was greeted by my long lost dog Casey and her new boyfriend Rudy. Can life truly be this perfect now? Casey spends most of her days barking at Pelicans to get off the dock and Rudy keeps a watchful eye on her every move.

It was overwhelming at first. My new friend from weeks earlier was now my new business partner, Captain Bill. Bill had a real lore for the ropes of the restaurant and bar business; like me, he just needed a break in life. Within days I was interviewing dozens of prospective waitresses and barmaids for the grand opening of Jesse's.

It was incredible having Derek and Suzie around. I never knew that Kirk had an identical twin. It was almost eerie being around him at first. It took a few weeks before he finally invited me out on his boat, or should I say yacht, for a little "one-on-one-get-to-know-each-other time." He bought the boat from Captain Bill for more money than Bill was asking. Bill used every penny to get himself out of debt and when I received my check for a million dollars from Kirk's life insurance policy, I knew the business that Derek and Suzie had bought for me would result in a huge long term success.

It was the first time I had been alone with Derek. Well, sort of alone. Remember my buddy Cole? He became Derek's first mate and was paid handsomely to maintain Derek's boat for him. We headed out for some fishing that day and a few cold beers. Derek and I sat in the two fighting chairs on the back of the boat, while Cole headed for the gulf -stream waters in search of game fish.

I remember how it all unfolded. I was sitting next to him and experiencing a surreal feeling of being with Kirk. Derek and Kirk were identical alright, except for their hair and Derek's moustache. Even their voices were exactly the same. I wanted to share so many things with Derek about his brother. It seemed strange that I would know his brother better than he had.

I looked over and said,

"You know. Your brother was an incredible guy. He was my best friend in the whole world. Maybe it explains why I finally feel so good again, about life. When I'm around you and Suzie, It's like things used to be. Only now.... I know myself better and I can accept things."

I had nearly forgotten, I had planned for days to give Derek Kirk's watch, which he had loaned to me before I mistakenly went to

Indiana for that sales presentation. It seemed like decades ago. Talking about him again reminded me.

> *"Oh, by the way, this watch I'm wearing, it's your brother's. You should have it. I feel funny wearing it now."*

I took off the watch and handed it to him. Derek took it from me and held it in his hand and looked at it in silence. Derek wore an arm brace on his left arm and never took it off. I never asked him what it was for. It didn't seem to bother him very much. I wasn't sure if he was a watch wearing kind of guy, but I thought having something belonging to his brother, might be kind of cool.

Just then Cole spotted some big fish on his screen, he shouted down from the crow's nest controls for us to get ready and get geared up. In an odd tone, Derek looked over at me, eye to eye, and asked if I was ready. Then he took off his arm brace and put the watch on. That's when I knew. I looked at his arm and there it was...the football tattoo that he had gotten, with me, in Vegas. It still gives me chills when I think about that moment.

He looked at me, smiled and said, *"Hey Jesse. I missed you."*

When I reflect back on good and bad times in my life, there are not years or days that come to mind, there are moments. They are solitary fleeting moments that mark chapters with montage images poised on the turning paths of our existence. This was certainly one of the moments. A moment where nothing more needed to be said, understood, questioned or explained. I will never forget it. We live for moments. We become our moments.

We fished for hours, laughed and even cried a little. At times, we acted as though we were sweating and needed to wipe our eyes, but we both knew they were tears of released anguish. Aristotle had it right when he described true friends as two individuals sharing one soul. We never talked about what had happened, it didn't really matter. All was good. Suzie gave me the entire story, later that night. It was still too difficult for Kirk to talk about and I never brought up the subject again.

Wow, what a whirl wind. And so, here I am. Life is great. Actually it always was. I just never knew. I was so obsessed with trying find myself and defining my identity, that I overlooked the real answer all along. It was a calming acceptance of who I am, not who I thought I was or wanted to be. It can't be taught, learned or counseled, it needs to enlighten from within you and on its own terms and its own process.

In the end, it wasn't hard work, an education, a spiritual moment or even luck that brought me to my rainbow. It wasn't position, power or money that rewarded me. It was friends, true friends, like the friends you had when you were ten. Why could they so easily accept me for who I was, while I struggled in finding myself, for most of my life? Because, they just did.

Chief O'Donnell had met a lady friend who managed the kitchen staff. She made the finest jambalaya in Louisiana and he ate at the bar every night, with her by his side. During the day, he was in charge of security for the entire marina. This basically meant, he would walk along the docks at night and check on the boats. It took him no time at all to know every single boat owner and he would often go out on excursions with them, along with his female companion. Often Rudy and Casey would tag along, too.

While sitting on the outside deck sampling our new menu and sipping on a Margarita, soaking in the beautiful day, Cole walks out from inside the restaurant and says,

"Hey Jesse, come on, it's time."

I walk inside to find O'Donnell sitting at the bar with a remote in his hands pointed to the television and watching a news video of a remorseless Agent Alden, handcuffed and walking through a blizzard of snow amid dozens of news hound cameras.

"Come on, Chief, Cole says it's time." O'Donnell points the remote to the television and presses the power button.

"How do I look?" he asks.

I look at him and smile,

"You look great."

We walk out of the restaurant door and down to the beginning of the dock. O'Donnell stood there and proudly waited. He's dressed in a white formal police captain's dress jacket with a bow tie and his hat under his arm right arm to his side. His hair is slicked back and his handlebar moustache is waxed, perfectly groomed and shaped. With a twinkle in his eyes, he turns to smile at Suzie who had just locked her arm with his. They look at each other and then turn to face down the long dock.

The Chief had always dreamed of walking down the aisle escorting a beautiful bride. Every pylon on the dock was adorned with a bouquet of yellow roses and a long white carpet had just been rolled out in front of them. Suzie was wearing a stunning white chiffon dress that flowed in the warm breeze and a yellow sash around her waste, which matched the white and yellow Daisy flowers in her hair. Together they slowly walk down the picturesque aisle, lined by well-wishers on the stern of every docked boat.

At the end of the dock, Kirk is standing in endless awe of her beauty waiting to take her hand. When they meet, the Chief extends her hand to his and kisses her, before stepping back. Captain Bill performs an emotional service about friends, love and eternal happiness. They had each written their own vows to proclaim their fate to be together for eternity.

The emotions of the moment are eclipsed only by the ring ceremony. Chief O'Donnell steps forward and hands each of them their rings to exchange with each other. The Chief had commissioned a jeweler to design two exquisite rings from Kirk's old football ring. Hers would be a brilliant diamond in a delicate, but stunning Tiffany setting and his, a solid circle of strength.

Only Kirk and Suzie fully understood the meaning of recreating something from their past. A moment which symbolized two hearts combined into one. The ring, which was once only an identity for Kirk, in his early years, became the clue that exposed the truth, freed him from his lonely soul and united him with his destined love.

When the service ends, there are numerous champagne corks popping and horns blowing from every boat in the marina and from dozens more, anchored and watching from the harbor's bay.

When it is official, the party begins. The sound of a Dixieland band trumpets from the restaurant's balcony, playing "When the Saints Go Marching In." It was the same band I had met at the bonfire party. They now had a full-time gig, working for me. Oh yeah, remember the law intern I met in jail? I always kept her business card. I called her and invited her to the wedding as my guest. She had learned of my acquittal and accepted my invite.

It was definitely celebration time. Suzie and Kirk step onto their yacht and wave to their new friends and to their old friends. Suzie throws her bouquet of flowers to a group of young girls watching nearby and throws kisses to everyone else.

The boat pulls away from the dock and motors into the setting sun. The handsome honeymoon couple stands hand-in-hand, raising a glass to each other and then to the delight of all, turn and share a passionate kiss.

Dozens of streamers and balloons are attached to the stern of the boat, blowing in the wind. As the boat drifts away, all that could be seen are the decorations on the back, the silhouetted embraced couple, and the gold stenciled name of their beautiful yacht....

"Dirty Laundry"

Epilogue

Kirk and Suzie's friends continued the wedding celebration well into the night and when complete darkness befell the docks, I invited everyone into the restaurant to continue the party inside. O'Donnell locked up the marina office and grabbed the marina's portable radio receiver and clipped it to his belt and with a flashlight in one hand and a glass of champagne in the other, headed up to the party.

Before he could reach the top of the stairs, a call came across the radio calling for the harbor master. The daytime harbor master had long left the marina and gone home. When a call came over the radio at night, often O'Donnell would respond to the caller. O'Donnell considered not answering the call, but then thought that it perhaps could be Kirk.

He put down his champagne glass and flashlight, unhooked his radio and raised it to his mouth.

"This is Harbor Master New Orleans 14." O'Donnell paused for a moment and waited for a response. The voice on the other end was a man with a heavy accent.

"Harbor Master 14, this is the vessel Phoenix requesting dockage for the night."

O'Donnell responded,

"Negative, I am sorry we cannot accommodate," and then O'Donnell placed the radio back onto his belt and walked into the restaurant. There was some continued chatter on the radio, which O'Donnell ignored.

O'Donnell entered the noise filled room of partygoers and was immediately whisked away by two young ladies, one on each of his arms. They lead him directly to the dance floor, in front of the dixieland band and forced him to jump into a congo line dance. O'Donnell's laughter could be heard across the room. The band had handed out tambourines, kazoo horns and whistles to everyone in the restaurant and most wore party hats and, of course, the customary Mardi gras beads. It was a grand party and one I will never forget.

After about an hour of revelry, I invited O'Donnell outside for a Cuban cigar which Kirk had given to me before the ceremony. It felt good to step out. It was a clear starlit night and the cool ocean air was refreshing to breathe and the placid silence was a welcomed change. Within minutes, O'Donnell's radio signaled another wireless call. Again, it was the vessel Phoenix requesting permission to dock at the marina.

I asked O'Donnell,

"Who the hell wants to come into the marina at this hour?"
O'Donnell raised his eyebrows and shook his head,

"Beats me, but they're pretty persistent."

"Why don't you offer him Kirk's slip? He and Suzie won't be back for a least a couple of weeks."

The marina rarely welcomed transient boaters. For the most part the marina was occupied by permanent resident boat owners. It was only when one of the slips was vacated by a resident on an extended excursion, that any room for visitors was even possible.

O'Donnell agreed,

"All right, I guess so. They must be desperate or they wouldn't be calling back this late. They better be big tippers."

O'Donnell grabbed his radio and keyed the transmit button,

"Phoenix, come in, Phoenix, do you read me? This is New Orleans Harbor Master 14."

The same man with the accent responded,

"Copy, this is the Phoenix, go ahead 14."

O'Donnell raised the radio and announced,

"We have one slip available for short term. Identify your vessel, out."

The man replied,

"Thank you very much; we are five minutes from red jetty 6 and aboard a 55-foot racer."

O'Donnell gave the boaters the instructions to find Kirk's T-dock and told them he would meet them there and they could toss him the boat's docking lines.

I stayed with O'Donnell for a few more minutes and finished my cigar. In hindsight, I wish I had followed my friend down to the dock, but I didn't. When I saw the spotlight from a boat entering the harbor, I told O'Donnell I would save a seat for him at the bar and I went back inside. O'Donnell walked down the dock and waited at the end for the boat to slowly approach the fixed bumpers.

The boat was a long and powerful cigarette-style racing boat and not one this area very often would see. It was the type of boat that was more popular with the jet set crowd in southern Florida, in waters off the coast of Miami or Fort Lauderdale.

As the boat drifted closer, the figure of a large muscle-bound man wearing a clean white tank-top shirt, standing on the bow of the boat, came into focus. Even though the long racing boat was coasting at a no-wake speed, the sound of the huge motors was an unwelcome interruption to the ordinarily quiet and peaceful serenity of the marina.

The man tossed the lines to O'Donnell, which he quickly secured to the dock's davits and then the captain of the vessel cut the sound of the powerful and rumbling engine. The smell of high octane fuel lingered and consumed the normally pleasant salty seaside air. When O'Donnell looked up, another man had emerged from the quarters below the boat.

The stranger looked down at O'Donnell on the dock and greeted him with a big smile.

"Gracias, Chief O'Donnell, it is so kind of you to help."

O'Donnell looked up at the man and asked,

"How do you know who I am?"

The stranger slightly opened his jacket to reveal a shoulder holster holding a silver handgun. He laughed out loud at the Chief's question and then lowered his voice.

"Senor Angel Lopez sends his regards. He told me you would be very cooperative."

The man looked over to his partner on the bow of the boat and said,

"Juan, please show the Chief onboard. I am sure he would love to take a ride with his new guests."